UNSPORTSMANLIKE CONDUCT

GODS OF THE GRIDIRON: BOOK 1

SHANNA SWENSON

UNSPORTSMANLIKE CONDUCT
Shanna Swenson

www.shannaswenson.com

For permission requests, write to the author at shannaswen@gmail.com

Edited by Jennifer Soucy

ebook design by: OliviaProDesign

Gods of the Gridiron logo designed by:
Books and Moods Designs

ARES- THE GOD OF WAR

"Magnanimous, unconquered, boisterous Ares, in darts rejoicing, and in bloody wars; fierce and untamed, whose mighty power can make the strongest walls from their foundations shake: mortal-destroying king, defiled with gore, pleased with war's dreadful and tumultuous roar."

—*Orphic Hymn 65 to Ares (trans. Taylor) (Greek hymns C3rd B.C. to 2nd A.D.)*

FOREWORD

This book was inspired by my love for football (and obviously Greek mythology too) which started at the ripe age of *thirteen*.

All it took for me was to see the legendary QB, Brett Favre, #4 for the Green Bay Packers take the field and I was hooked—line and sinker. I've been a diehard fan ever since.

(Go Pack Go!)

What followed was an obsession with football players, the game, and numerous book ideas that started before *Abundance* was ever thought up. These ideas have been in my head for far too long, and now they finally have a "field to play on."

The main MC in this book, Travis Redmond, was originally inspired by former RB for the Packers, Travis Jervey, #32.
I hope you enjoy the exciting start to this four-book football romance series.

To note: These books are written in order as part of the series, although you can, it is **not recommended they be read as stand-alones.**

Some books in this series may have subjects that are sensitive to some readers; reader discretion is advised.

This book mentions characters that connect with the *Sin and Secrets* series by Shanna Swenson, Nicole Rodrigues, Kali Brixton and Cara Wade. (The prequel novella, *RISE*, premieres in November)

FOOTBALL TERMS

Here are some terms to familiarize yourself with for the series, if you aren't familiar with football:

Offensive players—

QB- Quarterback (the team leader—throws/hands off the football to an RB or receiver)
C- Center (hikes the ball to the QB and blocks)
RB- Running back (a running position; the QB hands or pitches him the ball)
WR- Wide receiver (the QB throws him the ball; he catches a thrown pass)
TE- Tight end (can act as a blocker or receiver depending on the play)
OT-Offensive tackle (Runs blocks for the offense and protects the QB during pass plays)

Defensive players—

DL- Defensive line (Defends the line, blocks the progress of the ball)
LB- Linebacker (goes after the opposing team's QB and ball carriers)
DE- Defensive end (defender with same duties as above, can act as a lineman or linebacker depending on the play)
CB- Cornerback (covers the opposing team's receivers)

<u>Other terms to know—</u>

TD- Touchdown (6 point score, can be scored by anyone who has possession of the football and breaks the goal line)
INT- Interception (when the ball is caught by the defense of the other team)
FG- field goal (when the ball is kicked through the uprights for a 3 point score)
Down- One of four chances to advance the football 10 yards (ex: Fourth and inches, means fourth down and inches to obtain the first down)
End Zone- the area where a score is made, the rectangular end of the field (between the end line and the goal line)
Red Zone- the area between twenty-yard line and the goal line
GM- General Manager- responsible for players contract, hiring and firing of coaches

*For the **real** #21*
I love you, my yankee boy

***

*For all those who've ever been bullied, you **are** good enough, you are beautiful, and you are worthy!*

PROLOGUE

Travis Redmond sat at the bar, beer in hand, feeling like the biggest loser in the NFL. He'd gotten formally suspended *this* time after he'd pulled his helmet off and gone nose to nose with a player on the field, during a game, in front of eighty-thousand plus fans.

Yeah, he'd been wrong. Yeah, he'd been angry. Yeah, he'd been throwing the game...intentionally. And Pollux Reed had called him out for it.

But dammit, he had no idea what Travis was going through, why he'd done what he had. He was tired of the talk behind his back and when Reed had mumbled that bullshit under his breath, Trav had seen red and went at him before he could even think.

He'd only been playing for the Atlanta Gladiators for a month now and he was being scrutinized, his motives questioned—like they'd been before the Stallions had traded him. But no one understood what was happening, what a shit-show his little brother had gotten the two of them into. There were some dark and shady men at the center of this whole scandal, and if Travis didn't play his cards right, Tucker's life was at stake. He had to do what they said, had to subtly throw the games, had to keep the facade going; the alternative was unthinkable.

For now, Travis was simply biding his time. He looked back over to Hank, the bartender of Gunslingers, the current bar he was in, here in his hometown of San Antonio, Texas. He'd needed a break from all the heat he was in, back in Atlanta, using the excuse to come out and visit his family and catch up with his former teammates.

Tonight, Trav was meeting up with a friend he used to play with on the Stallions—his former QB, Judd Gilbert. He'd be heading back to Georgia in a couple days' time.

Travis checked his phone again, all too aware of the eyes that kept coming back to him. He was as inconspicuous as a famous football player and record-breaking running back could be in his backwards ball cap and shades, despite that it was so dark in the place that he could barely see. The tight-ass Nike t-shirt and jeans probably didn't help hide his appearance. Judd hadn't texted him back yet, although Travis had been at the bar for about twenty minutes now, waiting.

"Is it true? Were you throwing that game like they said?" Hank asked, leaning over the half-empty bar top, polishing a beer stein.

"What the fuck do *you* think?" Trav grumbled and looked around. "You know me. You know I ain't like that!" It hurt that people had no more faith in him than they did...even if it *were* true.

"I know, but it sure don't seem that way. You shouldn't have fumbled that ball, Trav."

"What do you do for a living?" When Hank paused, Travis buried the hatchet. "You pour fucking liquor into glasses. Why don't you do *that* and stop telling me how to do my job? When you bust your ass on that field every Sunday, then we can talk. Until then, shut the hell up." Travis looked away, his heart hurting at the acid dripping from his lips. He had to make this seem legit though or Tucker was a dead man. They'd warned him and warned him and warned him. And Tucker was in their grasp now. They could put a bullet through his head in the blink of an eye if Travis acted suspiciously. They'd already sent him a pinky toe in the mail. He assumed it was his brother's but couldn't verify it for a fact. They could be bluffing, but he knew them too well; they hadn't bluffed prior to now.

Travis pulled his shades off and looked around, narrowing his eyes at the onlookers, almost growling like a cornered dog. *Yeah, it's me fuckers, Travis fuckin' Redmond! In the flesh*, he wanted to shout but took another sip of beer instead. *Back home and up to no good*, he thought to himself.

Just then his phone beeped and he checked it, seeing a text from Judd.

Judd: Hey, man. Sorry, I'm gonna have to bail tonight. Jerica is running a fever and Gemma thinks we should take her to urgent care. FML! I really hate this. I'll call you tomorrow. Maybe we can do lunch before you head out on Thursday?

Well, shit! Trav was on his own tonight...in a bar he didn't even wanna be in. His night just kept getting better and better.

Travis texted back with: **No worries, man. Hope she's alright. Talk tomorrow.**

He replaced his phone in his back pocket and looked at the opening door, seeing that it was raining out now as an impeccably dressed redhead with a giant umbrella stomped in, huffing.

Trav's eyes narrowed as he tried to place her. That face, mouth, and skin tone... He could swear he'd seen them before. When she looked up, her blue eyes grazed him robotically before zeroing in on the bartender.

"Excuse me, do you have a phone I could use?" she asked and got a scoff from Hank.

"Payphone's in the back, *lady*."

She sighed heavily and closed the dripping umbrella, swiping her black heels on the giant rug at the entrance of the door. She was clad in a striped, heather-gray pant suit with a cream silk top. She rifled through the big leather bag on her shoulder before tucking her unruly, long curly hair behind her ears. He heard her grumble,

"Fuck," as she pulled out a wallet and runaway coins began to bounce onto the floor with little pings here and there.

Travis understood; his day was just as shitty.

He decided then to move off his seat and assist her. He stepped forward and bent down to retrieve the three quarters, five nickels, and four dimes that had fallen out of her wallet. As her sapphire blue eyes fell to his, the woman's jaw literally dropped. Damn, she recognized him.

He was used to this. Being a professional athlete got a man all kinds of attention; some wanted and others not so much. He wasn't sure of the attention here but hoped she didn't draw too much his way. The heat of the chaos he'd already generated himself was creating steam around him, and he wanted to hug a wall at this point.

The shock on her face quickly turned to scorn. *Great! She not only recognizes me, she hates me. No scoring for me tonight.*

"Here, you dropped this," his voice plunged in annoyance as he thrust the fistful of change forward.

"Keep it! No one asked for your two cents anyway."

Ouch! Feisty. Well, she was a *redhead* after all.

"It's actually $1.40 to be exact," he smarted.

"Hmm, you could probably use it more than I could right now, Mr. Redmond."

He rolled his eyes. Maybe she was a jaded fan or the wife of an opposing player. Either way, he wasn't taking her money; to hell with her.

He slammed it on the bar top because his temper was the shortest thing on him. "You'll need it for the fucking payphone," he grated out even as she turned her back to him and walked in the direction of the phone and bathrooms. "Ungrateful bitch," he mumbled under his breath.

Travis sat back down at the bar and continued to nipple his beer, looking up at the television that hung on the back wall. It was set to SportsCenter, so he kept his eyes locked on it, listening to the play by play of past Sunday's games. The sportscasters began arguing predictions of the coming games, evaluating the players and their stats, and then started to debate Travis's future with the Gladiators. Again, anger seized him. What the hell did they know? His head coach, Greg Cavanaugh, and the owner of his team, Jerry Taylor, hadn't talked about cutting him. He was only suspended for two weeks, and it'd been for taunting, not throwing the games.

Travis sighed and leaned back on the bar stool. His guilt might be enough to kill him; the team didn't deserve to be done the way they were, nor his teammates. Travis wished things could be different, but there was nothing he could do. He couldn't go to the cops, he couldn't discuss it—with anyone—and he couldn't allow them to fire him. He had to keep this up, had to continue to keep his brother alive.

"Can I have a water please?" *Joy!* The stuck-up lady was back.

"Does this look like a Waffle House?" Hank snorted.

"C'mon, I'll pay for a soda. I—"

"Give her a damn water, Hank, and quit bein' a dick," Travis scolded with yet another scowl, getting one in answer. Hank huffed but did as he was told. "You're grumpy tonight and it's showing."

"Yeah, and with no damn help from *you*. You're supposed to be the town hero, Travis. You're really disappointin' us lately."

Yeah, that makes two of us, buddy, he thought but spoke instead to the mysterious redhead who'd sat down two stools from him. "You sure you don't need somethin' stronger?"

"I don't drink."

"Figures," he mumbled and sipped his beer again.

"Yeah, well maybe if you didn't drink so *much*, you could keep your damn hands on the football." The redhead smirked, and Travis frowned over at her. Who did she think she was, talking to him like that? What Hell had she come from to torture him like everyone else was tonight?

"Like you'd even fuckin' know," he retorted back. She probably didn't even watch football, he bet. She just went along with what the man who'd put that big rock on her finger told her to do.

Travis rolled his eyes and looked back at the TV, getting nothing else out of her for a minute. As soon as this beer was done, he was saying, "Fuck off" to all of 'em and getting the hell out of Dodge while the gettin' was good.

The redhead rifled through her giant bag once more and sighed at the cell phone in her hands, drawing Travis's attention again.

"Fuck," she mumbled under her breath and threw it back into her purse.

Trav's brows went up in question, but she looked away quickly, as if his stare was abhorrent. She'd be pretty if she would stop being such a cunt. There was something about her though that, again, made him feel as if he knew who she was.

"You from around here?" he finally asked, curiosity getting the best of him, and moved lithely onto the stool beside her. He was curious by nature; he couldn't help himself.

"Yes, *unfortunately* I am," she responded, running a hand through her mane of red hair.

"Unfortunately?" he smarted. "What? You too good to come from ol' San Antonio?"

"No," she replied back and rounded on him. "But I certainly wasn't banking on running into *you* again."

Again? When the hell had he run into her in the first place? He hadn't slept with her, had he? If he had, he was certain he would've remembered a set of tits and a pair of legs like hers.

He grinned. "I don't reckon I know you, darlin'."

"Oh, *yes*, you do," she retorted hotly and took a sip of her water. "You just don't recognize me. I mean, it's been almost ten years since we graduated."

Holy shit! He'd gone to high school with her? Who was she?

He looked her over and tried to rack his brain. High cheekbones, great tits, curvy hips, porcelain skin... Nope, he was drawing a blank.

But then again, he'd been hit one too many times in the head since high school.

"Got a name, Fireball?"

"Yes, Travis Redmond, I do. Too bad you don't remember it," she sassed, and he couldn't help but laugh at this woman's audacity. He was certain he would've remembered a sexy, feisty redhead; this lady was unforgettable.

"You're gonna make me work for it... Ok, fine. Maybe it'll be fun." His grin was like the cat that ate the canary for a moment before he spied her engagement ring again. Damn! She was engaged, he'd forgotten. Too bad too, because he could've had loads of fun with this sassy, little ginger. Each one he'd ever taken to bed had truly been straight fire, and tonight, he needed that kind of fire to forget all his problems.

"Oh, I—" she stammered as she went to remove the ring from her finger. "I—I'm not—"

"Sure. And *I'm* not one of the NFL's leading running backs."

"No. Actually. He—he, uh—"

"Sure, he did." Travis went to turn, annoyed by the woman's sudden separation from her fiancé on his account.

"He was fucking his secretary. I just found out yesterday. It's one of the reasons I'm here. Along with work. I needed to get away." She blushed, her face as red as her hair. Tears hit her blue eyes. "The affair is big news now. The media got wind of it this morning," she mumbled, looking down.

"Bummer." He understood how the media took a story and ran with it. "So, your fiancé a politician or somethin'?"

"He's the mayor of Atlanta."

"No shit!" She lived in Atlanta, too? "Wait, ain't he a bit *old* for you?" The mayor was, indeed, an old dude.

"I guess it doesn't matter much anymore, does it?" She smirked sarcastically, and Travis's eyes fell over her face.

She had a light dusting of freckles, which her foundation covered, rosy cheeks, an aquiline nose, and no-nonsense blue eyes.

And in that moment, she looked as run-down as he did. He took pity on her and felt bad for calling her a bitch behind her back.

"Hank, get us two shots. Make 'em lemon drops."

"No," the pretty woman protested, shaking her head. "I can't. Really."

"Oh, c'mon. Have a drink with your old classmate. We're celebrating a reunion. Just a round or two. It won't hurt ya. Besides, there ain't enough liquor in those things to even get you good and buzzed."

She cocked her head, trying to get him to understand, but he persisted.

"Just one. Maybe two. I *swear*, I'll get you home in one piece."

"Oh, I know exactly what you'll try to do… if you're anything like what you were back in high school. But my car needs a tow and the wrecker's gonna be a while, so I'll have one, maybe two with you. But I am *not* going home with you, Travis."

"Deal!" Travis grinned and motioned for Hank to get the shots. "But I gotta ask? Have we slept together before?"

She shook her head dramatically. "I'd never sleep with you. Not in a million years."

"Right, but you'll sleep with the damn, old-ass, bald guy you were engaged to," Travis snorted. The woman didn't confirm nor deny the accusation but she sure as hell was gonna marry the asshole, so there was that.

"So, are you gonna tell me your damn name so I can get reacquainted with you or are you gonna continue to keep me guessin'?"

She laughed, like genuinely laughed, and Travis was taken by how beautiful she was as her face lit up.

Wow! How had he forgotten a woman who looked like that?

"Skyla."

"Skyla?" Travis was combing through every neuron to try and remember this lady, but he couldn't place her to save his life.

"I wore glasses, had braces, was overweight," she elaborated. "Skyla Larson from Bio."

"You're fuckin' kidding me!"

Travis was literally dumbfounded as he recalled the chubby, strawberry blonde he'd had Biology with. The girl he remembered was shy, practically mute, and tripped over her own two feet constantly.

"No way! You are *not*."

"Am too." Skyla's brow rose.

Travis's eyes roved over her. She'd honed that fleshy pubescent body into a slender masterpiece, taken those ugly-ass glasses and braces off, and now she was fine AF, and he told her so. "Damn! You're smokin' fuckin' hot now, Skyla. What'd you discover? P90X?"

She rolled her eyes but gave him a smile. "Thanks, Travis. That means a lot coming from you. But not only did I discover P90X and clean-eating, I also grew the fuck up... unlike some of my classmates."

Travis laughed. Damn, this was entertaining and got his mind off the fear that his life had become since his brother had come to him three months ago, pleading for five million dollars and protection. "You grew *up* alright." Travis's eyes focused on her big breasts, and he remembered that she did have those in high school—Braces, buck teeth, and big tits. It was starting to come back to him now. "You were never sarcastic though, and I can't say I like that about you."

"Good thing I don't give a shit *what* you like."

"Burn, baby." He smirked. "Is the rest of you as scalding hot as that tongue of yours?" He gave her a crooked grin.

"Wouldn't you like to find out?" she asked and thanked Hank for the shots he placed before them.

"Yes! I would indeed," Travis answered and raised his shot after Sky grabbed hers. "Here's to reconnections."

"Here's to facing our fears."

Travis frowned even as Skyla smiled. What the hell would she know about fear?

She downed her shot like a pro, and Travis couldn't hide his surprise. He followed with his own and pulled a lemon wedge to his mouth, sucking it as he set his shot glass down.

"Why do I suddenly get the feeling I've been the butt of many of your jokes over the years? And why the hell does it seem like you've done that *many* times before?" He motioned to the empty shot glass on the bar top.

Skyla's brow rose, as if she were keeping a dark secret. "Nope, we aren't going there. Let's just say, I discovered who I was in college."

Travis's grin deepened. "Pray tell exactly what you discovered. Was it your vagina and how much it likes to swallow cock?" His own brow went up.

"I'm not even honoring that with an answer. I swear to God, you haven't changed at all. It's like I'm looking at the sixteen-year-old version of you all over again."

"You didn't even *know* me. You talk like we were together."

"I knew enough," she grated as she looked at her watch. "I can't believe I have to sit here with you for another half hour. Talk about fucking torture."

"Oh, c'mon. I'm not that bad...am I?" Travis frowned again. When she just looked him over, he said, "You didn't answer my first question."

"Butt of my jokes? No, but I'm sure your ears were burning from all the swearing I threw at you."

Travis was taken off-guard. He didn't remember mistreating this woman in any way. In fact, he'd taken up for her on more than one occasion and informed her of this to which she responded with, "Yeah, yeah, I know how you jocks were. You made fun of anyone who wasn't like you. At Brevidge High, if you didn't fit in with the jocks, rednecks, goths or nerds, there wasn't a place for you. It's such a totalitarian view. *News* flash, I don't fit into a box."

"Whoa, easy there, McFly. You act like you were bullied so badly—"

"Don't," Skyla growled and flicked her finger into Travis's face. "Don't act like you even remember. You were there living your glory days. You weren't in the girls' bathrooms, you weren't having to listen to the bullshit and stupid drama. You were too busy scoring touchdowns and getting into girls' panties and didn't have a damn care in the world. Meanwhile, because I was more concerned with my GPA than fucking *GAP*, I was ridiculed constantly. I wanted *more* than to be someone's damn arm candy. Thank you very much." Skyla's voice was high-pitched, echoing inside the bar so loudly that the glasses could have rattled.

Travis was floored by her admissions.

Sure, Skyla might have been picked on here and there, by boys and girls alike, but he couldn't remember her ever actually being hurt by someone. Then again, damn if she wasn't right. Travis had been too concerned with trying to score with Brittany Balboa and making the varsity team his junior year than anything else...and he'd done both.

He felt bad all of a sudden, for there were unshed tears in Skyla's eyes and the pain of these memories tore into him. "Jeez, Sky, I guess I didn't realize how bad high school was for you. I'm sorry."

"You're not half as fuckin' sorry as I am." She began to rifle through her giant purse again, looking for tissues, he assumed, as a tear ran down her cheek.

Hank placed another round of lemon drop shots down in front of them; he must have sensed they needed them.

"Here," Travis offered and pushed her shot towards her. "To high school being over."

"*Fuck* high school," Sky shouted and shot the lemon drop back. She swallowed with a grimace and found the tissue she'd been searching for. She blotted at her eyes and looked back at him. "It wouldn't have been so bad if it weren't for you."

"Me?" *What the hell did I do?* he thought and frowned, getting a cynical laugh out of Skyla.

"Isn't it obvious, Travis?"

Travis looked around thoughtfully, then shrugged as his eyes fell back on her. "No. I don't know what you mean. I was *nice* to you in fact, if I remember correctly..."

She huffed and rolled her eyes. "I had a huge-ass crush on you, idiot. Didn't you know?"

Travis almost choked on the shot he'd flung back. His eyes went wide. Skyla Larson had a crush on him? When? How? *Why?* Hadn't she just said—?

"I know what you're thinking," she stated with a giggle. Uh oh, the alcohol was starting to take effect. "She was a dork, she didn't even think about boys, she was too busy with books." She had changed her voice to sound manlier, but it made her sound like Bullwinkle the Moose, and Travis couldn't help but chuckle. "But dammit dude, I had it bad for you. So bad."

He'd like for her to show him how *bad*. A million sexy thoughts flooded his mind as he fantasized grabbing her up and blowing her mind as he fucked her senseless. It had been a while for him.

"*Oh* no. Don't even think about it, stud. I'm not sleepin' with you. I already told you." She scolded, waving a finger in the air.

"Oh c'mon, you had fantasies about me. Surely there's a part of you that's still curious." He couldn't help but grin again.

She smirked and shook her head. "Not in the least. I made something of myself...without climbing the ladder that way."

"Me too." He jeered back and crossed his arms over his broad chest.

"How about assistant DA?"

Travis's eyebrows shot up. That's right! She *was* ADA Larson, he suddenly realized.

"Well on my way to becoming DA, eventually...if I keep playing my cards right."

"That's an impressive accomplishment, Sky." *And sexy as hell*, he thought. This woman was feisty, curvy, and probably commanded a courtroom the way she was commanding his semi-erect cock at that moment. He was getting her into bed if it was the last thing he did tonight. "So, why the *fuck* was your ex-fiancé cheating on you? What an idiot!"

"You think?" she frowned even as she motioned for Hank to refill their shots.

Travis smiled. *Yes, drink up darlin', I'm gonna have you naked and on your back before the night is through.* "Hell yes, woman. Have you looked in a mirror recently?"

"Looks aren't everything, Travis. Gah, I thought you'd gotten over that shit. You'll never learn. I swear, you're still a child."

"I can assure you, Sky, I got a Dirk Diggler-sized johnson in my pants that says otherwise." He leaned in even as he got another giggle out of her. She sure loosened up when she got a couple shots in.

"Dirk Diggler, huh? I'm surprised women don't run in the opposite direction then. I know *I* would." She laughed.

"Alright, well maybe I'm exaggerating a bit. But still, there's nothing about me even remotely childlike." If she were a piece of steak right now, he would eat her up with just the look in his eyes.

She smirked. "Didn't mean to damage your ego there, beefcake. You've grown a beard and bulked up a bit since I last saw you." Her eyes moving over his body made him feel like he was being engulfed in licking hot flames of desire. "You're even bigger in person than on TV." She gripped his bicep and attempted to squeeze the thick, taut muscle. "Hmm," she murmured as her small hand rested there.

When Travis's eyes came up to hers, he felt a jolt shake him as if Cupid had shot an arrow right through his heart. Fuck, he wanted her. He wanted her with an ache that wouldn't wait. The need to take her to the bathroom and claim her was so strong he had a hard time resisting it.

She must have seen it, for she quickly pulled her hand down and looked around bashfully. So, she liked bulging biceps, huh? Perfect. He flexed the arm she'd just been touching for good measure, watching as her eyes widened and her jaw dropped. He would bet her panties were damp with desire, and he almost growled in yearning.

"You like muscles, baby doll?" he asked. "I got more." He moved his free hand down his chest and abs, watching her eyes follow down to his tenting crotch. His cock was itching for love in that moment, as gnawing as a toothache. Just as he started to grab for her hand to let her feel what her eyes were doing to him, she shot up from the stool.

"I—I uh, I should go check and see if the tow truck is here." She cleared her throat and pulled the heavy bag up to her shoulder.

"I'll walk you out," he said as he stood too and pulled a hundred-dollar bill from his wallet, throwing it on the bar top. "Keep the change, Hank." He nodded to the bartender and ran after a retreating Skyla who was heading out the door.

CHAPTER ONE

S kyla Larson attempted to rein in her breathing and her pounding heart as she stepped from the bar and back out into the rain. This wasn't happening. This night had gotten so much worse than she ever thought it could.

First, she'd been humiliated seeing Sampson Steinberger on TV with his arm around the young, blonde secretary he'd been fucking behind her back for far too long. Then she was forced to come to San Antonio to investigate a string of crimes believed to be connected to the Italian mob family she'd been investigating. And, of fucking course, she just *had* to run into the one person she'd prayed to never have to see again—Travis fucking Redmond.

He'd been the one man she'd never been able to get off her mind, no matter how much distance she put between herself and him, and damned if he hadn't been traded to Atlanta—of all the mother-fucking places on earth—from the Stallions. And who but *him* would she run into the first time she'd come home to San Antonio in ten long years! It was as if fate was fucking her in the ass. *Ok, bitch, I hear you!*

"Fuck!" she yelled out into the dark night sky. *Why?*

Travis had been her high school crush. Gorgeous and untouchable even as he haunted her dreams with hot, raw sex almost nightly. The dreams had been so vivid, his hands so intimate and familiar roaming over her flesh, but she'd never felt worthy of him. Sky had been fat and insecure, a social outcast who cowered in the shadow of his illustrious glory. She'd come a very long way from those days she'd tried so hard to forget, but seeing him here in the flesh, more handsome and powerful than ever, and she became that undeserving, timid, reticent girl all over again.

"Motherfucking shit!" she screamed again. She'd swore more in the last forty-five minutes than she had all year, and it was his fault.

She looked around the dismal night, cursing the rain, her mood, and the damn blown tire a hundred yards down the wet road. She started to walk, only to have her shoulder grabbed.

"Hey, wait up, Speedy Gonzalez."

"Dammit, Travis, fucking leave me alone. Can't you take a hint?" she threw back over her shoulder as she shrugged his hand off and continued trudging along.

"Easy there, Fireball. I just didn't want you to be all alone walking out of a bar at night. Don't you watch the news?"

Fireball. Ha! She was only feisty with him...and bad guys in the courtroom. Otherwise, she was as easy-going as a Sunday morning. Perhaps that's why Sam had been fucking his damn secretary because Skyla was too easy-going, too even-keeled, too complacent. Perhaps *Fireball* needed to stick around and stir some shit up!

"I know what bad guys do, I help put them behind bars, remember?" she smirked.

"So tough, it's hot as fuck. I'd love to tangle with you."

"Not so fast there, Rocky. I know tai chai, karate, *and* krav maga."

"Nice. A woman who can kick my ass. Keep talking, baby, you're making my dick hard."

"Jesus, you're impossible. Get away from me, you freak."

"Oh, you haven't seen a freak yet, darlin'." He laughed and the sound of it rippled through her, all the way down to her sex.

Skyla picked up her pace but knew he was a running back and would outrun her long after she gave out.

"Where we going, by the way?" Travis asked and plucked the umbrella from her hands, her skin burning where his broad shoulder brushed hers. She inhaled sharply.

"To my rental. Waiting on a tow truck, remember?"

"Yup. Just wanted to know how far."

Skyla pointed to the SUV barely forty yards up the slight hill before them, the sound of the rain beginning to lull her annoyance. The road was quiet and empty, the land mostly flat with some trees, cacti, and dead grass on this chilly November night.

When they got to the SUV, Travis held the umbrella over her head while she fumbled with the keys and unlocked the door. She thanked him, despite that she wanted to tell him to hike back to the bar and go away. He assisted her in and she closed the door as he ran around to the passenger side. In a flash, he was in her car and closing the umbrella, setting it into the back floorboard.

"This looks far more comfortable than the bar bathroom," Travis began and looked her over with renewed interest.

She gave him a withered look and crossed her arms over her chest. "Give it a rest, Travis. I already told you—"

"Yeah, yeah, lighten up, would you? I'm just teasing," he protested. "You need a good fuck, though, to loosen that cork shoved up your ass."

"I'm sure that's the answer to all your problems, huh? Well, us adults have to actually face reality instead."

His eyes flashed red. "You don't know the first thing about my problems, big shot."

"And you don't know the first thing about mine so shove it."

He laughed, and the sound of it tickled and infuriated her at the same time. "Man, that temper of yours is as hot as the rest of you. Red hair always starts the hottest fires."

She took a deep breath in and counted to ten. Why the hell did he have to follow her out there in the first place? She listened to the

SHANNA SWENSON

sound of the heavy rain on the roof of the car and waited for her heart to calm down. It didn't, of course, for she was so close to him, in her car alone with him, and her senses had never been more heightened.

"Sky," he said softly and the hair on her arms stood at attention. She'd never understood the overexaggerated response his deep, sexy voice had always had on her body; it awakened some deep primal instinct within her, her mind sailing back to those memories she'd tried unsuccessfully to stuff down over the years.

"What's the matter, Sky?" Travis asked as he turned in his desk in front of her.

She hadn't been able to stop crying as she left the bathroom to go to class. It had continued as she took her seat, even as she wiped the tears from her cheeks. She simply shook her head. He couldn't understand. He'd never been made fun of a day in his life. It wasn't Skyla's fault her single father wasn't rich like his and couldn't afford the best clothes.

"Hey, talk to me?" he beckoned, his perfect blue eyes speaking to her soul as they stared back into her own.

She was held captive by them, a prisoner to him. How could he not see into her soul? See the secret she kept from him. She relished in his presence, lived for this class because she saw him every day, got to sit so close to him, see his sexy big frame in front of her. She'd memorized every inch of his hairline, every curve of his muscled back, every mark on his flawless skin.

"I—" she began, his request too enticing to not answer. "My shirt came from Walmart," she admitted and blushed, horrified, because she couldn't for the life of her understand why she'd divulged this information to him. He'd think she was an idiot, poor, even more undeserving of his attention than she already was.

He smiled big at her, his sexy dimples popping into view beneath his scruff. "I like Walmart clothes, myself." Was he kidding? Surely he must be. "These shorts came from there, you know? And guess what, I don't care."

18

Then his eyes narrowed. "Did someone say something to you about that?" His concern touched her and made her heart literally melt.

I can't tell him. He'll pity me even more than he already does.

"Trav. Ugh, don't talk to that fatty. She shops at Walmart!*" Brittany Balboa interrupted, and Skyla's bubble burst in an instant.*

"I do too, Britt. What the fuck?" he smarted over at the gorgeous blonde pouting up at him. She immediately canned whatever she had been about to say and turned forward, scowling. "Don't worry about what she thinks. I like that color on you. It brings out your eyes." And with that, he winked and turned around.

And Skyla's heart soared on a cloud of perfection that lasted through the entire sixth period...that was until Britt ridiculed her again after class.

THE DARK VOID she felt then spilled over into the moment now as Skyla attempted to hold in the emotions that threatened to overtake her. *Dammit, that was a decade ago, I have to let it go!* But it was easier said than done when it seemed as fresh as yesterday. She gulped, looking into the same eyes that had both calmed and excited her that day so long ago.

"I need to get out of this car," she whined and reached for the umbrella, only to be stilled as Travis's hand halted her own. She pulled in a shaky breath, unable to stop the tears that threatened her eyelids.

"Do I make you nervous?" Travis asked, confused.

Nervous. Angry. Horny. Reflective. Miserable. Pick one, asshole, she wanted to scream. But knew it wasn't his fault for what his paramour had made her feel all those years ago. Skyla knew her anger was misplaced, but he was here, not Brittany. Therefore, Travis was to be the one to deal with the wrath that had built up over the years beneath her skin, a volcano ready to erupt after lying dormant for too long.

"Don't touch me," she hurled and could've recoiled at the shock on his face.

"Jesus Christ, you're bipolar," he threw back and jerked his hand away. "Fine. Have it your way, crazy bitch."

"You know what? I *am* crazy! Because of assholes like you!" she retorted and grabbed for the umbrella.

He didn't stop her this time as she took it and got out of the car, not understanding why she was so furious with him and why she was completely overreacting as she was. Were her hormones off? Was she about to start? No. She was simply sick and fucking tired of being pushed around by men. Never a-freaking-gain.

When she stopped at the front of the car, she looked back into the windshield at Travis who continued to sit in the passenger seat. She couldn't see him but knew he was probably stewing over how she'd talked to him. She felt bad, as she probably should. But she also felt justified. He was a hot-headed, self-confident legend who was used to getting his way and having women drop their drawers for him at his beck and call. *Well not this time, jerk off. Not this girl.*

Skyla Lynette Larson was done with letting people make her feel less than what she was. She had proved herself over and over again and no longer cared what they thought of her. Fuck people. Fuck Brittany. And fuck Travis Redmond.

As if sensing her challenge, the passenger door opened and the man whom she'd always felt was larger than life approached her.

She was suddenly overcome by his powerful presence, stunned by how big he was right there in front of her—so tall, so broad—and literally stepped back. He grinned, glad for his mightiness. Her eyes narrowed, angry that he could best her. God, he was so *fucking* cocky.

"You over your little temper tantrum, darlin'?"

"Fuck you," Sky stated back, feeling a power all her own.

"Fucking is exactly what your sassy little ass needs. Let's go back to the SUV, and I'll do you that service," he offered. Whether he was serious or not made no never mind. She was over him. He needed to cease and desist.

"Travis, I—" she began, only to stop talking as a big vehicle's lights blinded her. *Oh, good, the tow truck is here.* "Thank God!" Now, she wouldn't have to deal with this smug, brazen bastard any longer.

She looked at the truck door that opened and stepped forward, only for Travis to step in front of her and approach the burly man with a grease-stained shirt first. She didn't protest. If it made him feel more like a man to help her, then she wouldn't object. There was a part of her that was grateful he was being a gentleman and making sure she was safe out here by herself.

"Howdy," the tow truck driver began. "Someone call for a tow?"

"I did," Sky stated, coming to a stop beside Travis. "I got a flat."

"A flat?" Both men turned to look at her as if she'd lost her mind.

"You called a damn tow truck for a flat tire?" Travis asked, incredulously.

"Yes! I did. I wasn't changing the freaking thing in the rain." She shrugged.

Travis took a deep breath in and shook his head at her. "You didn't tell me that. I thought it was dead. Jeez, Sky."

The tow truck driver put his hands on his hips, puffing his chest out. "Well, you wanna tag team and we'll get this tire changed out for this young lady?" he asked Travis.

Travis nodded and turned to follow the other man to the side of her vehicle.

Together they began working on the deflated rubber blob clinging to the rim, and Skyla felt bad for being such a cunt to Travis Redmond, who really had never personally done anything to her. He was just a good target for her rage because his life had always been perfect: Perfect family, perfect genes, perfect football record—save til now.

Skyla wasn't paying attention as another car's headlights came up the hill, but the hum of the engine quickly faded into the distance as a loud blast assaulted her ears and rattled her entire body. She screamed as she watched the tow truck driver's head literally explode on his shoulders.

"Sky, move!" She heard Travis's voice and felt his stocky body hit hers as he moved them around the side of the SUV. He pushed her to the wet ground as the whoosh of a bullet flew past her ears. She felt his big arms around her, his heavy frame against her back and bottom. She screamed again and Travis's hand covered her mouth. "Shh," he whispered. "Get to the truck." He pointed up to the open door of the tow truck and picked her up as if she weighed nothing. "On three, we're gonna run for it. I'll put you in first, then I'll get in. Ready?" he asked, looking into her eyes as he held her tightly to his muscular chest. She wasn't sure she was. She was overcome with panic, her logical mind shooting off in a million different directions, but somehow her brain told her to listen to him and do as he'd said. She nodded and was rushed to the truck door, terror seizing her as the sound of bullets rained through the air.

Travis picked her up and pushed her in. She crawled over the bench seat and watched him follow and slam the door quickly. He put the diesel in drive and gunned it. She gaped as she looked back and felt Travis grab her head. She was pulled down to the seat, her cheek hitting his massive thigh as the sounds of gunfire blasted the back window. She pulled her legs in as glass shattered around her and felt the shards, like a thousand pin-pricks, rain over her legs. "Keep your head down."

Sky's head reeled as her adrenaline soared with the reverberations of truck racing car. Travis kept his cool, somehow, as he drove, jerking the wheel to outmaneuver the vehicle behind him. Soon, the only sounds were that of the rain pelting the windshield and bed of the tow truck.

Apparently, the chase was over.

Sky shivered and felt something hard jab against her cheekbone. She gasped when she realized what it was, bolted upright, and shoved Travis's big shoulder.

"Gross, you pig!"

"Oh can it, Red. I can't help how my body reacted to the combination of adrenaline and your head in my lap."

"Oww, dammit," she yelped as a glass shard on the seat dug into her right palm.

"Careful," he insisted and sighed.

"Ok, first off, what the fuck was that?" Her rational mind had returned.

"*That* was Geraci's retaliation. One of many to come, I'm afraid."

"Hold up! You mean *Giovanni* Geraci?" she asked, dubiously.

"Yes, ma'am."

"What the hell have you gotten yourself into, Travis?"

"You wouldn't believe me if I told you."

"You have exactly thirty-seconds to tell me," Sky retorted, crossing her arms over her chest and glaring at him.

"I *will* tell you, but right now, I've got to get us out of this truck and into a different vehicle. We're sitting ducks."

"Oh, no!" Skyla huffed. "There is no 'we' to all this. It's just you."

"And that's where you'd be wrong, Fireball. Like it or not, you're now running from him too. Unless you wanna be 'swimming with the fishes,' you gotta hide."

"I'm here to investigate a crime, I'll have you know."

"Yeah if you can survive until morning."

"Stop talking, my damn head is killing me." Sky held her fingers to her temples, trying to quiet down the migraine coming on.

"There." Travis pointed and turned onto the highway from the two-lane road they'd been on. "We'll head north, ditch the tow truck, and hit a hotel for the night."

"Jesus, Travis. We can't just steal a car."

"Where's your phone?" he asked and grabbed for her purse.

"It's dead. W—what the hell are you doing?" she protested as he took it from her grasp and opened his window. "Travis!" she cried even as he tossed it out the window along with his own that he suddenly fished out of his pocket.

"Like it or not, we have to get off the grid."

"I'm an assistant DA, I can protect us. I could've made a phone call, if you'd have given me—"

"Look, you don't know this man like I do. He won't stop until we're dead. Get that through your fucking thick skull. You're not in Atlanta anymore. We're on our own right now." Travis took a deep breath in. "He's gonna kill Tuck; I just know it—if he isn't dead already. Jesus, I should have seen this coming. Dammit!" He slammed his massive palm against the steering wheel, causing Skyla to flinch.

Sky was quiet for a time, taking in the fear in Travis's face, the anxiety in his muscles, the seriousness of the situation.

"Jesus, Trav. Does this have anything to do with you throwing the games? What's going on?"

"It makes so much sense," he continued as if she hadn't spoken. "They've been watching me... Of course they were there. They saw me talking to the assistant DA of Atlanta." He laughed without humor, and Sky couldn't stop the shiver that ran up her spine. "Who knows you're here?"

"I—" Sky huffed. "My boss of course—the DA—and my friend Joanie."

"Good. They'll have to know you're in trouble when you don't check in, right?"

Right, but why did his eyes still look so uncertain. "Why do we have to hide?"

"Just until we can get away from their reach. Then we might have a chance."

"I just need to make *one* phone call, Travis."

"Don't you see that they're watching us? Let's say you do get to a phone to make that call. Did you not see what they just did to the tow truck driver? That'll be you before you can communicate what's going on. You get me? They're reach is unending. Trust me!"

Sky sighed and looked away, knowing it was true. Geraci, of *course*. He was the powerhouse of the Atlanta crime ring. He did the empire's "dirty work." But she knew there were more bosses than just him. There had to be. Especially for them to have all the eyes and reach they seemed to have. Now, he knew she was here in San

Antonio. He'd be covering the things up she'd come here to investigate. There would be no evidence now. Dammit!

"Sky, why are you here in San Anton?" Trav asked, as if reading her mind.

"Trying to link crimes to a mob boss."

"Jesus Christ. It all adds up now. I bet they thought you'd come to talk to me. Fuck. We gotta get out of here."

Travis took the next exit off the highway and pulled into a Love's Travel Stop.

"I want you to listen carefully. I'm gonna go swipe some keys, and I want you to go grab us some food. I don't give a fuck what it is: Doritos, canned goods, Powerade, whatever. Make sure it's nonperishable for a little while, nothing we have to heat up or keep refrigerated, just in case. You've got a total of five minutes."

"But—" Sky began.

He gripped her cheeks and looked deeply into her eyes, holding her as captive as he had in class all those years ago.

"Sky, do you want to die?"

"Trav—"

"Do you *want* to fucking die?" he insisted.

"No!"

"Then do what I'm telling you."

A part of her wasn't sure if she should trust him or not. Wasn't he throwing his games on purpose? But she'd always trusted him and had to hold to her gut instincts now. A man was dead, and they would be, too, if she didn't do as he told her.

"Ok," she agreed, and he let her go.

TRAVIS WAS LOSING his calm as he moved into the bathroom of the Love's truck stop, anxiety tore threw him as he looked around and approached a urinal. At least he *did* have to pee. He took his time unzipping his pants and relieving his bladder as he assessed the current situation. He waited for his moment when the smaller guy beside him—the one he'd followed inside from the gas pump—was off-guard and they were all alone as he zipped his pants up and made his move.

It took one second to step up behind him, and Travis gritted, "Give me your keys and don't look at me." He held the guy's head straight ahead with his left hand and opened his right palm for the man to acquiesce.

"Please. I got kids."

"And you'll see those kids again...so long as you hand me your keys." Much to Travis's surprise, the dude did as he'd asked. "Thank you. Now, I'm gonna move you into that stall. You'll stay there for five minutes. Don't come out until then. If you do, you'll regret it. Remember your kids."

Travis guided the stranger to the stall, which he opened and moved into. He closed the door and Travis headed off, keeping his capped head lowered as he quickly walked out of the truck stop.

Sky was standing just outside the automatic door with three filled bags. Travis nodded to her and hit the lock button on the fob in his hand. The lights of a black Kia Sportage flashed, and they both moved to it as he then hit the unlock button. Travis was grateful the owner of the vehicle had done as he'd asked as they peeled out of the parking lot and headed out, back onto the highway.

"Where are we going?" Sky asked.

"I have a house in Lubbock."

"We can't go to your house. They'll look there."

"It isn't listed."

"It doesn't matter."

"Crap, you're right. Then where?" he asked and increased his speed as he headed north.

Sky was quiet for a time before she said, "My father's buddy has a cabin in Estes Park, Colorado."

"Jesus, that'll take forever to get there."

"Yeah, fifteen hours or more."

"Can anyone track you to it?"

"No, the cabin's been there for a long time. They wouldn't know that I know him. He isn't famous, he isn't related to me. He hasn't been there for a time."

"How do you know he still has it?"

"I just know. I went up last year for some alone time."

"Do you have a key?"

"No. But it doesn't have an alarm or anything. It's old, been there for fifty plus years."

"So, we're just gonna break in?"

"Do you have a better idea?"

Travis shrugged. No, he didn't. And Colorado wasn't a place that Geraci would necessarily look for them. It was out of Texas and a long way from Georgia. It might be a great place to hide. Estes Park was in the Rocky Mountain National Park.

"Alright. Let's go."

"What about this car? Won't the man report it stolen?"

"Yeah, but by the time the cops get to Love's, take the statement, and begin the search, we'll be far from San Antonio. Besides, I'll switch the tag next time we stop."

"Why does this seem so shady?" Sky huffed and looked over at him.

He took in her frightened expression, her unruly hair, and her beautiful face. He answered honestly, "I don't like this anymore than you do. I'm just trying to get us to safety so we can live to see tomorrow."

"Why is Geraci chasing you, Travis? How the hell did you get involved with him?"

"It wasn't me. It was my brother, Tucker."

"He's a very bad man."

"No shit, Sherlock," Travis smarted, his bite harder than he'd intended. Just the thought of something happening to his little brother was more than he could bear to think of and right now, his mind was wired and reeling from all that had happened in the last thirty minutes. He sighed, "Sorry. I know. Jesus. But what was I supposed to do, Sky? They threatened to kill my brother if I didn't do what they told me to."

Travis grew quiet as the road soothed his senses, the sounds of the tires on the asphalt quieting his fears for the moment.

Sky didn't speak, just looked at him. Her hand rested on his on the steering wheel and he glanced back over at her. Finally, she said, "I'm sorry."

"Thanks," he said and turned his focus back to the road. He didn't want to talk about Tuck, didn't want to think about what they were doing to his brother, if he were indeed still alive. All Trav could do was pray that Geraci was still using Tucker as leverage, pray he wouldn't be stupid enough to kill him just yet.

"We've been on to Geraci for a time now, the entire organization. We've been attempting to get enough information to indict him. It's just a matter of time, Travis. We have a mole in their system. Perelli wasn't the only caporegime. We believe there are three more bosses, Geraci included."

"Three? Jesus."

Travis recalled the name Vincent Perelli—and his death some seven years ago when *The Devil's Playground* burned down. Supposedly, one of Perelli's men had killed Vince, then himself, after lighting the strip club up, killing several others in the process. But thank God, Perelli had been taken down. He'd been a head crime boss, drug runner, money launderer, and sex trafficker. Travis had never gone to the club before it'd burned down, but he'd heard about the bastard and his shady activities following the news coverage of the fire. It irked him to know that there were three other men like Vince in Atlanta, and that his own brother had somehow waltzed right into the lion's den and brought Travis, and now Skyla, with him.

"I'm sure my brother had no idea what he was getting himself into when he went to Geraci's boy, Sal."

"Why did he go to a bookie?"

Travis shrugged. "He was a gambling addict. He bet on sporting events, including my football games."

"Which is how he got *you* involved?"

"He got me involved after he asked for five million dollars and for me to protect him against them."

"Oh my God! Five million dollars?"

"Yeah, he owed them and with serious interest."

"So, you gave it to him?"

"Fuck no!"

"It's not like you don't have it," she scoffed and looked out the passenger window.

"It wasn't about the money, Sky. It was the principle. That asshole was bribing my brother, and I didn't want criminals taking my hard-earned cash," Travis retorted heatedly. "Not that I have to fuckin' explain myself to *you*, ADA."

His mood darkened and he didn't want to discuss it anymore, tired of hearing her belligerence toward him for the time being. The miles flew by as he sailed down the road, skirting right under the speed limit.

Almost an hour had passed with silence between them before Sky dug into a bag and fished out some chips and salsa—of which he made a snarky comment about how difficult it was going to be eating *that* in the car—and a couple of Arizona teas. He gave her a grin as she handed one over, unable to continue his scowl at the familiarity he drew from her.

"Arizona Lemon tea? You remembered, huh?"

"Of course I did. You brought one in every day."

He thought back to Biology, not recalling much beyond Mr. Bennet's goofy laugh, barely passing, and seeing Skyla, always giving him a soft smile behind those thick-framed glasses of hers.

"You really paid attention to me, huh?" He could almost blush. It was endearing that she'd been so into him that she knew what he drank on a daily basis.

Sky looked down and reached back into one of the bags. "Five minutes wasn't a lot of time to grab things, but I tried to rally."

"You did good. Three bags worth is impressive."

"I watched a lot of *Supermarket Sweep* back in the day."

Travis laughed heartily. "I remember that show. But I'm sure a gas station isn't set up the same. Way to come through, Skyla."

The smile she gave him back hit him hard in the chest and stole his breath. God, her smile was arresting, pulling her lips up and sharpening her eyes. "Wow, you're stunning, lady. Were you always so gorgeous? Was I just simply blind?"

She looked down again, and he frowned; she tended to do that a lot. Then he reminded himself that she'd just been cheated on by her fiancé. And she'd been ignored by the boy she'd crushed on for four years in high school; she'd reminded him of this fact several times already. Travis felt as if he'd somehow wronged her. He hadn't known she was infatuated with him then and he realized that even if he'd known, it wouldn't have changed anything. He was too busy chasing the hard-bodied and vibrant cheerleader Brittany and wouldn't have seen how amazing Sky was through his lust-filled teen boy eyes. But he still felt bad about it. The grimace on her face was tangible.

"So, how long were you and Sampson engaged? And what the hell did you see in an old fart like him?"

"He wasn't *that* much older than me..." she trailed off. From what little Travis knew of Sampson Steinberger, the man was old enough to be her father. He was bald and seemed like a real hard-ass.

"I mean, I can't even imagine how shitty the sex was. I'm surprised he can even still get it up at his age." Travis realized his attempt to lighten the mood was spoiling Sky's as she got even quieter. He felt like he was being an ass and despite that it hadn't been his intention, he apologized with an, "I'm sorry."

"Don't be. I wouldn't know how the sex was, I didn't screw him."

"Oh Jesus, don't tell me you sucked his wrinkly old balls?" Travis made a gagging sound.

"No. I didn't," she stated, seriously.

"Ok? Was this gonna be a marriage of convenience then or what?"

Sky sighed. "No. I mean, we messed around. But never went all the way." She got quiet after that, and Travis decided to drop it. He didn't want to think about Sky and the old man. It personally made him sick to his stomach...and he suddenly got furious about that bastard touching her.

"Why don't you get some rest. I'll wake you in a few hours to drive when I stop for gas."

She gave him a curt nod and laid her head on the headrest as she reclined the seat back a little.

It wasn't long before Sky was asleep, her head falling to the window as Travis adjusted in his seat a little. He let the road carry him through the sullen night, the tires eating the pavement as they continued north toward Lubbock on I-10. He turned the radio on low, to keep himself grounded, passing some trucks on the left and watching as the grass changed to desert.

It was well after midnight when he decided to stop for gas at a Shell station off the highway just north of Eden. It wasn't far from an old Walmart where he planned to change out the tag on the car to evade both the cops and Geraci's men.

When he cut the engine off, Sky shot up in the seat, alarm paling her features as she tried to reassess where she was and what was happening.

"Shh, it's ok, we're just stopping to get some gas. You need anything?"

She nodded and said, "Bathroom."

They both got out of the car and Travis locked it, placing his sunglasses on and adjusting his ball cap for anonymity. He wished Sky had the same luxury but hoped there were no cameras—or, at least, no need to hide in the long run once they got safely out of the state. He let the gas pump as they headed inside.

He nodded to Sky and watched her head to the bathroom as he

paid for the gas with cash and was grateful when she emerged quicker than he'd expected.

He looked around outside before they both got into the car he unlocked, seeing a big rig and a little sedan, nothing out of the ordinary. He drove around to the Walmart, parking quickly beside a car towards the back of the lot.

"What are you doing?"

"Changing out the tag."

He got out and did just that, hurrying to remove the tag from a sedan with Colorado plates, grateful he'd selected this car and this lot. He then did the same with the tag on the Sportage and swapped the two. When he got back in, Sky frowned at him.

"Do you think they know where we're headed?"

"No. I don't. How could they?"

Sky shrugged. "Want me to drive?"

"I'll be ok, for now. If you want, go back to sleep for a little while longer."

She nodded once more and leaned her head back onto the window, propping up on her elbow. "Do you think the tow-truck driver had children?" she asked randomly, her voice softer than he'd heard it prior to now.

Travis sighed heavily, feeling guilty about the man who died so close to him. Trav had seen the rifle coming out of the passenger side of the black Buick and had begun to move even as he saw the man's head split into a thousand bloody pieces. He wasn't sure he'd ever be able to erase that scene from his memory banks. Sky had been to the left of him and he'd grabbed her and pulled her around the back of her SUV and to the ground. He'd never been more grateful to see that the diesel truck was still running and the driver's door still open. Now, he simply worried about the fact that they'd left the scene of a crime and their DNA and fingerprints were gonna be all over the tow truck, making them look like suspects.

Oh well, Sky was the assistant DA; she'd find some way to get them out of this…he hoped. He finally looked back over at her pale face and gave her an understanding grin. He extended his hand and she took it. Her palm was soft in his own and he was awed by how small her hand was. His dwarfed hers, making her seem even more vulnerable in that moment. When he looked into her blue eyes, he saw tears there and it hit him right in the gut.

"It was supposed to be me." He swallowed audibly.

Sky was shaking her head. "No. You're too valuable to them still. They were making a statement, that's what they do. I—I just— Every time I close my eyes I see…" she trailed off.

"I know." Travis sighed again. "Sky, I'm really sorry about all this. I never…" Travis stilled his thoughts, unable to explain how awful he felt about the goons chasing them, the dead man, and the need to flee for their lives. Then thought of a way to make her laugh. "Hey, you remember that doofus who always came to class with a huge stack of books? He smelled like garbage and talked to himself. Got all excited, like he might be ADHD."

"Yeah, he walked funny and was more than likely Steven-Hawk-ing-smart."

"Yeah, maybe even smarter than you." Travis winked, and Sky gave a little laugh. "I ran into him one day in the hall. It wasn't on purpose, mind you, but would you believe when I did, his books fell to the ground and he put his dukes up like he was gonna fight me?"

"Really? Because you made him drop his books?"

"Yeah, I mean, I guess. I thought for a minute Dork-Brain Loheizer was gonna kick my ass."

At that, Sky belted out in laughter, sexy and hearty. And Travis grinned, glad he could take her mind off the murder they'd witnessed. He squeezed her hand and held it in his for a time, taking comfort in the fact that they were hopefully headed to safety and could call for reinforcements once out of Texas. Trav felt some comfort in knowing the tags didn't reflect a stolen vehicle any longer, but it wouldn't be long before the officials put two and two together.

"For what it's worth, Skyla. I'm glad it's you that's in this with me."

Sky scoffed and shook her head, rolling her eyes. "Thanks for saving my life, Travis."

"You're welcome. Get some rest so I don't have to drive the next twelve hours, would ya?"

"Fine," she grumbled and closed her eyes, still holding his hand.

Travis smiled and gunned it.

"WHAT THE HELL are you talking about?" Norm Jeffers, the DA of Atlanta, said into the receiver of the payphone he'd been paged to call the mole on. "Sky is *missing*?"

"Yes, we lost them. She and Travis left the scene of the crime. I'm not sure which way they're headed, but it's only a matter of time before Gio finds them."

"Shit! How soon before you can wrap this shit up, Mathers?"

"We're close, sir, I just need his confession. I'm hoping Skyla can help with that."

"What are you suggesting, agent?" Norm hissed, not liking the tone in Casey's voice.

"We both know what I'm suggesting, sir."

"Dammit, Mathers. I'm not putting any more people in danger."

"It may be the only way to finally end this. Geraci believes Travis met with her on purpose. He wants them both."

"Can you stall?"

"I already did by stopping the chase when they took off in the tow truck, but Gio's boys are scanning every satellite and camera as we speak. You know they have connections everywhere. They *will* find them."

Of course Casey Mathers was right. He'd been with the crime family for almost two years now, undercover. "What do I need to do?" Jeffers asked, frustrated to hell and back.

"As smart as Larson is, I'm sure she's going to try to contact you as soon as she can. You need to have your men in place and ready to go when we come to take them back to Gio's. I'll be ready on my end. Tell Sky I'll give her the code word 'Angel,' and she can use it if something happens before the time comes to raid."

"Is this gonna work this time? This is my assistant DA you're talking about here...and one of the leading running backs in the NFL."

"Gio isn't stupid enough to kill them, Jeffers. Surely, he would see they're much more valuable alive."

"How's the brother?"

"Weak but alive. I've seen to it. I'm not watching him kill anyone else."

"What about that trucker?" Jeffers grated sarcastically.

Mathers sighed heavily. "Unfortunately, collateral damage, sir. I'm sorry. I obviously didn't know that was going to happen."

Jeffers rubbed his forehead with his thumb and index finger. "I'll make sure his family gets all the benefits I can. But Mathers, this needs to be over and done with. As soon as possible. Geraci has *got* to go down."

"I'm doing my best, Jeffers."

"I know. Dammit. Get Sky back and fast. And preferably unharmed."

"You know I can't make promises, but I will do everything in my power. Just be ready when she calls you."

"May God be with you, agent."

"And with you too, sir."

Mathers hung up the phone and returned to the black Lincoln.

CHAPTER TWO

S kyla awoke with a gasp, seeing the man's head shatter in slow motion. "Pull over," she cried out and sought the door handle.

The car wasn't completely stopped before she was trying to get out and evacuate her guts. Sky heard Travis swear as he hit the brake. The car jolted to a stop and she threw herself from it, puking toward the ground, bile burning the back of her throat as her stomach emptied itself of its own volition.

"Fuck, Sky," Travis scolded as his palm came to her back. "That's one way to get yourself killed, as if we need any more reasons. Ever heard not to jump out of a moving vehicle?"

His smart mouth made her mood even more foul, and she shoved at him as she wiped at her lips. "Get away from me," she whined as she fell to the ground, the trauma and anguish and fear of the last hours finally taking their toll on her. Hysteria racked her body as she took in deep breaths, and felt Travis's hard frame pull her against him even as she fought him. "Don't touch me. I need…" she exclaimed but wasn't sure what she was trying to say. She realized the danger they were in; her nightmare had brought reality crashing into her. If they were caught by Giovanni Geraci's men, they were more than likely gonna end up that way too. "He's dead because of us. It's our fault. It's—"

"Shh, c'mon, Sky. We can't do this right now, honey, ok? We're still not safe."

Sky looked around, as if she was just made aware of where they were and what was happening. The area around her was different than San Antonio, and she wondered if they were being watched. She shivered.

"Get back in the car. We're not far from the border."

"The—the border? Damn, how fast are you driving?"

"As fast as I can."

She looked up and for the first time, she saw fear in Travis's blue eyes, which made her shiver even harder.

"C'mon, Sky, you gotta hold it together, baby. Please?" he begged and took her hands in his. "Get back into the car, ok?"

Skyla nodded and let him pull her back to the Sportage. She attempted to dry the silent tears at her eyes as the sting of defeat pulled at her. She wondered if they were gonna survive this, if they were gonna die, be hunted down...and if they *were* caught, how much they were gonna be tortured until the relief of death came to them.

Geraci didn't play, not unlike his counterpart Vince Perelli. These were men who were greedy, money and power-hungry players; if you didn't play by their rules, you were an enemy. Enemies of the crime family were not treated with mercy, but with cold, hard deaths akin to medieval torture methods. All the previous files filled her mind and her heart swelled with terror, sickness tore at her guts, and she tried to hold back the gag that came.

They'd sold young girls into sex slavery, slaughtered innocents, made examples of people who deceived them. There was no end to their means of retribution, and now Skyla and Travis were on the wrong side of it. They wouldn't stop, they wouldn't rest until she and Travis were hung up by their toes and made to pay for their supposed misdeeds against them. No amount of begging, bargaining, or threatening would matter. They were walking dead people.

Which was why she had to make that phone call and soon.

Travis let her calm down, although it took far too long as the panic leached through her veins like a dose of heroin; but, when she finally did, they were about to cross into New Mexico.

"I need to make that phone call, please?"

"Sky, I don't know if—"

"If they're following us, then we have to let Norm know where we are."

"You let him know where we are and they're only gonna find us *fucking* sooner. We *have* to wait until we know they aren't on our trail."

Sky calmed her heart and tried to think logically. They hadn't seen the vehicle she and Travis had transferred to, didn't know which direction they were headed, but that didn't mean it wouldn't be long before they found out. Travis was right. They had to hide their tracks, camp out, and wait for help.

It had to work.

Four hours went by slowly as they made a quick stop for gas once more and dined on some protein bars and Mountain Dews, passing the time with scavenger hunts and playing "Punch bug."

"This diet is for the birds," Travis joked. "My coaches would kill me."

"Well, beggars can't be choosy," she reminded him. "Besides, it could always be worse." She pulled out a bag of Funyuns and laughed at his reaction.

"Oh, man, it's been years since I had those."

"Right?" she giggled. "I couldn't resist."

They crunched on the salty snack and stared in awe at the Rockies when they came into view. Skyla was grateful to be crossing yet another border between Texas and those gangsters chasing them. She felt a sense of safety, even if it was only momentary.

The last year had been a cat-and-mouse chase as Jeffers tried unsuccessfully to catch Geraci at his game. It'd been difficult; Geraci was careful, and despite having a spy in their midst—Sky didn't have a *clue* as to who the agent was—the chase was slow-going. According to Jeffers, this person had been in the ranks for over two years. It didn't look as if they were any closer to shutting the crime boss and his organization down; although, Jeffers didn't relay all the information he knew to her. The less people who knew, the better, he'd said. The only reason she knew about this inside job was because Jeffers had to tell her in private one day after some files came up missing and she questioned a fellow lawyer's loyalty. It comforted her to know that they had a man on their side among the bad guys, but she personally couldn't imagine the constant fear of having Geraci suspecting one of his own, when or *if* that time finally came.

She'd heard all about Perelli's sick games and prayed Geraci was a pussy cat in comparison. Now, with what she'd seen firsthand, she feared Geraci was just as bad. Power and money made men like them invincible, turning ordinary men into self-imposed gods. And these gods had run Atlanta for a long time now. They had to be shut down. Good had to triumph over evil.

"What you concentrating on so hard over there? I smell something burning," Trav smarted.

Sky rolled her eyes. "Funny," she said and watched a hawk circle over their heads in the bright sunlight, grateful for the day's warm rays on this early morning.

Travis yawned big, and Sky scowled over at him; she hadn't even volunteered to drive yet. It was her turn.

"Hey, when we get to the border, let's fill up and I'll drive for a little while."

"No, I'm good. I don't even know if I'm gonna be able to sleep." Trav looked resignedly over at her and she understood all too well.

"Well, you can at least try," she offered and ended the

conversation.

They'd made it to Trinidad, Colorado when they stopped at a QT. They filled up, emptied their bladders, and Trav grabbed a couple coffees and biscuits. He was the one who was shielded most from suspecting eyes with his sunglasses and hat, so Skyla began to head out the door, only to be stopped when she saw the face of Sampson Steinberger on the television. He was crying, or trying his pathetic best to, and she approached so she could hear what he was saying.

"I'm utterly devastated and can't believe this is happening."

The screen then flashed to a picture of Travis, in the crimson and gold uniform of the Gladiators, running a play. He was carrying a football and rushing into the end zone for a touchdown.

Sky's mouth dropped as the caption read, "NFL RB Travis Redmond wanted for questioning. Assistant DA Skyla Larson missing." Sky gasped out loud but immediately shelved it so as not to draw attention to herself.

She looked over at Travis who was paying for their breakfast and silently made her way outside.

She had to make that phone call to DA Norm Jeffers, and she had to do it as soon as possible.

TRAVIS IMMEDIATELY PICKED up on Sky's mood as he handed her the coffee cup. "What?"

"Uh, nothing, I uh—"

"Skyla, what's wrong? You got 'Holy shit' written all over your damn face."

"Our suspicions were correct..."

"About?"

"About being implicated in the murder. Only you look like a suspect who kidnapped me. The news isn't saying it officially, but you're wanted for questioning and I'm missing."

"Motherfucking shit!"

"Don't worry. We'll get your name cleared. But we're still being hunted so we have to keep driving, right? We stick to the plan."

"This is bullshit, but I fucking knew this would happen. Son of a bitch."

"Hey, don't worry. We're gonna bring this motherfucker down. He's done ruining lives. It stops with us, ok?" Sky looked hard into his eyes, fierce blue eyes that sparkled with the promise of victory.

"Well, *you* sure changed your tune, ADA Larson."

"Oh shut up," she scoffed and put the car in drive.

"No, it's hot as fuck. Is that how you are in the courtroom. Feisty and sassy? Like you are in the bedroom?"

She gaped even as she brought the coffee cup to her lips—to avoid his eyes he knew—and turned back onto I-25 North.

They were quiet for a few minutes as he handed her an egg-and-bacon biscuit, his stomach growling hungrily.

"Sorry, I wanted something hot in my belly."

"I appreciate the gesture." She grinned over at him before taking a bite of her biscuit.

They ate and took in the sunshine and mountains, grateful for a reprieve from the figurative darkness in their periphery. It was a beautiful November day, and Travis suddenly remembered all the vacations he'd spent here in Colorado with his family when life had been good. His mom and dad had brought him and his brother to Vail and Aspen many times as children; Travis loved skiing and snow-boarding. He'd always been quick on his feet and had great hand-eye coordination. His father had never been prouder than when he'd committed to LSU in his senior year of high school. He'd always strove to make his old man happy, despite what a hard-ass he'd been during Travis's teen years.

From the outside, they'd always appeared to be the perfect, loving family. His father had been a Harvard graduate, his mother, a San Antonio socialite who made Martha Stewart look bad, and Travis was the golden child; but inside their immaculate six-bedroom mansion, an entirely different story played out.

Tyler Redmond had been a no-nonsense business man with a penchant for perfection; the top had never been high enough to please him, and they all eventually got fed-up with trying to meet his unobtainable expectations. Tyler had started going on drinking binges by the time Travis was fourteen and came home cursing everyone out. He got physical at times, and Travis became the whipping boy to save his mother and brother from the angry fists of a violent drunk. Trav's mom, Fiona, finally left his dad when Travis graduated from high school. After Travis left for college, Tuck had taken the brunt of the beatings, and somewhere along the way, it had broken him; he'd gotten into trouble with drugs then gambling later on.

Travis felt guilty about that now, looking back. His mother should have left his father sooner and perhaps Tucker would've been spared. Trav and his mother, Fiona, had always had a strained relationship. They were so different, and she never seemed to understand him. He hated when she compared him to his father, for he was nothing like that belligerent fuck. He'd protected her from the flying fists and lashings—or had he?

He'd seen proof of the bruises over the years and finally confronted her one day when he was sixteen, getting a, "We all have a price, Travis. Let it be." As time went on, he began to learn exactly what she meant by that. The cost was going to be his downfall. The cost for fame, fortune, and freedom.

He must have been thinking aloud for Sky's hand came to rest on his forearm and he jerked, startled at being pulled from his reverie. "I'm sorry. Are you ok? You got pale, as if you realized something. It frightened me."

Travis shook it off and gave her a grin, not wanting to alarm her. "Nah, I'm good. Just enjoying my biscuit, wondering how long we'll have to camp out in this cabin before we're rescued by your boys." He winked and took another bite of the calorie-laden, sorriest excuse for a southern indulgence he'd ever had. *Hey, at least it's hot,* he thought.

"Hopefully not long. This cabin isn't gonna be like what you're used to though, I should go ahead and tell you."

"Oh?" he asked, his curiosity piqued as she blushed.

"Yeah, it's very small and barely has running water. Not fancy, Mr. Big Shot."

"Oh, well in that case, turn this car around and head back to San Anton," he mulled exasperatingly, getting a laugh out of Skyla.

"I'm serious. You're gonna be disappointed."

"You know what? If it has a bed I can sleep in and a bathroom, you won't get a single complaint out of me. Boy Scouts' honor."

"I'm holding you to it. Just don't say you weren't warned."

"Duly noted, doll face." He chucked her chin and got a swat back, laughing before he asked, "So, you spent a lot of childhoods at this place?"

"Yes." She smiled and it lit her up, making her even more beautiful than she already was. "My father and I came up to fish Lake Estes and fell in love with the Stanley Hotel. My dad's a huge Stephen King fan. Plus, his buddy Terry had the cabin, so it was cheap to spend our summer months here."

"Your dad was pretty frugal, if I remember correctly." Travis fished, crumbling his wax paper up and tossing it into the bag they'd designated for trash.

Sky's eyes warned him, but he'd always been curious about what made her father so damn eccentric. According to his own father, Lorenzo Larson had as much money as they did. So why hadn't he showered his daughter with the money he hoarded following his wife's early demise?

"Frugal, eccentric, a nut job, choose your words, Travis," Sky smarted. "He was a brilliant man with a broken heart. Either way, money isn't everything."

Travis held his hands up in surrender. "Hey, I'm not judging. Just curious."

"My father didn't talk about money or my mother, so you know as much about it as I do."

Her demeanor changed and she got quiet once again.

Well, that went well, Travis, he scolded himself. *Now that you've pissed her off, you can get the silent treatment.* "Well, I guess that's my cue to shut the fuck up and take a nap."

"Couldn't have said it better myself." Sky's brows went up and she smirked over at him.

"Wake me when you're ready for a reprieve." He settled into the too-small seat and leaned back, letting his mind drift to imagine this trip as a pleasure cruise where he and Sky were on their way to a luxury cabin with a hot tub. He smiled, visions of a naked redhead with porcelain skin and freckles dotting her curvy flesh filled his mind. He moaned and let himself indulge.

"AND I TAKE IT, you're on their trail?" Geraci asked into the cell phone.

"Yes sir, we picked it back up in Lubbock."

"Hmm, why Lubbock?"

"Redmond has a house there, we're gonna go check it out."

"You think they would be dumb enough to go to a property he owns?" Geraci smarted.

"It is on the way, sir, better to be sure," Mathers answered back.

"I've always appreciated the way you think, Kane. By all means, leave no stone unturned. And make sure you make a statement." Geraci growled.

Mathers knew Gio was pissed, but he was going to give ADA Larson every second he could to get somewhere safe before he brought the war to her, playing as dumb as he could. He'd not checked back in with Jeffers or his boss, Arnold, as he'd been on the road and hadn't had the opportunity. For now, he could buy time, which was exactly what Larson needed more of.

"Will do, sir. I'll check in with you at 0900," Mathers stated and hung the phone up. "1245 Autumn Drive, Biggs, and step on it," Mathers grumbled, playing his part to a T.

They were on their way to wreck Travis's house, leaving breadcrumbs for the cops. He knew the FBI would be hot on the trail, and knew his boss well enough to know he was waiting. They would see real fast that Redmond was, and had been, a pawn in this game for a while. Geraci and his crew were going down.

The final countdown had started; time to throw the first punch.

SKY SMILED as they closed in on the old cabin in the woods at the top of Eagle Mountain Lane, just above the ridge from a tributary and lake. It was about halfway between Drake and Estes Park, very remote, and for once, she was grateful for its unremarkable allure. They parked out front and Travis whistled.

"Woo-wee, you weren't kidding. This is out in the boonies."

"Gorgeous, isn't it?" she asked as she looked around at the abundance of trees, barer than she was used to seeing with it being late fall as opposed to summer.

"It's perfect, Sky."

She could breathe easily, knowing that even though it wasn't luxurious, it would do for the time being to keep them somewhere safe and away from the predators hunting them.

"So, you're sure there's no alarm?"

"Positive, it's the same way I left it last summer." She moved up the front porch steps and looked the door over, seeing the old wood and locks hadn't changed. "Hope you're good at breaking and entering."

"Ha," Travis laughed. "Negative, Ghost Rider. I could probably shove my way through the door but picking locks, nope."

"Well, damn." Sky began to rifle through her huge purse that held everything from screwdrivers to hairspray, thank God. She was grateful she had it with her when the shit had hit the fan, especially when she reached in to find a bobby pin and smiled in triumph. "Ha ha!"

It took ten good minutes of picking, swearing, and getting pissed before she was able to jimmy the lock. She was a bit shocked by her skills and had been two seconds from telling Travis just to bust the door down before the lock gave and she turned the knob.

The hinges creaked as the door opened and the familiar musty, woodsy smell assaulted her nostrils. It took her back to her childhood, and she smiled as she entered, setting her bag on the small wooden kitchen table.

"It needs some airing out but it's got potential," she stated with content.

"The Property Brothers would have a field day in here." Travis looked around at the rusty wood-burning stove, peaked ceiling with large wooden beams, and the old leather couch that looked like it had survived a bear attack with clear disdain.

"I told you it wasn't a damn Hilton, Robin Leach."

"Hey, I'm glad it's here. Not complaining, I swear." Travis took his shades and hat off, stretching his arms up.

"Sure, sure. The sheets are clean and there's running water, so shut it, Moneybags." Skyla moved over to the sink, grateful there *was* water and it was hot. *Thank God!*

"The little things are always the most important." He looked at the far bedroom and pointed. "Well, first things first, Ms. Larson. I'm taking a nice, long shower. Wanna join me?" Travis bobbed his eyebrows at her.

"In your dreams." She rolled her eyes at his confidence, not shaken at all by their predicament. "I still stand by what I said at the bar, Travis. Nothing has changed."

"Oh, everything has changed, Fireball. It's just a matter of time before you change your mind and cave to me. My natural charm will win you over in no time. Besides, being forced to live in close proximity like this with me, I've got that on my side too."

"You're so full of shit that your eyes are turning brown. Do you actually hear the stuff that comes out of your mouth sometimes?" Skyla shook her head in bewilderment at his unwavering cockiness.

"This mouth can do things to you you've only dreamed about, darlin'. These hands. This cock." He grabbed himself suggestively, and it was all she could do not to slap that smirk off his gorgeous face.

"Only *you* would be thinking about sex at a time like this. Go, shower so that I can too. I want to get to a payphone and call Norm, then I want something hot for dinner."

"Me too, sexy lady. Me too."

With that, Travis licked his lips, slowly, sexily. Sky felt a tingle in her lower belly that spread to her sex, and she almost whimpered aloud. She wouldn't tell Travis Redmond to save her life, but she wondered suddenly too if he wasn't right about what he'd just said. Being stuck in this cabin with him was going to be hard...and the sexual chemistry was undeniable.

She'd felt it practically sizzling her last night at the bar as she'd moved her hand over his big bicep and the tribal tattoo that covered it. She'd never felt anything more wonderful than the smooth expanse of his perfect skin and wanted him with such a hunger that it had frightened her. How could she even think of being intimate with any man after she'd been jilted so by her fiancé?

It'd hurt when she'd suspected Sam of infidelity, and it scarred her heart permanently when she'd seen it for certain. Not only had she seen it, but all of the world too; her heart had literally broken in two at the betrayal. He hadn't even had the decency to tell her in person; she'd found out through the media. Not that she hadn't known, deep down.

Sky had felt something was off. He'd been spending too much time at the office, came home too late on far too many nights. But she'd held out on him, refusing to sleep with him, and for good reason. Now she was glad she'd saved herself more heartache. The pain of it and all that had happened over the last twenty-four hours took its toll as Skyla felt tears sting the back of her eyes. A man was dead, and all she was thinking about was herself. But it trumped the fear she felt running from Geraci's men.

She shut and locked the cabin door, then ambled into the small den. She grabbed the blanket off the back of the couch and surrendered into the exhaustion that seized her heart and mind in that moment.

Skyla awoke hours later with a start as Travis turned the lamp beside her on.

She gasped even as her eyes roved his half-naked frame, clad only in a burgundy towel wrapped precariously around his hips.

"Fuck, Travis, what the hell are you doing?"

"Sorry, I fell asleep on the bed after my shower and just woke up. It's getting dark outside."

"Shit!" she whined and began to remove the blanket only to stop as her eyes fell over Travis's gloriously naked torso. "Jesus Christ," she muttered beneath her breath and gulped as his muscles rippled with each breath he took. His chest was broad, his pecs large and chiseled not unlike his washboard abs and cut arms. He was the perfect sculpture of a god, in every sense of the word. She suddenly wondered what those muscles felt—and tasted—like.

Travis stood still and let her evaluate every exposed inch of his flesh, the black tribal tattoo that covered his left pec and the expanse of his arm. Then her eyes moved back to his face, which seemed to be as surprised as she was. She knew she was practically drooling, her mouth agape, but God help her she couldn't come to. Was she still dreaming? That had to be it. This wasn't real and soon she would wake from this sultry dream to a cold, harsh reality. A reality of a woman who'd never felt like she'd been enough for any man, who intimidated the few she'd had. A woman who'd always longed to be wanted, loved, and worshipped by a sexual beast like Travis Redmond but never had been, all because her insecurities outweighed her confidence.

She stood and let the blanket fall from her, entranced by the cool, blue eyes that held her, once more, captive. She'd never wanted to be a prisoner any more than she did right then. The allure of his warm body pulled her in, like a beacon in the dark. Her palms came to rest on either side of his face, on his bearded square jaw. Her eyes roved his plump lips, that straight nose, and serious brows, back to his perfect eyes. Eyes she'd prayed to get lost in. Eyes she was now lost in. Eyes that saw past every flaw, every doubt, every fear. She gulped again and moved her hands to his shoulders. God, he was so broad, so tall, so *powerful*. She was a mere mortal to the mighty "Ares," as he was called by his teammates, and now she knew why. She wanted to be overcome by him, feel his hard body dominating hers, feel him ramming her into a fantasy where nothing existed but the two of them.

Travis shivered even as he inhaled sharply at the touch of her hands on his skin. Her fingertips hovered over his deltoids, down his shoulder blades, to his biceps and squeezed. When she moaned aloud, he growled, and she'd never been more aroused in her life than in that moment. She longed to throw herself into his big arms and beg him to take her to Mt. Olympus, where he reigned in his realm of gridiron legends.

The allure of letting herself go had never been stronger. They were on the run after all and might die before all was said and done, and dammit, she felt as if she'd not lived until this very second being in his presence. She bit into her lip to keep from beseeching him to *show* her what he'd been saying earlier about his mouth and hands and cock, her half-sleeping brain still in La-La Land.

"Sky," he warned and stepped closer, not quite touching her but close enough to make every hair on her body stand on end. His eyes closed as his head moved down toward hers and she saw that she wasn't the only one losing control. Would it be so bad to give in to her darkest, deepest desires? Would it be so wrong to let the controlled woman loose for just a night? Just long enough to have the one man she'd always wanted with a fire that had never burned out.

Then something snapped into place—her logical brain. The body who'd been had far too many times by far too many assholes finally intervened. Her puffy cloud of pink popped into a raging red inferno: *He's a player, you fool! He eats women for breakfast. Fuck him and you'll only have a heart even more broken than it already is.*

And just like that, Sky moved back and pushed his chest away. "Go put some fucking clothes on, will you?"

The hurt in Travis's eyes cut her but not as bad as she knew the venomous bite of his charming ways would poison her entire system, creating a domino effect of tragic loss for years to come. She couldn't allow him in. Many men had damaged her psyche, but Travis Redmond would break her beyond all repair. He growled again, a tantrum of a man used to getting his way.

"You're a fucking shifty bitch, you know that?"

"And you're a selfish pig," she shot back and begged her heart to calm itself down. It simply swooned over his retreating form, the muscular back and firm ass moving back to the bedroom.

When he returned in his Henley and jeans, her heart rate hadn't quite calmed, but her mind was set as she said, "About damn time, now it's my turn to shower."

"So, I guess we aren't going into town to make the call?"

"I mean, it's getting dark. We should probably wait until morning, right?"

He glanced out the curtained window at the setting sun.

"I only say that because it's harder to find this place in the dark, and I'm not certain how far town is from here." She shivered and not because she was cold, but Travis didn't realize that.

"Alright, that's fine. Go shower, I'll start a fire and take inventory of our supplies." He nodded then gave her a soft smile.

The sweet side of her longed to apologize to him for acting like a prick-tease earlier, but the cynical bitch within wanted him to suffer as she had over the years for her unrequited love for him. She gave a terse nod back and retreated to the shower.

The bedroom was just as she remembered: stacked logs for walls, a queen-sized iron bed centered between two curtained windows with a colorful quilt for a comforter. A vanity sat at one wall, a dresser at another. The bathroom had been updated year before last to house a clawfoot tub which she intended to use at some point, a separate room for the toilet, and a stone shower. She slid her clothes off and draped them on the counter, turned the shower on, and stepped in. The hot water felt good against her skin and she moaned aloud, letting it lull her senses.

Travis Redmond—of all the freaking men in the world she was running from Giovanni Geraci with. Fate was a damn evil cunt sometimes, and she planned to have words with the bitch about this. Travis had haunted her hopes and dreams when she was still an impressionable teen, being raised by her outcast, lunatic of a father. He was a good man but so smart most people in town considered him to be weird, especially after her mother died of a congenital heart defect at a young age, when Sky was just fifteen. Skyla was smart and introverted too, not unlike her father, and got made fun of by boys and girls alike. Travis was one of the few who didn't directly make fun of her, and took up for her, but his unintentional rejection hurt as bad as the ridicule did.

She'd tried to let it go after ten years of pent-up anger, but seeing him again, being stuck with him like she was, had brought all those buried emotions to the surface. Sky was afraid she might end up like a volcano and erupt on him before all was said and done. It wasn't his fault, she knew that. He wasn't to blame for what had taken place, but that didn't take the pain of it away. It was oozing, festering, coming to a head. As she got out of the steamy shower and covered herself with a towel, she realized she had two options: she could lance that wound or she could let it continue to build. It was high time she decided.

"HOUSTON, WE HAVE A PROBLEM," Travis began as Sky came back into the den from the bedroom.

"Oh?" she asked, her big lips plumping in question.

"Yeah, that other bedroom you said he had. It's not there."

"What? It is too. It's right there." She pointed to the north end of the house and approached the closed door. He followed. When she opened the door, she gasped. "The bed. It's—it's gone."

"I don't know that it's so much gone as it is buried under all that furniture, those damn boxes and dust, so looks like I'm sleeping on the couch."

"You're too big for the couch, you take the bed." Sky looked up at him.

"Oh, no. I'm not gonna be *that* prick," he retorted and her brows went up in question. "The prick who acts like an ass and takes the bed. It wouldn't be very gentle-manly of me to do that, so I'll take the couch. Thank you very much."

Sky shook her head. "Travis, I insist."

"Nope, not happening, missy. You already think I'm a number of things that I'm not. I'm not givin' you anymore fuel to light your big-ass fire."

"Oh?" Skyla crossed her arms over her chest. "Go on, please? I implore you. Please tell me where I'm wrong about you?"

Damn her, she was so fucking self-righteous, it really stuck in his craw. Before he could answer, Miss Thang continued, "Cocky play-boy, thinks he's better than everyone else, can't take a hint, show-boaty, arrogant, full-of-himself asshole."

"Bitchy, cork stuck so far up your ass that it's giving you a headache, know-it-all, prick-teasing, brain bigger than her tits, can't let her fucking hair down for a second because God knows she might have an *ounce* of fun, ball-buster," he retorted back, ticking off on his fingers.

"Ha," she huffed, incredulously. She took a step toward him, finger in his face. "Has it slipped your mind that we're being hunted down like animals? How in the hell am I supposed to find *any* fun in this, Travis?"

"Has it slipped *your* fucking mind that we both saw a man's damn head blown off, his life ended in an instant?" he yelled back. "Excuse the hell out of me that I wanna enjoy the last few hours of my own life...in bed with a beautiful woman."

By this time, they were within inches of one another, Travis's nose almost touching hers, his lips a breath away. Her big breasts heaved against his chest, and he could feel his cock growing in response to their imposed closeness. Sky looked up at him, her mouth open in surprise. "You—you think I'm beautiful?" she asked, oblivious.

"Skyla, I've said it several times now. Why in God's name do you *not* believe me? Whoever told you that you weren't?"

Her blue eyes burned into his, taking his breath from his lungs and he reeled, unsure why she was still so damn insecure. She was slender, beautiful, smart and sassy—and had a passionate fire burning within her that could spark a conflagration, if only she'd just let someone in. He realized once more that she was hurting, hiding something that happened to her, a damaged spirit beaten down by society, by herself, and by a past she couldn't let go of. She was a grown woman now though, not a teenager with teenage problems and flaws; she'd overcome her own battles, so why wasn't she embracing this instead of crawling back into the shell that had held her captive?

Sky's eyes closed and she squeezed them shut, a tear running down her cheek. Travis fingered it and brushed it softly away, cupping her cheek as he angled her head up. "Sky, look at me." She shook her head, her lips quivering, holding in emotions he didn't comprehend. "Please?" When she didn't, he said, "Darlin', I realize your fight isn't with me. You're lashing out because you've held shit in for a long time, ok? You're not the only one here who's been hurt by people in your past, though, so please stop acting like it."

Her eyes shot open, realizing what he was trying to say and her brows drew. Anger took over again. "What the hell would you know?" she grumbled.

"Oh, I *know*. Far more than you'd ever think, in fact. But guess what? You've never asked me about my life, now have you? You've just assumed I'm like everyone else who's ever hurt you, that I'm just some soulless asshole with no conscience. News flash, baby. I'm not."

He released her and moved off to the kitchen, grabbing the remaining chips and salsa, Vienna sausages, a box of Fig Newtons, and a bag of Reese's pieces as his stomach growled.

"Dinner's on me. But you're buying tomorrow night." He grinned as he sat the items down on the coffee table and beckoned her to the feast of junk food before him.

She smiled big and came over, tucking her hands between her legs as she sat beside him and looked down. He felt an apology coming on, but before she could demean herself any more than she already had, he spoke again, "Look, I know emotions are high and have been for some time now over the last day. Just know that I'm not the man you assume me to be, and give me the benefit of a doubt. Could you, please? I know I'm not perfect by any means, and I have a short temper and a big head, but I'm still a human being with feelings like you."

Skyla sat quietly for a long time, rolling his words over in her mind before she looked up into his eyes. "You're right. I haven't even given you a chance, have I? I stereotyped you."

He nodded, but didn't want to make her grovel. "It's what people do, Sky. I'm a rich man who's had his life handed to him on a silver platter, right?" When she looked back down at her lap, he continued, "Wrong. I've not always had it so easy. I've worked my ass off to get where I am today. I'm a fighter. I enjoy what I do, love to travel, and dine on fine foods. I'm passionate and sometimes my passion tends to overstep my rationale. Perhaps you and I aren't so different after all, are we?"

When her eyes came back up to his over the firelight, he saw something new reflecting in their cerulean depths—respect, realization, renewal—and she stilled.

"Now, I don't know about you, but I'm starving, so can we eat and stop bantering like a bunch of enemies? I thought I was your lab partner, dang it."

She laughed and the sound warmed him even as the chill of the whistling wind coming beneath the windowsill made him shiver. "It's drafty in here, huh?" she asked. She rubbed her arms and he grabbed the blanket, draping it around her shoulders.

"Here. Let me throw another few logs on the fire." Travis walked over and did just that, feeling the heat radiate from the old stove. "There we go."

He moved back to the couch and opened a can of sausages, handing them over to Sky. His fingertips touched hers, scorching his skin where they did so. He shivered and watched her eyes as she froze.

The sparks between them were irrefutable, and he wondered if their lust would burn as hot as their anger toward one another did. If so, they were in for some scalding hot nights in the sheets. As ice-cold as this woman appeared to be on the outside—the resting bitch face was strong with this one—he knew it wasn't so. Like the red in her hair, she reeked of pent-up fury that he craved to unleash as much as Poseidon loved releasing that damn Kraken. The allure of taming this banshee was as strong as that of opening Pandora's box; Travis knew once unwrapped, Skyla's passions would ignite a raging inferno that might consume everything in its path, including him.

He wanted the challenge, craved it, wanted her to be putty in his hands, poking the beast and drawing out the essence of her. But he was afraid, too; of exactly what he wasn't certain, but there was something in her eyes that warned him away. *Play with fire and you get burned.* He knew the warning signs, but damned if he didn't enjoy striking a match and seeing the embers dance.

Tangling with her promised to be the most thrilling test yet. And Travis made up his mind that he was up to the challenge. *I will have her before all is said and done. She* will *be mine.* And God help him if she pulled him into her web, for he might just be helpless to escape once entrapped by her.

CHAPTER THREE

S kyla awoke the next morning to the feel of a hard body against hers and something digging into her bottom.

She tried to recall the night prior and remembered being carried into the bedroom. She jolted and felt a hand squeeze her breast, an arm covering her chest.

"Travis! What the hell?"

"Five more minutes," he grumbled and gave her breast another squeeze. "Mmm, so soft and firm at the same time."

"You bastard! This is sexual harassment, assault, and battery." She smacked at the hand on her bosom, but the big palm grabbed hers and she scoffed.

"Oh, just relax, baby. Isn't this comfy?"

She felt a nose nuzzle her jawline, right below her ear, and shivered as his hot breath fell on her neck, aware of how her entire body tingled.

"Comfy isn't the word I would use to—" The palm at her breast suddenly covered her mouth and she felt his other arm pull her closer into his chest, the sharpness against her ass digging in deeper. She gasped even as a moan died in her throat. Holy shit! If that was his erection, he was hung like a freaking mule. She tried to calm her pounding heart and swooning sex as her body absorbed the feel of his muscles on her back and his hard member shoved into her ass cheek.

"This feels so good, Sky," his voice sounded equal parts playful and aroused. "Imagine how much better, if only my cock was just a few inches down and to the left."

The thought of feeling that hard shaft buried deep inside stilled her thoughts—and her protests. God, how enticing it was. The temptation of letting his hand fall back to her breast, letting his fingers bring her nipples to even harder peaks than they already were, feeling his lips on her neck as he plunged deep inside her and unleashed the inner sex goddess lurking just beneath the surface. God, how she wanted it. Wanted him. Had always wanted it to be him who'd unlock the side of her she'd never fully exposed to anyone.

His hand suddenly moved off her mouth, and she fought the urge to rub her bottom against his rock-hard member. All it would take would be one movement, one moment to lose her inhibitions, one glance back into those captivating eyes of his to let the vixen loose. His nose touched her earlobe with such tenderness that she sucked her breath in. She bit into her lip, fighting hard not to cry out in pleasure. Her entire body quivered in unrequited lust, and her womanhood screamed at her to move his hand down to quiet the ache he'd awakened inside her.

Oh Travis, how I've died inside waiting for this very moment, the teenager inside her blubbered. But the mature woman stood solid as a rock, daring her to give in. *Go ahead, idiot. Let him use you and discard you like his former lovers. He won't stick around, and I'll be the one left to lick your wounds clean, only this time it might just kill you.*

She gasped and pulled away quickly as if she were escaping quicksand. He released her and let her stand up. She turned, planting her hands on her hips, and wasn't prepared for the drop-dead gorgeous sexually-primed god who lay in the bed she'd slept in. Her senses reeled at the man who'd mastered the word sexy, unsure how she wasn't melting into a puddle of desire right onto the old wooden floor at that moment.

Dear God, have mercy on me, she thought as her eyes betrayed her.

Travis lay bare-chested with the sheet and quilt covering his hips, brown hair all mussed, looking as if she'd just rocked his socks off in every sense of the word. His sensual grin was devious and his eyes did things to her insides that she hadn't known were possible without having sexual relations beforehand.

"Wh—" her voice wavered, giving her away; Travis's smile deepened. She cleared her throat and tried again. "What are you doing in my bed? I thought we agreed—?"

"We did, doll, but I got cold out there by myself." Oh God, his pouting lips might just give her an orgasm.

"Well…wh—why are you naked?"

"Oh, Fireball, I ain't naked."

She closed her eyes against the body that set her own aflame in scorching hot lust. She pointed to his naked torso. "Y—you're *half-naked!*"

"Sorry. That's how I sleep, darlin'. In my skivvies." Damn him and his sexy as sin grin and fuck, his dimples. "I can take 'em off, if you prefer."

"Tr—Travis," Sky cleared her throat again, attempting to control the thoughts running through her mind was impossible. "You can't do things like this." She got out finally.

"And why not, baby?" he cooed, knowing exactly what he was doing to her starved sex. "Why not indulge?" He said the word indulge as if his voice were made of straight satin. If she wasn't jumping right into bed and kissing the sugar right off his sinful lips, she was dying.

She simply held her breath and counted to ten. Then he did the unthinkable. His hand moved beneath the sheets and he looked to be touching himself. "Look what you did to me, Skyla, you naughty girl." He moaned and closed his eyes.

Fuck, fuck, double fuck. NO! *Do something*, her sex screamed even as her mind screamed the same. But she couldn't pull her eyes away from the forearm hidden under the quilt, the covered hand doing taboo things as it moved, and the flex of his rigid muscles as he stroked himself beneath the covers. She prayed for the sheet to fall, to expose his member to her, for him to tempt her just a little further, to invoke the sex goddess he was slowly unfurling.

"Oh, baby, tell me you don't want this too. Tell me you don't wish this was your hand on my hard dick right now. Your mouth. Mmm, fuck that feels so good. I wish it was you instead."

She fought within herself, a woman torn. One part of her wanted to say fuck it, shuck her clothes and join him, the other wanted to run and cry and hate herself even more than she already did for wanting him as much as she still did. This was high school all over again, nothing had changed. She was still the naïve, scared girl with low self-esteem and the urge to hurt herself as much as others had.

She turned and fled to the bathroom.

TRAVIS IMMEDIATELY STOPPED HIS MOVEMENTS; bewilderment, embarrassment, and anger set in as Skyla ran to the bathroom. When he heard her hurling into the commode, he added self-loathing and resentment to that list.

"Sonovabitch," he swore as his erection waned painfully in his palm. *Well, that didn't go as planned*, he thought.

He hadn't lied about being cold and uncomfortable on the couch, so he'd thrown another couple logs into the stove and headed into the bedroom around two AM. Sky had been sleeping peacefully there, and he'd decided to join her; it was too inviting for him to resist.

She'd curled right into his embrace and he'd tucked her sleeping head into his shoulder, falling into the most restful sleep he'd had in weeks. She'd felt soft, and good, and right in his arms.

He'd woken to his usual morning wood and couldn't stop the pull to tease her, even as he'd known she wouldn't acquiesce. But he'd never—in a million years—expected this reaction from her.

Travis never had a woman run away from him and puke instead of turning in his arms and taking what he had to give. This was a new feeling, and he didn't quite know what to say or do. He was completely taken off-guard. To say that he was put off was an understatement, to say his feelings were hurt was accurate, and to say he felt degraded as a man was spot-on.

He made sure he was out of the bedroom when Skyla came out of the bathroom. He was also dressed and ready to go with his mouth shut and his tail tucked firmly between his legs.

He tried giving her wide berth as he planted his sunglasses on his nose and set his cap on his head, determined to stay to the task at hand.

Her eyes were puffy and her face red, he noted. He grabbed the keys from the table, mumbling, "I'll drive."

Skyla didn't argue as she nodded and looked for a house key, finding one in the kitchen drawer and handing it off to him to add to the keyring. He tried not to appear rattled by the feel of her fingers on his, but dammit if he couldn't remember how good her ass felt against his hungry sex. He could all-out roar, a lion caged against his will.

Soon, they were out the door and in the car, heading down the road. The silence was all-consuming, the calm before the storm. Just as Travis was about to turn the radio on to still the insecurities bubbling inside him, Skyla spoke. "I'm sorry about..." Her eyes closed and she appeared to be in deep pain, pain that Travis didn't understand. And perhaps that was the problem here. He didn't understand a lot of Skyla's reactions to him. Maybe it was time they laid some shit out on the table and sorted through it.

"I didn't realize I repulsed you quite so much," he said softly, disappointment lacing his tone.

"*Repulse* me? You?"

"I heard you vomiting, Skyla."

"You *would* make this about you, wouldn't you? Geez, your self-ishness has no end." She shook her head incredulously.

Travis braked to a stop, slamming the car into Park and turning to look at her.

"I was convinced that you were *this* freaking close to coming back into bed with me," Travis held his hand up, showing an inch measurement with his thumb and index finger, "then you run off to the bathroom and get sick. What the hell am I supposed to think, huh?" He threw his arms up in defeat.

"I wasn't sick because I was repulsed, Travis. I was sick… because…because I can't believe I'm still so damn in love with you, after all this time."

Travis couldn't hide the shock on his face. Did she just say that she was in love with him? He frowned, unable to respond, his brain was frozen, his heart hummed and he couldn't breathe.

"Yes, I said it. Please don't make me repeat it," Sky whispered and lowered her head, her lips quivering. "I'd hoped I could just suppress my feelings and they would go away eventually. I'd prayed it was simply puppy love, that when I grew up I wouldn't still feel the same way I did back then. For a time, I thought I'd forgotten all about you, about my love for you…but then…" She gulped hard, and when she looked up at him, a single tear fell down her cheek. "Then I saw you in the bar and…" She covered her face with her hands and sighed heavily, the weight of the world on her shoulders.

Travis felt a piece of his guarded heart rip away. Had anyone in his twenty-eight years ever cared so much about him? Had any woman he'd had a relationship with, any woman he'd slept with ever shown this much emotion toward him? He couldn't remember, and the pain of the reality hurt. This woman had pined for him, dreamed about him, adored him, and was in love with him despite that she didn't even know him, had never shared his bed, felt his passion. He was truly in awe.

"I tried to fight how I felt. Tried to keep it at bay. But spending this time with you has only solidified my feelings even more. I'd thought it was just a teenage girl phase, but..." She didn't finish even though Travis knew she would say, "It wasn't."

He was speechless for the first time in his life. How could he possibly respond? He let her sit there in her audible reverie until she looked like she might die from embarrassment, her eyes cowering before his, like a meek servant in the presence of a great king. He had to say *...something.*

"Sky, I—"

"Please, just don't, ok? Don't ruin this by saying something stupid back, alright?"

He frowned. She wasn't even giving him a chance to speak. He wasn't gonna say anything stupid. Well, it sounded better in his head. Never mind. She was right. Of course she was. Dammit! He exhaled and looked out the window at the gray sky and brittle bones of the dead trees surrounding them and engaged his heart to come through.

"I'm flattered, Skyla. Truly, I am."

With that, he put the car in Drive and headed down the mountain, feeling a tugging begin in his heart that he'd never quite felt before.

"Larson! Oh thank God, I was getting so worried," DA Jeffers said.

"I'm sorry. I felt compelled to wait until we were safe before attempting to call so I could give you my coordinates." Sky stated into the phone.

"Of course. I would expect no less from my diligent girl." Sky's boss gave a hearty laugh and she felt an immediate calm.

"Any news on his whereabouts?"

"They ransacked Travis's house in Lubbock. The agents found it torn to shreds. Nothing of value was taken though so the police are aware that something is amiss. Looks good for expunging

Redmond's record. No worries on that end, by the way. We'll just get this whole thing squared away then he'll be taken care of. For now, my dear, I want you both to hold fast and bunker down until I can get our boys in place and ready for the showdown. There's something you're gonna have to do though, Sky. You aren't gonna like it, I'm afraid."

Her stomach lurched just at the thought of it. "What?"

"They're gonna take you, both of you."

"What? No! Please?" The thoughts of facing that maniac in person terrified her.

"We need you. You're the final piece to the puzzle."

"Me? Why?"

"You're to interrogate him. The final interrogation, so to speak. Get him to confess to the murders, the fraud, the racketeering, all of it, including what's been going on with Travis's brother. We need it all, and you're gonna get his confession on tape."

"But I'm not wired."

"No, you aren't. But our mole is, and he'll be right beside you the whole time."

"How will I know who he is?"

"He'll give you the code word 'angel' to identify himself and to use for when you're ready for us to come in."

"Sir, with all due respect, these men want us dead. How do I know I won't be immediately killed?

"You won't. Geraci sees you both as viable assets, I've been assured. We'll be live the entire time and if I suspect anything, don't worry, I'll pull the plug on those bastards."

Skyla was reassured by the fact that DA Jeffers had her welfare in mind and would take care of her. He wanted this to be over as much as she did. He also didn't want anyone else to die, he'd said it many times. Sky had to trust him, trust his judgement, and do her job to finally get Geraci taken down; she had to be the one to do it.

"Ok, sir, I'll be ready."

"Trust your gut, Larson. I'm ready for your coordinates. This line is secure."

Sky spouted out the latitude and longitude of the cabin and waited for verification.

"Larson, one more thing. The abort code is Santa. Do you copy?"

"Ten-four. Abort code is Santa. To justice, may she forever reign."

"Good luck, Skyla, and Godspeed."

Sky hung up the phone with a sigh and got a crooked grin out of Travis. "I didn't realize y'all use so much cop jargon."

"What, ten-four?" she giggled.

"Yeah and coordinates. I felt like I was listening in on a military conversation I wasn't supposed to or something. I kept waiting to hear the terms 'target' or 'squadron.'"

Skyla couldn't help but laugh at the handsome stud waiting at the car before her, his hips propped against the driver door and his huge arms across his chest. She wanted to lean in and feel the comfort of his arms around her. But she reminded herself that he wasn't hers... and probably never would be, so why tease herself? Even if it was awfully inviting.

He seemed to sense her hesitancy and tilted his head at her. "You're not gonna let things get weird between us now, are you?"

She looked at him confused. "Weird?"

"Yeah, just because you're in love with me doesn't mean I'm gonna stop flirting with you...or bantering with you! Because I'll be honest, I'm gonna be stuck in a cabin with you for a few days and I'm gonna need to pester the shit out of you and attempt to lure you into bed with me before we're rescued by your people. Consider it a personal goal of mine."

She shook her head at him, as if he were the dumbest man on earth, a glutton for punishment. "Travis Redmond. I would expect no less. But don't think I won't rebuke you and possibly kick your balls up into your throat if I need to."

"Sweetheart, you've been in control of my balls for the last two days and guess what?" His sexy brows raised in challenge. "I'm taking them back. Starting right the hell now."

Suddenly, he grabbed her and pulled her into his chest, enfolding her in his steel-wrapped arms. She whimpered even as one of his big palms slid down to her waist and the other planted in her hair, holding her captive to his sorcerous ways. She was the puppet on his string, a slave to his charm, under his control, and Lord help, she never wanted to be freed.

He turned them, her back hitting the car even as she shivered from the warmth of his big frame pressing into her own. She looked up into azure orbs that left her immobile before her eyes fell to his lips, lips she suddenly realized he was about to kiss her with. She gasped and began to protest before her remonstrations died, his mouth crashing to hers in a glorious clash of passion, domination, and submission. She grunted as his lips slanted across hers and his mouth opened. His strong tongue slid in as stealthy as the serpent into the garden of Eden, and Sky was spellbound. Her head reeled, her body hummed, and her lips kissed Travis's back ardently, as if he were breathing life into her. She took it, inhaled it, and gave back, moaning as he deepened their kiss. His lips and tongue tangled with hers in glorious fury, a harmonious dance of lovers old and young, a symbolism as old as time itself; when he pulled back, Skyla's entire soul vibrated as if struck like a chord.

She sighed, licking her lips and tasting lust, power, and sweetness, and dammit if she didn't want more. He sensed this and gave her a satisfied smile, licking his lips in turn and goodness if she wasn't ready to jump his bones right then, she never would be.

But there was more that needed to be discussed before she just gave herself to him, she realized bashfully, and looked down.

"I knew you weren't all talk, ADA Larson." He leaned in, moving her hair off her neck with the hand at her scalp and whispered, "I can't wait to taste your other set of lips and fuel that fire inside you with my own. Maybe tonight you'll give in?" He arched a brow and pulled away, grinning as he tossed the keys to her. She caught them, even as she felt she was falling into a puddle on the ground. "Here, you drive. I'm afraid my focus won't be on the road."

"Let's make this quick, huh?" Travis said, taking Sky's arm as they walked into the small grocery store. "We just need the basics: toilet paper, soap, and condoms."

Skyla laughed in both humor and sarcasm before scoffing. "What, so you have something to jerk off into? Because that's the only action *you're* getting tonight."

"That's what you think." He winked. "I haven't begun to unleash the full extent of my charms on you yet. You'll be swooning, my little southern belle."

"Ok, *beast*." She rolled her eyes, as she grabbed a cart and began wheeling it towards the freezer section. "I can't do another bag of chips. I'm thinking something hot for dinner."

"Yes, hot and spicy with red hair. Sounds like a feast to me."

Travis pushed his luck and grabbed a handful of ass as Sky stopped in front of the tater tots. He heard her gasp, and she spun around to stick her finger in his face. He was two seconds from pulling it into his mouth and sucking on it seductively when she pulled it back.

"Dammit, Redmond, I swear to God." Her cheeks flamed and he was satisfied to no end. "You pull that shit again and I'm gonna have you on the floor begging for mercy."

"Oh baby, please? By all means, punish me for my wicked ways."

He knew he was flirting with a fine line but could care less. That kiss he'd given her on the curb had made his mind and heart soar. The flavor of that little fireball fueled the lust building inside him that he yearned to quench. He wasn't sure if it was because she'd told him she loved him or if he was half-crazed from their brush with death the day prior or what. All he wanted was to make her his, and he intended to pull out all the stops in order to do so.

"You could *try* to be a bit more inconspicuous. We are hiding out, you know?"

He looked around, realizing they might be drawing attention but saw this little place didn't have many visitors, which he was grateful for. He smiled obediently and set about looking for food. He grabbed up a couple boxes of Stouffer's mac and cheese and some chicken pot pies.

"Travis? What—?"

"It's cheap and convenient."

"It's disgusting. I was gonna cook something."

"You can cook?"

"I'm southern, of course I can cook." She gave him a withered look.

"Then by all means, baby cakes." He bobbed his brows. "Win the way to Ares's heart."

Sky rolled her eyes. She did that a lot lately. He shrugged and moved over to a shelf with boxes of pumpkin-spice donuts. He grabbed one and threw it into the cart too. He was in need of a hard workout and a proper meal, but death put things into perspective; he'd be damned if he wasn't at least having one more donut before that grim bastard came for him.

"Wow, you eat like shit."

"Not on a regular basis," he retorted and touched his chest. "Obviously."

"*Ob*-viously."

He smirked at her constant annoyance with him. He knew deep down it was because she wanted him. It had to be.

"So, what's your specialty, Chef Larson?" he asked, coming to a stop in front of the fresh meats.

"What are you in the mood for?"

"You really want me to answer that question?" The look he gave her was downright feral as his eyes slid from the top of her copper-gold locks, down to her heels. He didn't fail to notice her gaping mouth as he separated the distance between them. "I thought I'd shown you already, Fireball. But I'll be glad to show you again." His hand cupped her cheek and his breath fell over her face.

"Can I help you?" The butcher walked up then, a middle-aged fat man with a cleaver and a big smile.

"N-no, we uh, we're just—" Sky stuttered, quivering as Travis's finger lingered at her earlobe.

"She was checking out my meat," Travis quipped with a wink at Skyla and got a blush from the butcher.

Sky's jaw dropped in shock. Travis had a hard time holding his laugh in as she pulled away and swatted his hand. She thanked the butcher and he ambled off. Sky rounded on Travis again, her cheeks as red as her hair. "Travis! You are disgusting!"

"Am I?" he chuckled.

"I can*not* believe you just said that."

"I was messing—"

"Again! We're in hiding. What if he'd have recognized you?"

Travis sighed heavily. "Fine. I'll behave. Just until we get back to the cabin."

"No, you're gonna behave even then."

"We'll see about that, Fireball." Travis grabbed up a pack of prepared meatballs, seasoned, formed, and ready to cook. "How about some spaghetti and meatballs? Can't go wrong with a classic like that."

Sky shrugged. "Sure. I have a great recipe for sauce."

"Perfect."

They set about grabbing the remaining items needed, enough food for another several meals, including vegetables, eggs and cheese, toilet paper, soap, and even some wine before heading to check out.

"This looks pretty good," the cashier stated when she glanced at the wine. "Might need another bottle, though, if this blizzard comes through."

"B-Blizzard? What blizzard?" Sky asked.

"Oh, it's all over the news. They're calling it a doozy. Might have the roads messed up for a week."

Travis's mouth tightened as he looked to a frowning Skyla. He didn't say a word, just moved back to the wine section and grabbed another couple bottles before coming back to the register.

"That'll be $132.35." The lady said and looked to Sky, who began rifling through her purse only for Travis to intercede.

"I got this one, baby doll." He pulled two hundred-dollar bills from his wallet.

Sky realized her folly too late, groaning as she pushed her credit card back into its slot.

Once they took the cart out to the car, she apologized. "I'm sorry. That would have given us away. Dammit. I—"

"It's ok. No harm, no foul."

She just nodded and they unloaded the cart with the bags before Travis pushed it into the carousel.

"Blizzard, huh?"

"Yeah, what the hell? I have to be stuck in a cabin with you for a week? Kill me. Now, I know why you got wine."

"I got the wine for you, Fireball. I'm gonna need it to get you good and loose."

"Oh, God. I'm gonna need some duct tape too."

"Sounds like fun." Travis laughed even as she shoved at him.

"Keep it up, and I'll lock myself in the bedroom."

"I'll just break the door down."

"So, you plan to take me no matter what?" Her blue eyes narrowed.

"Only if you're willin', baby." He winked again.

God, he loved getting a rile out of her.

"Do you honestly believe that women swoon for your crap? Because you're not funny."

"I have an irresistible charm, soon you'll be overcome. It's just a matter of time." He threw his arm over the back of her headrest as she shook her head and cranked the car.

"Charm, huh? Is that what they call an ego as big as yours?"

"Once you see what I got in my pants, you'll understand my big ego."

She laughed again and he couldn't fight the smile on his face. "You'd do well to keep it in your pants; I might be tempted to cut it off."

"Ok, Bobbitt, but don't cut it off before you sample the goods. You'd only be punishing yourself as well as dozens of other women who have yet to partake."

They came to a red light just as Skyla's hands came up to cup her face. "Please, just stop. Seriously. It's off-putting."

"Sure it is."

"I *hate* your cockiness."

"No, you don't. It's part of my allure."

"You weren't like this in high school."

"I thought you hated high school. Make up your damn mind, woman. You're all over the place."

"Can we just play the silent game for now?"

"No, I want to get to know you more."

"What could you possibly want to know about me?"

Travis frowned as if she were being dense. "Everything."

That gave her pause as she looked over at him to see if he were being serious. "Why would you want to know now, when you didn't back then?"

"Jeez, Sky, would you *please* stop comparing me to the teenage version of myself that I barely remember? I know that seems like yesterday for you, but some of us have moved on and grown up over the last ten years."

His words seemed to rile her up even more. "Oh, I'm sure you barely remember. You were too busy living the life of a god even then. Well, some of us have had to live with scars you wouldn't even understand."

"Here we go again," Travis huffed. "Have you seen a therapist for this shit, Skyla? Seriously?"

"Fuck you, Travis, you have no idea. I have, actually. Thank you very much, asshole."

Travis softened his tone. "So why are you stuck on high school, unable to move on past the *horrible* things that happened to you? Please tell me if you were mistreated. Who hurt you and how badly?"

He paused at the anger suddenly pinking Skyla's cheeks. "I'm not telling you anything else. You love tormenting me now as much as you did then."

"Whoa, hold up! What the fuck are you talking about? I didn't torment you at all." He scowled.

"You faked being nice to me. It was all a show. I know your games, Travis. She told me."

"Hold up! *Who* told you what?"

"Brittany."

"Brittany?" Travis racked his brain to try and remember Brittany ever being cruel to Skyla. Sure, Britt had her snobby moments like any teenage girl, but what were these *scars* Sky was talking about and why was she so hung up on the past?

"She told me you were pretending to be nice to me. That I was an ugly, fat slob that you wouldn't give the time of day to. I remember all of it. Just because you've chosen to forget, doesn't mean I get to."

Travis's heart and mind reeled. He'd never pretended to be nice. He'd never pretended at all, in fact. And he'd never told Brittany anything in regards to Skyla. Ever. He would never call Skyla names like that. But he realized Sky was believing something Brittany had told her and nothing he said right now was going to change that.

She ignored him as they rode. He was quiet, just trying to figure out a way to get through to her, make her understand that he wasn't the bad guy in all this. Brittany was. And he couldn't understand why. What did Brittany have to gain by being so nasty to Skyla? And how bad had it really been? What lengths had she gone to to torment Sky?

Travis had a nagging feeling he wasn't going to like the answer to that question.

CHAPTER FOUR

"Cow. Do you eat all *the ice cream, that's why you got globs of it hanging off your skin?"* Brittany *sneered and pinched Skyla's side* hard, getting a wail out of her.

"Stop, please?" Skyla begged.

"Stop," Brittany mocked, laughing back at her other two girlfriends.

"You know what I want you *to stop doing?" she asked and shoved Skyla back against the bathroom wall. "Stop looking at my boyfriend like you do. He'll never want something like you. He wants me. He likes my body. Not your fat ass. He wouldn't give you the time of day."*

"I—I don't—"

"Shut up, you pathetic slob. That's what he thinks you are, you know that? He told me." She jeered even as Sky's heart burst into a thousand pieces. "Yeah, he thinks you're ugly, and he just pretends to be nice to you, so stop talking to him and looking at him. He's mine. You stick to your books, that's what you know. Let me do what I know." Brittany winked. "Travis Redmond."

With a laugh, she gave a final shove and smacked Skyla's cheek, leaving her a mess of tears and snot as Sky fell to the floor of the bathroom. She trembled in anguish and dejection. Travis thought she was fat and ugly?

73

Her heart felt like it had been literally shattered, tiny shards cleaving to her ribcage, piercing through her flesh. Her stomach twisted and her eyes burned. The boy she loved thought she was disgusting. But why was she surprised? She didn't look like Brittany, as Brittany had said. Brittany was blonde and beautiful, perfect skin, lean and fit. Skyla was freckled, pale, unattractive, overweight...the list went on and on.

When the bell rang, she popped up, she had to get to class. She ran to a stall and grabbed a wad of toilet paper, wiping her eyes and blowing her nose. She took a final glance at her puffy eyes and red cheeks before running out and heading three doors down to Biology.

She barely made it before the bell rang again and avoided Travis's seeking eyes, for she couldn't bear it if he saw her like she was. Brittany's words echoed through her brain and her entire soul felt torn in two. She barely listened to the teacher's lecture as she tried hard not to yearn for a new life, a new body, a new start. She'd hated herself so long she didn't even know where to start anew. She let the pain of the incident come close to destroying her before deciding that she wasn't going to let Brittany get the best of her. She was going to change herself, make herself better in every sense of the word, make herself a woman worthy of Travis Redmond. And she was going to start today.

SKY SHIVERED as she recalled that awful day. The day she had let the bullying take its final toll on her mind and soul. Even as she'd punished herself later that night, she'd made her mind up to stop being the victim, stop allowing herself to be affected by the words of someone like Brittany Balboa.

"Sky?" Travis asked as his hand settled on her shoulder. She shivered again and recoiled from his touch; it both burned and excited her senses. "Hey." He called and moved her hands from her eyes. His beautiful face came into view. "I never said those things. You have to know that I didn't. Brittany told you that to make you feel bad."

"She succeeded," Sky replied, feeling dejected once again as her head fell and she lowered her eyes.

"Brittany Balboa was a bitch. And now she's twice the size you ever were with three evil kids."

That thought didn't make Sky feel better. It didn't matter. For Brittany had every justification to say the words she had back when they were in high school. The girl had been utterly perfect.

"Skyla, I'm sorry...but I never thought that about you. You need to know that. I liked you. You were kind and smart, and I loved your smile. The one you never give me now because I'm being punished for something someone else did to you."

"She was your girlfriend. And I was just the pathetic girl pining my life away for you, the one who'd never get to have you. She loved rubbing that shit in my face."

"Again, *I* didn't do that."

"No, miraculously you were oblivious. She would ridicule me every day in the bathroom. When I started losing weight, she found something else to rag on me about. It was never-ending."

"I swear, Sky, I had no idea."

"It's easy to turn a blind eye when there were so many other important things in your life going on. More important than me."

"Ok, go ahead, punish me. If that makes you feel better. I'll be your whipping boy for my ex-bitch's mistakes. Let's hear it."

"No." Sky shook her head, turning her face to look out the window of the parked car. She noticed the gray skies and how cold it appeared as the wind blew past the trees. "You're right. I need to move on. It was ten years ago. None of us are the same people we were. It's just—"

"What would you say to her, right now, if you could?" Travis asked, his face more serious than she'd ever seen it.

"No, Trav—"

"Seriously, out with it. It'll make you feel better."

Sky thought for long moments, drawing memories of being bullied for months on end by Travis's beautiful but cruel high-school girlfriend. It didn't matter now, she knew. But the pain of Brittany's words and what Sky did to herself afterward couldn't be overcome so easily. Time healed all wounds, but scars had also been left, scars from both the words and Sky's cutting.

"Ok, fine... B—Brittany. I'm not...ugly. I'm not fat, not anymore. I've worked hard to get where I am. To prove myself to you. To prove myself to...well, to myself. To prove myself worthy of any man. Especially Travis Redmond, who wouldn't have wanted me back when I was fat. Your words have hurt me, scarred me, taken so much from me. But they also pushed me to work hard, to be better, so thank you."

Travis frowned. "Thank you?"

"Yeah..."

"No." Travis huffed. "Say, *fuck* you, Brittany. You fucking bitch."

"No. I forgive her."

"Fuck that. This went on for months you said. She was a damn bully. I knew she was mean, but this is something else. You deserve an apology."

"An apology I'll likely never get, but that's ok."

"No, Sky, it isn't. I freaking hate bullies. You had enough to deal with. You were a teenage girl who'd lost her mom and that was how you were treated? Naw, she's a bitch, just say it."

"It was a defense mechanism."

"For what?"

"She was insecure about something."

Travis's brow went up. "You're right. We all have them, don't we? Me, thanks to my dad. I threw myself into football because it was my escape from his drunken beatings."

Skyla was stunned by his revelation. She never would've suspected Tyler Redmond of abuse. Travis hadn't made it known and why would he? No one else was knowledgeable of this dark secret of his, she was certain. It made his accomplishments seem all the more inspiring.

He continued, "Brittany's parents were loaded. She had it all. She had to take out her insecurities on someone, I guess."

"And that someone just happened to be me," Sky finished and

took his hand in hers, giving him an understanding smile, seeing beyond that beautiful exterior to the strong soul within. "Brittany might've had her own skeletons lurking in her closets. We'll never know." Skyla shrugged lightly.

"Well, I'm apologizing on her behalf. I'm sorry you had a shitty time in high school. But darlin', we ain't in high school anymore. We're about to be snowed-in, in a cabin far from civilization, so in the spirit of forgiveness allow me the honor of apologizing to you in the only way I can. With my rockin' body."

Skyla couldn't help but laugh. God, the man was so unbelievably vain.

"There, finally! Now can we unload this car and get these groceries in?"

She nodded and wiped her tears, following Travis's lead while he began to grab bags. She moved to unlock the door and let him in first as she attended to the few bags he'd left behind. When she sat the last bag on the table, she turned to close the door and lock it, shivering as the blistering wind whistled in. It had gotten exceptionally cold in a matter of hours.

She turned to the bag only to be stopped by Travis as he gently gripped her shoulders.

She gasped but looked his handsome face over, seeing a softness in his usually overconfident blue eyes she'd not noticed before.

"Hey, you know I can't undo what she did to you. I can apologize for her, but I can't take the sting away or change anything from the past, especially when I didn't know what was happening."

Sky scowled and nodded. "Travis, it's ok. I—"

"But what I *can* do," he interrupted, "is attempt to make it up to you."

"It's not your place to do that."

"Ok, well." He gave her a beaming smile, showcasing those dimples she'd always swooned for. "Let's say, I want to. Allow me the honor of an attempt to make your high school memories better?"

Sky gave him a confused look, unsure what he had up his sleeve.

"You didn't go to junior or senior prom, right? Your mom was sick that first year, so you missed it."

Skyla blushed a dozen shades, looking down even as Trav's finger moved beneath her chin and tilted her face back up. Tears stung her eyes as she stared into orbs as blue as glacier water. "Yes, but she insisted I go. I wasn't asked by anyone either year...of course. But she begged me to go stag, so that I could experience the spectacle. I knew I would be laughed at, so I declined."

"Anyone who was stupid enough to laugh at you deserves a punch in the face...that goes for Brittany too."

"You wouldn't punch a woman," Sky contended.

"Ok, no, but I might have encouraged you to punch her," he joshed. "My point is, I think we need to redo prom. Tonight."

"What? How?"

"Well, I got a radio and batteries, here. And I'm sure we can find some clothes in the drawers. They may not be fancy, but we can pretend, embellish a little." He winked.

If she hadn't been so in love with him already she might have fallen then, for the twinkle in his eyes had never been so brilliant. She smiled big, grateful for his kindness. It touched a place in her heart...and somewhere low in her belly too.

"Would you like that?"

Sky nodded as a tear fell down her cheek. He swiped it away and leaned into kiss the cheek he'd just set on fire with his tender touch. He whispered, "Well, first Ms. Larson, I need to ask you to go with me."

"O—Okay."

"So, Skyla, I was wondering... you wanna go to prom with me?" Travis's smile was mischievous as he pulled back some to look into her face, far more handsome than she ever remembered it being when he was a teenage boy.

She couldn't fight the tremble that started up her spine and she licked her lips as his eyes fell to her mouth. She couldn't speak so she nodded again.

"Since this is an impromptu prom, we can dance and cook…and maybe after we'll let our bodies party too." He winked again and she shoved at him.

"You need to behave. My father would never approve."

"Good thing your father is far away; you're not a teenager anymore, you know? Besides, I can't let those condoms go to waste."

"And just like that, you killed the mood…moron." She rolled her eyes, moving away to unpack the bags and put the groceries away.

"I'll just reset it. I'm an expert where women are concerned."

"Yeah, well, not this woman. This woman isn't like the others. You can't sweet talk your way into my pants, even if you take me to 'prom.'" She crossed her arms over her chest.

"No?" he asked, taking the meat from her grasp and gripping her wrist. He ran his finger down the inside curve of her arm and up into her sleeve. She stifled the moan at her throat. "You wearing panties made of steel?"

Sky laughed. "No."

"Then trust me when I tell you, I'll get in 'em. If my words don't melt them right off first."

"You seriously think you're God's gift to women, don't you, Travis Redmond? Your head is really that big."

"They *both* are." He flashed his pearly whites again and she jerked her arm away, moving to the fridge. "I intend to have you, Skyla. I may even ruin you to other men once you get a taste of what I can do."

Skyla turned and laughed big in his face, even as he began caging her into the chilly fridge, her back hitting the metal. "What makes you think I even *want* to sleep with you? How many lovers have you had by now?"

"Less than you'd assume."

"Double digits, I'm sure."

"Possibly." He shrugged, nonchalantly.

"I bet you've lost count, haven't you?"

"No."

Sky's eyes narrowed, attempting to read him. "You'd probably just lie to me, wouldn't you?"

"I'm a lot of things, Fireball. A liar isn't one of them."

"I beg to differ, *cheater.*"

The smile faded from his face and his lips tightened into a line. He pulled his big inked arms from beside her head, and even though she was more comfortable with the distance, she felt a chill that had nothing to do with the cold air blowing on her back. She wanted to apologize but held her ground.

"You, of all people, Skyla, know how it feels to be called names. Especially when you aren't what people assume you to be."

"Trav—"

"I'm, uh, I'm gonna go shower and change. You got this?" he asked, his face red.

Sky simply nodded. She'd never seen Travis so angry and didn't know how to respond. He paused and sighed heavily, as if intending to say more but then he shifted, his retreating back all she was left with.

"Great job, Sky," she said aloud to herself. "The one man who's been interested in you in a long time, wants to sleep with you, and you push him away. Classic."

She turned and continued to put the groceries away, suddenly feeling like the biggest bitch who ever lived.

WHEN TRAVIS CAME BACK into the kitchen his hair was still damp from his shower. He wore an old flannel button-down and a pair of sweat pants he'd found in one of the drawers. He'd topped it with a leather jacket.

"Well, look at you, you found clothes to fit you."

"You didn't mention Terry was such a large man." Travis pulled the sweat pants out and they fell a little. He rolled them down and pulled them up his hips, tying the drawstring at the elastic waistband taut. "I mean I'm six feet, two twenty. He's gotta be a good twenty or thirty pounds heavier than I am."

"Yeah, he's not small." Sky turned and looked him over. "But you fill out his clothes nicely." She grinned as she looked him over, her eyes hovering on his chest and shoulders, which the shirt hugged tightly despite the bagginess in the waist.

"I mean it's not prom attire but comfy at least. I figured our clothes needed to be washed."

"Good call. Guess I'm wearing an equally as comfortable flannel and sweats, huh?"

"There were some smaller clothes in there. You might actually have more options." Travis stepped up behind her and put his arms around her waist, tucking his chin against her shoulder and inhaling her lilac-scented hair. "Mmm, that smells delicious."

"I—I, uh, I figured I'd start the sauce while you were showering. It needs to simmer."

"I was talking about you, Fireball. Not the sauce."

He noticed Sky still and flicked her ear with the tip of his tongue, feeling her quake in his arms. He knew he was being pushy, but it was difficult to be so close to this woman and not be drawn to her, despite her warring emotions. She was a fierce lioness who stopped at nothing to shelter her heart, but there was also a vulnerable side that called to his masculinity. An overwhelming need within him to protect her, comfort her, and claim her.

"Travis, I should apologize."

"Water under the bridge." He interrupted and moved the hair off her neck, letting the waves fall through his fingers as he twisted it in his fist. "I don't want to talk about the past, only what the future holds. Tonight, I envision wine and candles and the sounds of my name on your lips as I take you again and again and again." His mouth lingered on her pulse point and he watched her tremble, loving how she responded to his touch. He sighed before gently kissing the peachy flesh there that beckoned to him as he fisted her shirt at her waistline. "I bet you're gonna feel amazing."

"Tr—Travis, please. I—"

"You're right. Music and wine first."

"I also want to change."

"Yes, that too." He released her and turned her slowly in his arms, watching her uncertain eyes look him over. He could see the inner fight within her and wondered if she would give in to his advances. "Make it something less conservative. More skin." He winked.

Skyla scoffed. "How is it that you're so confident?"

"Years of training, being the best, and having women throw themselves at me." He shrugged.

Sky looked down, almost reproachful, as she disentangled herself from his arms. "Must be nice," she quipped and began to walk off. "Watch that sauce, don't let it stick."

"Oui, madame." Travis gave the sauce a quick stir with the wooden spoon Sky had been using, letting the aroma of tomatoes, basil, garlic and oregano assault his hungry belly, which growled in response. He set the spoon aside and moved off to look for a skillet to brown the meatballs in, finding a large cast iron one and pulling it to the gas stove. He decided to make himself useful, hoping to impress Skyla. He didn't understand why but he wanted her to see him as more than a big-headed athlete with an ego as fat as his wallet. He wanted her to look at him in admiration. He wanted to earn her heart, earn her love, earn her loyalty.

When she came back in, he'd turned the radio on, fished out a pan for their garlic bread, a bowl for their salad, had started the meatballs and was washing the produce. She stopped and her brows went up, she was surprised to say the least. He didn't want to admit his heart was soaring.

"Wow! You're efficient."

"Wow, you're stunning." He smiled and looked her outfit over. A gray pair of sweatpants that were much smaller than his, presumably a woman's, a tight white tank top beneath an unbuttoned pink flannel and fuzzy socks with little ducks on them. "Honey, we match. And here I thought I was gonna have a hard time finding a corsage."

Sky smiled big, her mouth lifting and perfectly straight teeth showing. Travis swooned and grabbed her up as Frank Sinatra belted out to them, a song about not asking him to dance. She giggled sweetly as he pulled her against him and spun her around the kitchen, the smell of Italian food filling his nostrils. His heart swelled as the two of them connected on this cold Colorado night. Travis hummed the song as his feet moved and he twirled his date to the rhythm of the music. He dipped her at the end and pulled her back up, aligning her to his body, noticing she was the perfect height and fit just right, there in his arms.

Her blue eyes held him as another song took them, this one slower and with more sexual promise. Sky swallowed hard as her eyes fell to his lips and his hand moved to her waist, stroking her through her shirt.

"You're a good dancer, Sky," he said and gave her a grin.

"I took lessons in college. Ballroom."

"That's interesting. Did you learn anything *sexy*?" he asked and she huffed. She moved off to turn the meatballs and he felt a little dejected, bereft without her there. He sidled up beside her and began drying the lettuce off with paper towels. "I was just kiddin'," he stated.

"Why are you so confident? Seriously, where does it come from?"

Travis shrugged. "Defense mechanism, right?" he smirked.

"Perhaps, but you make it look and seem so easy."

"It's just who I am, Skyla," he defended.

"I envy you," she whispered, almost so softly he barely heard it and his eyes snapped over to her. She was looking down though, focused on their food and he frowned. She was being honest. Her self-esteem was in the toilet, and his was soaring high. He'd never had an issue with liking himself and didn't understand why she did. It was perplexing.

He decided to bring the mood back. "Well, this is gonna be delicious. I'm starved. How about I break out the wine?"

He moved to the cabinet where they'd placed the bottles of red blends, grabbed one, and began to search for a wine opener. He finally found one in the drawer next to Sky, loving having an excuse to touch—and frazzle—her even further. He was breaking her down even more and she would be his little indulgence soon enough. He couldn't wait to be buried deep inside her, hearing her scream in pleasure as he screwed all that sass right out of her.

When dinner was done, they plated it up, lowered the music and lit candles to place on the table. Trav had to admit, this was pretty romantic for an impromptu dinner in a remote shack in the woods, while they were hiding out. It turned him on and amped him up.

He bit into a juicy meatball first and moaned aloud, his appetite for food almost as strong as his appetite for the spirited little ginger seated next to him. "Alright, is it too soon to propose to my prom date? Fuck, Sky. This is amazing. You'll have to tell me the secret recipe."

"Can't. Thus, the secrecy. I'll require the blood sacrifice of your first born in exchange." She winked.

"Well, fuck me sideways. Did you just make a joke? You mean to tell me ADA Skyla Larson has a sense of humor? Damn. Who knew?"

"Funny. I have a great, albeit dry, sense of humor."

"You don't say. I hadn't come to that conclusion at all," he smarted back.

"Oh, can it, Redmond, and eat your food," she scolded, playfully.

He did and enjoyed every bite of it, filling his belly as they talked about Skyla's work, her cat, Khaleesi, Travis's affection for snowboarding and football, and the dark subject of Geraci.

"Years now, huh?" Travis asked as she told him how long they'd been onto the mobster.

"Yes. We've been so close. Yet somehow, he always has one up on us."

"Yeah well, not this time. You got a man on the inside, right?"

"Yes, and we've not been sure how Geraci's been evading us, but we think we've figured it out."

"Oh? Top secret."

"No, a dirty cop."

"Shit! Really?"

Sky nodded and sipped her wine, her words slurring just enough to hint that she was starting to get a buzz on. "Can we change the subject, please?" She shivered as the power flickered and the wind whistled harshly by the door, causing it to quake.

"Sure. Let's talk about sex instead."

"Ugh. You're so hung up on that topic."

"And you're not hung up on it enough. You know women are supposed to be in their sexual prime in their thirties? Perhaps you just need the right lover, Sky. A sixty-year-old isn't gonna do it for you, Fireball."

"Psst, he's not sixty. He's fifty," she whisper-yelled.

"Whatever. Same difference."

"And I'm not thirty yet. I got two more years, thanks so much."

"Close enough."

"Obviously he's doing pretty well." Sky snorted. When Trav frowned in question, she continued. "He was fuckin' his secretary, remember? He *apparently* didn't have a problem sexually."

"Yeah, well, he's dumb."

"Blondes have more fun," Skyla stated cynically.

"So they say. I like what they say about redheads myself though," Travis fished.

"Why do you think he cheated?" Sky skated right over his ploy, staring off and downing her drink before looking back at him. "Can a man really be loyal to one woman? Is that possible? Or are all of you just promiscuous swine who only think about one thing day and night?"

Uh oh! Perhaps the alcohol was a bad idea.

"I believe men can be loyal." Travis steepled his hands, wary that he needed to proceed with care. "I think once a man finds the right woman, it's possible." It wasn't a lie, after all; despite how his father had treated his mother, Travis believed in true love. He just hadn't found it yet.

"How many times a day do you think about sex? Is it really thousands like they say?"

"I don't know who 'they' are, but…yeah, it's a lot," Travis admitted.

Sky looked off once more then pulled her hands to her face, covering it. When she finally pulled her hands down, she looked miserable. "It's because I refused to sleep with him."

"Who? Sam?" Travis asked. Sky just nodded in response. "Why?"

"Dammit, because I wanted to wait until marriage."

When Travis literally balked, Sky snorted, "No, I'm not a virgin. Duh! I just… I've always given myself to men who didn't deserve me. Each and every one of them was some random quickie, involving far too much alcohol and not enough restraint. And this final time, I wanted it to be special, not just a roll in the hay that meant nothing." She huffed and pulled her legs up, wrapping her arms around her knees.

"But he was your fiancé. I'm sure it wouldn't have meant nothing… well…" Travis faltered. The man *had* cheated, so perhaps it was a good thing she'd held out on him.

"I guess it doesn't much matter anymore. He couldn't wait for me, so…" she trailed off and looked forlorn. Travis realized he had to say something.

"He's missing out." Travis held her gaze when her eyes finally came up to his.

"You don't even know, so you can't say that."

"I can see you have a fire inside you, Sky. You've got a wild little goddess in there that's begging to be unleashed. Come, let's free her."

Travis stood, moved to the radio and turned the volume of the slow song that was playing up. He recognized it from the movie *Dirty Dancing* and grinned to an unsure Skyla. He extended his hand and she looked at it as if she were deciding whether to jump off a cliff or run in the opposite direction. Finally, just as he was starting to lose every ounce of his confidence, she took it and stood.

He moved them into the living room where the fire was starting to die in the slightly ajar wood-burning stove. The blue, red, and orange flames danced together, crackling and flickering hungrily, similar to Travis and Skyla's intimate connection. He cupped her hand in his and splayed his other hand low on her back, loving her femininity and softness against his hard frame. He was acutely aware of her breasts pressing into his chest, her pelvis touching his, her thighs hitting his own as they swayed. He started to become aroused, not only at her closeness but the way her eyes stared back into his, the way her tongue kept darting across her lips. He felt his heart beat increase and his breathing accelerate.

His hand fell from hers and moved to join the other at her waist, he linked them, pulling her even closer as her hands slid up his shoulders to wrap around his neck. The head of his stiffening member brushed her thigh, and she gasped sharply. He, at first, feared she would be offended but she just looked surprised. He felt the need to apologize for his erection, almost as if he were with a virgin, the way she reacted to him and his body's responses to her closeness.

"Sorry. I, uh, it happens." Travis gave her a crooked smile. When her eyes fell, he silently reprimanded himself. "I mean, even if I attempted to rein it in, it's still gonna happen." *No, idiot. Try again!* "Fuck, I mean…"

"I'm a woman pressed closely to you, I get it," Sky muttered and looked away. Her eyes moved to the fire, insecurity dancing in them, and Travis felt his gut rip at the pain that was so evident there.

"No, Skyla." His hand moved to cup her cheek and turned it to face him. His finger traced her high cheekbone. "You're a *gorgeous* woman that I'm pressed intimately close to, and I want you. I want you with a hunger that I haven't felt before." It might be the truest words he'd ever spoken, and he found his head reeling from the realization.

Sky just looked up at him, in awe, in disbelief, in disgust…he wasn't sure. He looked her beautiful face over, the brilliant blue eyes that entranced him, her wavy copper-gold hair, the spattering of freckles across her cheeks, her small, pert little nose, her perfect lips —not too big and not too small. He let himself be drawn even further into her allure, for if she were an enchantress, he was a victim to her hex and he was going to absorb every second of this while he could.

Travis's cock grew even more prominent between them. He longed to rub himself against her and let her feel what her spell was doing to him. He grinned as his hand moved up her back, feeling her out while Sky continued to be mute. He'd left her speechless; that had to be a good sign.

When she finally spoke, her eyes were reverent as they looked his face over, falling to his lips. "This was all I ever dreamed of as a teenage girl, you know."

"Prom?" he probed.

"Being wrapped in your arms, having you look at me like you are now. This feels like a dream. Now, I know what Cinderella felt like at the ball."

Travis's heart swelled. It was nice to be someone's dream. Girls had always been drawn to him; he had an infectious personality—or so he'd been told. Travis considered himself a handsome enough guy with his dark brown hair, bright blue eyes, and dimples. Females loved his smile and his charm. But he'd always felt like a fun little toy for them, used and discarded afterwards. He wasn't the man they wanted for a husband, a fling for sure, but not husband material. He was impulsive, unpredictable, enjoyed the chancier side of life, unsettled. He wasn't stable enough for that life and if they got the wrong idea, he'd been sure to remind them of it too. He'd been the one to break up with Brittany when she'd suggested trying to transfer to the same college as him or somewhere closer to where he was their senior year in high school.

"Negative, sweetheart," he'd scoffed. "I'm going to college single, nothing personal. It was fun and all, but I'd like a clean slate." After all, he'd not wanted a dead weight on his shoulders to start his college career. And the likelihood of her getting into LSU was slim to none anyway, her grades had been mediocre at best. Plus, he'd grown bored of her and her attitude. She'd been a pretty girl, but she wasn't a nice person and that had started to grate on him. He realized now that she'd never been right for him and wished that he'd have noticed how alluring Skyla was and had always been. Spicy, passionate, full of life.

He realized suddenly he hadn't responded to her comment, and she was blushing, her cheeks reddening. It was so adorable he chuckled. "So, if you're Cinderella, does that make me Prince Charming?" She simply smiled and nodded. "Well, I'll be honest, Fireball, I don't know that Prince Charming had quite as broad of an imagination as I do. He's far too chaste for the things I have planned for you and I."

"You *would* corrupt good ol' Prince Charming, wouldn't you, bad boy?"

"Oooh, I like that nickname. Say it again." Trav's brows went up. "Only whisper it in my ear this time."

Skyla giggled wickedly, which made his cock jerk in response.

He moaned softly. "That sweet little giggle does wonderful things to me, Sky."

Sky bit into her lip, and Travis moved his hand into her hair, pulling her head closer to his, her lips closer for his taking. They were but a breath away from one another when a log in the open stove snapped loudly. Sky jumped in his arms, her forehead hitting his jaw, causing him to bite his lip.

"Ow, dammit," he muttered and covered his lip with his finger. When he pulled it away, there was a droplet of blood there. He licked it and frowned.

"Oh my God, Travis. I'm so sorry," Sky whined.

Travis couldn't help the laugh that bubbled deep in his throat. "Courtship can be painful, my dear, but I had no idea you were a sadist. Damn Sky, what else you got in mind?"

Skyla looked mortified and suddenly, Travis felt bad about messing with her so much, she really took everything he said to heart. She attempted to pull out of his embrace, but he held her. "I need to go get some ice or something. A wet rag at least," she reasoned.

"Just give it a second, love. It'll stop. You think this is the first time I've gotten my lip cut? Nah, I got men hurling their gigantic, padded bodies at me left and right. This ain't nothin'."

But Sky's bravado began to crumble, and Travis could see that this wasn't 'nothin'. "Oh, Sky, baby, c'mon. Look. It stopped bleedin'. See." Her frown tightened before her hands came up to once again cover her face. She tended to do that a lot lately. Hiding. In shame. From him.

"I'm so sorry. I ruined the moment, didn't I? I'm such a klutz."

"Oh, you are not. C'mere." He pulled her against his chest and stroked her hair, tucking her head into his pec. "There. There."

He comforted her unease, listening as the wind whipped hard against the roof and windows, sounding like a hurricane. They were completely fogged up now and he bet if he looked outside he would see snow falling.

"Sky, c'mon baby. It's really alright. I swear, I'm fine. You aren't a klutz." He coaxed her chin up to look at him. She sighed again, embarrassment painting her cheeks.

"I'm really, really clumsy though."

"Well, I'm really, really sarcastic. No one's perfect." He winked and got a smile out of her. "There. Look at that. See, all is right as rain."

Just then the power flickered and went out, leaving them in semi-darkness with only the soft glow of the stove.

"Glad I brought that extra wood in," Travis murmured and ran his hand down the back of Sky's head, following her long hair down her back. "See, even mother nature wanted us to have our moment."

With that, he leaned in and captured her lips, getting a sharp gasp out of her. But soon she leaned in and was melting into him. He absorbed her, loving how good she felt in his arms, how good her soft lips felt, how they tasted. He moaned into her opening mouth and let his tongue slide in. It stroked hers in rapid succession, eliciting yummy sounds from her throat. His cock grew harder between them and longed to be nestled inside her silky heat. His hand moved down her back to that plump little ass of hers and squeezed. Damn, it was nice and firm beneath the sweats. His other hand moved down to follow suit and gripped her other ass cheek, pulling her hard against his throbbing erection. He pulled back to breathe and moaned loudly. "Fuck baby, you feel so damn good."

Sky moaned before crashing her lips hard against his, reopening the cut on his lips, but he was numb to the pain, the blood. All he felt in those moments was a driving desire, a force stronger than anything to pull those pants off her and take her, mark her, make her his. He turned them away from the stove and moved slowly towards the couch.

She fell and he followed, gripping her and pulling her back against him, rubbing his need for her against her thigh as she wrapped her legs around his waist. "Oh Travis," she murmured as his mouth found her neck and nibbled while his hand cupped a breast. The sound of his name on her lips like that made his desire spike through the roof. Soon, he was gripping her thigh as he thrust harder against her, the need to bury himself inside her outweighing any other need he'd ever had.

"Sky, I want you. I want this. Fuck." He began pulling the flannel shirt off her shivering frame, attempting to pull the tank top up so he could see her peachy skin. Only he couldn't see shit; it was getting too damn dark, and he swore again.

Sky grunted as he pulled back. "What's wrong?"

"Nothin', baby. I just can't see, and I need to see you." He chucked her chin as he moved away, back toward the stove so he could throw another couple logs onto the fire and make it lighter in the room. When that worked and he could see well enough, he came back over to a wary Skyla, who covered her arms. "We can move to the bedroom, if you want, Fireball," he offered as his hand came to her cheek again.

"Travis, I—" Her eyes found his and he realized she didn't want this, not like he did.

Disappointment riddled him and something he'd never felt before—rejection. And this wasn't the first time. He realized that she might be in love with him and had hoped for this all her teen life, but that didn't mean as an adult she was actually gonna go through with it. She was older, wiser, and less naïve than she'd been as a young girl. For the first time in his life, Travis realized his track record in the bedroom might actually be his disadvantage now. He didn't know what to say or how to respond. He swallowed hard and looked down.

As if reading his mind, she said, "It's just so soon. I—"

"I'm being pushy."

"No."

"I am. I know I am. It's been a while for me."

"Oh?" she smarted. Uh oh. *Wrong thing to say, asshole,* his brain warned.

"Sky," he tried to remedy but it was too late, she was pulling away.

"Guess that's why you're wanting it so much, huh?" her tone was less smart than hurt, and Travis sighed heavily.

"Sky, I want *you.*"

"Any girl would do, Travis. You just said—"

"I know what I said. But— Dammit, Sky, I really suck at this kinda thing, you gotta know that!" He threw a hand through his hair and looked back at the tears suddenly falling down her cheeks like rain. "Baby, that's not true. Not just any girl would do, ok? Just because I haven't had sex in a month or so, doesn't mean that I would hop right into the sack with the first piece of ass who came along. I do have standards, ya know?" He tried to lighten the mood and elbow her, but it was no use; she was full-out crying now, and he cursed himself to Hell and back. Dammit, the alcohol was a bad idea. She was horny one minute, crying the next. "Sky."

"I'm sorry, I don't mean to be overly dramatic," she said, her words muffled behind her hands even as he tried to pull them away. "This has just been a rough forty-eight hours."

"I know, darlin', I know it has. C'mere." He pulled her back to him and settled her on his lap, cradling her into his arms and tucking her head against his shoulder. He let her cry, thinking about how harrowing this all had been: running from men with guns shooting at them, the fear of getting caught, hiding and keeping their guard up, knowing that this wasn't over. On top of that, Sky had been faced with a past she hadn't been prepared for when Travis had randomly shown back up in her life bringing old skeletons out of her closet.

Travis realized he was also exceedingly tense. He truly feared for his brother's life, knowing this entire time he'd been as frazzled as Sky had been; now, this was his attempt to escape the truth, live in the moment, and de-stress. That was what she needed, he suddenly realized and got an idea. "I know exactly what you need, baby. Here. Sit here for a minute. I'll be right back, ok?"

He pulled her from his embrace and sat her onto the couch then moved to the kitchen, grabbed two candles from the table and moved into the bedroom. He sat the candles on the sides of the big tub and started the water, making it nice and hot as he rummaged for some bubbles to add to the water. He found a bottle of body wash that smelled as spicy as his girl did and squirted it into the cascading water from the spigot. He smiled as it filled up and moved to grab a towel and washcloth. Then he went and got Sky. He picked her up, placing an arm beneath her legs and one behind her back. She blushed as he carried her like she weighed no more than a feather. Her arms wrapped around his neck and she looked into his face as he walked her past the bed and into the bathroom. She heard the water running and smiled as she realized what he'd done.

"You, my little Fireball, need to relax some and I'm gonna help a girl out." He winked as he set her down, her feet touching the floor as he released her. "Welcome to Spa de Ares. Where our priority is your pleasure." He grinned and she laughed.

"This is sweet, *Ares*. You shouldn't have."

"Oh, but I absolutely had to. Your frazzled nerves needed a good soak. So, by all means. Disrobe and sink in, madame." He grabbed her hand and brought her knuckles to his lips, kissing them gently. He watched her eyes dart to his and she bit into her lip. *Romantics eat your damn hearts out*, he thought to himself. Had he known winning her over would be this easy, he would've done so already and gotten into her panties even faster. There was more than one way to a touchdown, he knew, and grinned again. "I'll bring you another glass of red for your nightcap, Aphrodite."

"Aphrodite? Ha!" she scoffed. "I don't think so."

"Well, it's a good thing you aren't the Greek god who gets to decide the names of my consorts, huh?" he retorted and pulled her hard against him again. He got a gasp out of her and it thrilled him to no end.

Her eyes spoke to him and it was all he could do not to rip her clothes off and take her against the wall, right then and there. He held back though because he sensed her hesitations.

He kissed her hand again and, with all his willpower, stepped away, pulling the door closed as he did so.

CHAPTER FIVE

Sky sighed in contentment as she settled down into the suds of the bubble bath Travis had drawn for her. He continued to surprise her at every turn. Just when she'd decided he was selfish, self-absorbed, and an arrogant asshole, he came in and showed her an entirely new side of himself. It was refreshing and made her feel good, even if she knew it was only a matter of time before he got his way and took her to bed, inhibitions be damned. He'd come very close until she'd accidentally busted his lip. She'd realized how undeserving she still felt of him, although she couldn't say why. He'd had far more lovers than she had, she was sure, and last she checked, she was a decent human being who deserved to have a lover blow her mind. She was almost positive Travis would indeed do so—or at least she prayed he would.

She couldn't remember ever having a man share her bed who loved her body like she'd read in any romance novel. In fact, her sexual encounters had been wholly uneventful in their passion. The conquests she'd had in college had been drunken flings, not unlike the one she'd almost had with Travis moments ago before her senses began to kick in; she realized if she acquiesced to him, he'd see the scars she wasn't quite ready to show him just yet. She'd panicked and her insecurities had surfaced just in time to stop the disaster from happening, thank God.

Skyla imagined Travis would be different than her clumsy partners back in college. She'd had more than a few, but they'd all been the same—drunk or high and in a hurry to simply fuck their cares away. She'd always made sure they had protection, but it was a hurried few pumps and they were spent inside her, leaving her to wonder what the big deal was about. Sex had always seemed impersonal to her, despite that it was supposed to be one of the most personal, sensual things people could do together. However, Sky had immediately seen that with Travis that wouldn't be the case in their coupling. There was nothing about how he touched or kissed her that had been quick or hurried or detached in any way, shape, or form, and she longed to explore a different side of the erotic act she never had before.

Even with her ex-fiancé, things had been so messy and sloppy, his kisses overpowering—and not in a good way. Sky had realized right away she'd have to rein him in or Sam would end up being just like those men she'd sought to distance herself from, which was probably why she'd wanted to wait to do it again.

A knock came at the door and Sky gasped, covering her breasts as it opened.

Nothing could have prepared her for the onslaught on her senses and she felt her mind, body, and jaw go slack as her eyes were assaulted by one of the most beautiful naked men she'd ever seen in her life.

Ares, for that's who he could have been in the flesh, stood utterly nude in front of her, moving from the door into the bathroom with nothing but a tray in his hand, a tray with a glass of wine atop it.

"T-Tr—" She couldn't even speak his name; every sexual fantasy she'd ever had in her life had just come true.

He was even more alluring in real life than he'd been in her dreams. Tall, big, muscular. His chest was broad, his tattooed arms thick, his torso ripped in sinewy muscles, his big thighs the size of tree trunks. She saved his sex for last because she knew once her eyes fell there, she was doomed. It's girthy length was slightly erect and growing harder, bigger than she assumed it would be. When he stopped mere feet in front of her, she couldn't take her eyes off of it. She even whimpered, knowing she was powerless now to the sexual spell he had her under. If he wanted to fuck her that instant, it was going to happen and there was nothing she could do to stop him. She was his now—Ares—the powerful warrior god of the gridiron. She gulped and licked her lips.

"Fireball, if you keep looking at my dick like that, I'm going to unleash it upon you. And so help me God, I don't know if I can be held responsible for the havoc it plans to wreak on you."

Her eyes shot up to his then in both excitement and terror, and he grinned, the grin of the very Devil himself. She was truly fucked in every sense of the word. It was all she could do not to beg, for relief or mercy she wasn't sure. Her chest heaved and she looked back down at his cock jutting up at her, wondering what it would feel like in her palm as she pumped it, down her throat, inside her; she licked her lips again. Just as she was about to beg him to take a step forward and let her explore that fascinating part of him, he knelt down, obstructing her view.

She inhaled sharply, realizing her chest was literally heaving in anticipation.

"The elixir of the gods, my sexy Aphrodite." He motioned to the wine with his eyes. Damn that sexy as sin grin of his, those dimples. God, she wanted to investigate them with her tongue. Fuck. What the hell was he doing to her? Her womanhood vibrated with sheer lust.

Skyla realized she hadn't scolded him for coming in on her naked and in the tub but, try as she might, she couldn't and wouldn't; she wanted to see how far he was going to take this little game of his. She simply took the wine off the tray and downed it in three sips. She needed it to calm her taxed nerves. She was two seconds from standing and throwing herself into his tempting arms.

He took the glass from her and set both it and the tray on the bathroom counter before returning and cupping her face in his hands.

"Do you want to know how a goddess is worshipped?" his tone was as smooth and rich as molasses.

Oh, fuck yes. Worship me, my god, she thought but couldn't utter the words aloud. She nodded as he stood and moved behind her and into the tub. *Oh shit,* she thought. *This is happening. This is* really *happening.*

She felt his big, trunk-like legs settle on either side of her as she scooted forward a little. He sat down behind her, his hefty length pressing into her as he adjusted her in his lap. Her back hit his hard-muscled chest and torso and she blushed, wishing her body were even remotely close to being as toned as his was. Her thoughts died as his hand moved her hair off her neck and his lips brushed the curve of her shoulder, delicately kissing her there. Her heartbeat quickened as his right hand moved from her hair to her cheek, then her neck, gripping it lightly in his big palm. She swallowed hard, her entire body alight in licking, hot flames that threatened to draw her down to Hell's gates. His feet moved beneath her ankles, and he used them to spread her legs wider. She shivered and heard him chuckle as his other hand came around her side to cup her breast.

"Mmm, so beautiful," Travis murmured as his mouth moved to her collarbone and licked.

She gasped and moaned all at once, her senses overloaded with arousal. What was he doing to her, and what had he put into that wine? She realized he couldn't see her body with the scarce light of the candles, which gave her some relief and also increased the eroticism of this act as he went by feel alone.

He tilted her head back with the hand holding her throat as he continued to fondle her breast, pinching her nipple with his thumb and index finger. She felt his tongue lick up the back of her neck slowly and she shivered, whimpering again.

"Oh, Aphrodite. Do you know how badly that sexy little whimper makes me wanna fuck you?"

God, his voice. It was hot as hell and she wanted to reach around, grab his cock, and beg him to do so. "Tr—Travis—"

"Name's Ares, baby doll." His grip tightened on her throat and he growled in her ear, nipping her earlobe. She moaned aloud, her stimulation coating her insides. "I'm gonna worship this gorgeous little body until I make you come." She shivered as his hand moved from her throat down her chest, his fingertips trailing down her cleavage to her belly. She started to protest his hand going to her lower abdomen but thankfully, it jumped to her upper thigh. "What I really want right now is to jerk you out of this tub and spank your sexy little ass for sassing me so much today. Then fuck your brains out." His tongue licked at her pulse, making it thrum.

She moaned again as his fingertips tickled down her leg, stopping at her groin.

"But, my sexy goddess, I'll settle for sliding my finger inside you instead, if you'll allow it."

His hand continued to knead her breast, his fingertips squeezing her nipple as she moaned again. She moved her palm over his and interlaced it with her own, placing it in between her legs. He took the initiative from there and ran his index finger up her slit. She gasped as his fingertip settled on her clit. "Oh my God." She groaned.

"Mmm, you like that, baby?" His movements quickened on her flesh and she arched her hips against his hand. "Yeah? Let's see how you like this then." His hand moved lower and two fingers spread her folds. His middle finger entered her; she cried out as he hooked it before withdrawing it. "Fuck, Sky, you're making me so damn hard," he groaned as his hips rocked against her, his erection digging into her ass cheek.

"Oh, shit," she whined as his finger began to move in and out of her, the heel of his palm torturing her swollen bud as his other hand gripped her breast and squeezed. "Mmm, Ares."

Skyla's body wasn't her own any longer as pleasure seized every bit of her, settling into her core as Travis's fingers ravaged her sex. She moaned and whined and arched, letting his fingers, hands, and mouth become the only thing she focused on. Her head fell back, resting on his shoulder as he made her pleasure his one and only goal. She spread her legs further and rocked her hips with his movements even as his own hips hit hers and water splashed around them.

"My sexy Aphrodite. Come for me, baby." His mouth settled on her neck and he kissed her flesh with passion, using his tongue on her pulse point as his lips sucked softly. She shivered, her flesh pebbling in goosebumps as everything he was doing overwhelmed her senses.

Suddenly, her womanhood quickened around his pumping finger and she cried out as the pleasure intensified into a tumultuous climax where she was thrust into a world of exquisite torment, her release coming violently upon her. "Yes, yes, oh, shit, oh... Oh my God. Travis. Travis. Mmmm," she rambled as her orgasm assaulted her, her body quaking in spasms. He held her to him, letting her fall apart as he continued his caresses. His movements slowed once her climax faded, her walls continuing to clench hard around his finger as she came down from her sexual high.

Her vision returned slowly and her legs cramped from their position spread eagle atop Travis's thighs, but she lapped up the final contractions of her body and sighed as Travis's lips kissed her tingling neck and his fingers continued to play, one at her nipple the other at her clit. She gasped and shuddered, and he chuckled lightly into her ear.

"Mmmm, my, my, you *are* a little sex goddess, aren't you?" His hand moved back up her belly then and up her chest to her jaw and he turned her face to his. She leaned her head back and looked into his eyes, the flames from the candle dancing there, making him look as bad-ass as the part he'd just played. She almost moaned aloud then did as his mouth came down to kiss her, sexy and passionate but slow and unhurried, as if he had all the patience in the world.

His fingers continued to play at her nipple and he had her aroused again before his movements slowed and he stopped all together.

When she pulled back to look at him, his face was intense before he grinned, shaking it off. "That was hot as fuck, Sky," he said and looked back at her lips.

She blushed, aware of how wanton she appeared to be, opened up across him. "What about you?" she asked and motioned with her eyes downward.

"Oh, I'll get mine, don't you worry." He winked and leaned in to kiss her cheek. "Now, you relax. That was for you, Fireball. You needed the indulgence."

And before she could protest, he was releasing her and pulling away, leaving her feeling bereft as he stood and moved out of the tub. He grabbed a towel from the rack nearby and dried off quickly, covering his erect shaft before she had a chance to admire it again. She gulped, holding back the tears that threatened to come once more.

He was leaving, going to attend himself, since he *obviously* didn't want her doing it for him. That knowledge stung deep.

Travis moved forward and knelt down once more. He cupped her cheek and looked into her eyes, her sex tingling, wanting his touch again and again. "You want another glass of wine, darlin'?" he asked. She quickly shook her head. "Alright." He smiled. "Enjoy your bubble bath then. I know I did." He winked again and kissed her quickly before moving off and out the door.

That's when Skyla broke down into tears.

TRAVIS BARELY MADE it into the kitchen before he draped the towel over his cock and began to relieve himself. He leaned against the counter, one hand on his hard length, the other gripping the granite as he went to town on himself. He was maybe ten furious pumps in before he came, hard and violently, his hips thrusting against nothing. He shoved his face into his bicep and bit down to keep from crying aloud as he spilled his seed into the towel tenting him.

"Ahh, fuck, fuck," he groaned.

He jerked and grunted, coming down from his orgasm as his breathing returned and his mind whirled.

Skyla had worked him up so badly that he'd had no choice but to leave the tub and flee here to masturbate. Seeing her reaction to his naked form had been so arousing, having her eye his cock like it was a juicy steak had almost made him lose his mind; then feeling her orgasm right on his lap had nearly done him in. It was all he could do not to pull her on top of him and fuck her senseless, have her come as hard around his cock as she did around his finger. It had been the hottest fucking thing he'd ever heard in his life and left him salivating like a damn dog. He'd pulled every ounce of self-control he could manage looking down at her in the tub while she admired his erection. He'd never wanted so badly in his life to step forward and beg her to suck him off. He could imagine those sexy lips around him now as his hand continued to pump his member. Dammit, he was throbbing like a toothache again. She was doing ridiculous things to his manhood. He had to go back in there. He had to take her and quiet this damn ache in his balls to have her.

"Fuck," he said under his breath and began jerking himself off again with a fury he couldn't hold back.

He groaned in pleasure and came again, swearing as his mind and load was blown once more; Sky's moans flashing through his head as he ejaculated into the towel again.

"Oh shit," he whined as he came back down to earth.

He was in deep shit. What had this woman done to him and why was he so enchanted by her? He didn't know, but he was going to have to have her. Having sex with her was going to be even sweeter than fondling and fingering her had been; he couldn't wait to score.

He'd seen the hesitation in her eyes tonight, felt the insecurity of her body language, and knew he was being too pushy; he was going to have to wait. But a hot bath and the realization that she needed a physical release had been good ideas on his part. Hopefully she was feeling much less anxious now than she had been. Travis knew he certainly was as he cleaned himself up and breathed easier. It was amazing how sometimes a person just needed to get their rocks off to relax a little—mental health and all that.

He moved back to the couch to retrieve his clothes and dressed, feeling nice and chill for the first time since all this craziness. He moved back to the door and realized with a sinking feeling that it was locked as he turned the knob.

"Shit," he swore and realized Skyla had locked him out. What had he done *now*? He'd given her an awesome orgasm, dammit. Why was she shutting him out?

Fuck, why did women have to be so damn complicated at times? If they weren't pissed about one thing, they were pissed about another. He realized this was probably why he was still single but dang it, they were so hard to read and so fucking wishy-washy. Fine. She didn't want him in there, he'd stay out here.

He pouted even as he pulled a blanket over himself and laid down, settling his head on a pillow and contemplating what he'd said to insult or offend her. He racked his brain but came up empty. *Oh well*, he thought, *I'm sure I'll get to hear all about it tomorrow.*

He closed his eyes and smiled, flashing back to the sounds of her moans as her tightness squeezed his middle finger in climax. He couldn't wait to feel her around his dick doing the same. He made his mind up as he fell to sleep; he was taking her tomorrow. It was happening, as sure as his name was Travis Redmond.

CHAPTER SIX

Travis awoke to the sound of a pan clinking and the smell of something delicious cooking on the stove. He shivered as he pulled the blanket up to his chin and groaned. He felt like he'd just fallen to sleep but the brightness surrounding him made him realize it was daylight. It was a new day! Time to turn on the charm and find out why giving her an orgasm hadn't been enough to satisfy that fiery redhead he wanted with a passion that wouldn't wait.

He jumped up and shivered again, realizing the fire was almost out in the stove. He opened it, threw some more logs in and closed it, opening the flume to feed it.

He wearily eased into the kitchen, seeing a makeup-less Skyla scrambling some eggs. Her eyes looked a little puffy, and Travis felt bad all the sudden, not understanding why or how he'd upset her last night. He caught her eye and got a warning look. He stopped in his tracks and tried to smile at her. When she ignored him, he moved to the coffee pot. He'd be damned if he, Ares, god of war for the Gladiators pro football team, would cower to a woman half his size. He would stand tall to the mighty Aphrodite and have her falling to her knees before him before the day was up.

He decided his fate as he moved to the coffee pot, poured himself some coffee, and turned to watch her. She appeared to be sautéing mushrooms, onions and peppers in a skillet. Travis crossed his arms over his chest, bringing the mug to his lips, and waited for her to round on him and tear him a new one. When she didn't, and continued to ignore him, he let the anger rise within and finally lashed out.

"You wanna tell me what's got your panties in a wad this morning?"

Nothing. The little shit didn't even turn or acknowledge him in any way. Fury began to take hold.

He took another sip of coffee and moved up behind her, growling. "After what happened last night, I would expect some type of greeting this morning. Anything would be better than you pretending that I don't fuckin' exist."

She whirled then, face red and eyes narrowed into slits of sapphire. "Don't think that just because you fingered me that you have *any* idea about what's goin' on in my panties, Travis." *Poke the snake, you get the venom.*

"Ouch, I didn't want a thank you, Sky, but fuckin-A, what's your damn problem?"

"You! *You* are my problem."

He frowned, perplexed. Was he just imagining things last night or was she not enjoying everything he'd thrown at her? Who was this livid banshee hell-bent on ripping him apart?

His brow raised and he smirked, "Why the hell are all you women crazy? I mean, fuck, I thought I was being nice by drawing you a bath and giving you a much-needed sexual release, but I wake up this morning and realize I've wasted my time because you still fuckin' hate me as much as you did before. Please, enlighten me? What did I do that was so wrong?"

She rolled her eyes and turned. She was a true redhead—irascible, like a lit fuse—and right now her fury was so intense she was shaking.

"Just when I think I *finally* get you chicks, I'm thrown for a damn loop. Y'all wonder why us men are such dicks...because you tell us things are fine when they aren't fine and expect us to read between the lines. Guess what? We aren't mind readers. We actually really suck at it, by the way. We're doers, fixers. Our brains don't work like yours do."

He longed to touch her—hoping it might soothe her anger—wrap his arms around her waist, and insist she bring the sexy Aphrodite back. Just as the urge got to be too much and he moved to act, she finally spoke, with her eyes squinched tightly. "I wanted you to stay," she whispered. "I wanted..."

"Sky, I wanted to stay too, but... I didn't fuck you because I got your signals, loud and clear. Trust me, I wanted it as much as you did. Leaving you in that bathtub was the hardest damn thing I've ever done."

"But you came out here and *whacked* off," she accused, pointing her wooden spoon at him, and he almost laughed.

"Yeah, I did. Because I was about to bust a nut in there and needed to come."

"Ugh, why are all men so daft?"

"Daft?" he harrumphed, offended. "What, Sky? What do you want me to say to make this better, huh? I'm a man, dammit. I have needs too. I—"

She shook her head, lips curled in anger, and he wanted to explode at the frustration he felt in that moment. Nothing he said was gonna make this better. She thought he was daft...and dammit, maybe he was.

He took another sip of coffee and slammed the mug down onto the countertop. Sky shook as if he'd slapped her and a realization dawned on him. It smacked him hard across his head and he reeled. "Wait. You're *mad* that I came out here and jacked off? Why?" he asked and took a step forward. "You didn't want me to fuck you, so how can you be mad about that? Do you realize how crazy that is?"

She turned away from him and sighed heavily. "You can't possibly understand."

"No, I can't, not when I continue to be punished for the actions of others."

He realized her anger at him was a defense mechanism and tried to calm down, after all he really couldn't comprehend the pain that she'd experienced.

"My anger isn't directed at you." She verified his thought and turned, batting at the angry tears on her cheeks. "Dammit, I hate that I cry when I'm mad."

He pulled her to him by her wrist. Her face remained hard and closed off, but he forced it up with his thumb and index finger. "Sky, that's because you're not actually *mad,* are you?" She shook her head, her blue eyes looking hard into his. "You're...*hurt?*" he asked, trying hard to understand why she would be so upset at the fact that he hadn't forced himself upon her. "Please baby, you gotta spell it out for me. I'm 'daft,' remember?" When her lips turned up in a smile, he separated the distance between them, caging her in with his arms as his hands settled around her waist. He rested his forehead against hers and implored her. "Talk to me, my fiery goddess, tell me. Make this aggressive god inside me understand."

Skyla's lips quivered as she attempted to rein her emotions in, shame taking hold of her as his knuckles brushed her cheekbone. "I —I thought..." She paused, and Travis realized how difficult this was for her. He frowned again and leaned down to kiss her cheek. "That you didn't *want* me to do it for you," she stated quickly and looked up, disappointment marking her beautiful face.

"Now, why would I not want you to get me off?" he asked, and she answered with a cute little shrug. "Oh, Skyla. If you only knew how much I wanted it... Hell, it might've frightened you." He gave a humorless laugh and pulled her into his chest, cradling her head and kissing the top of it. "Want me to tell you exactly what I wanted last night, my sexy, little Aphrodite?" She nodded against his chin and he felt his need for her grow between them. "I wanted to fuck your mouth, your tits, and your pussy, baby. Then I wanted to pull out and come all over your perky little ass. Want me to keep going?" he asked again and pulled her back to see her face, which was as red as he'd expected, getting a laugh out of him. He chucked her chin again and looked her in the eyes, staring hard into them. "While I was fisting my cock like there was no tomorrow right here at this counter last night, I was imagining how amazing being inside your body would be and I came in two seconds flat, no joke. Now, does that sound like a man who doesn't want you to finish him off?"

Sky gulped and looked away for a second before shaking her head.

"No, it doesn't. I'm a man who wants you so badly that my erection seems to be constant whenever you're around. But I know you've very recently been jilted, and I wasn't gonna push you into doing anything you're not ready for. So I came out here and took care of myself that way you didn't feel *obligated* to return the favor. I was tryin' real hard last night to be a gentleman, baby doll, despite that I pride myself on being the bad boy." He smirked and stroked her cheek, leaning down to kiss her softly on the lips. "But whenever you're ready for Him, you're getting Ares. And try as you might, He's not letting you go until you've been thoroughly fucked. Every delicious inch of you." He licked her lips slowly with his tongue and stepped back, letting her digest his words as he moved to the stove to stir the veggie mixture.

She wanted "The Ram," by God, she was gonna get him.

SKY GAPED as she looked over at the gorgeous sex god stirring the veggies at the stove like he hadn't just soaked her panties with both his naughty words and enticing tongue. She'd never been spoken to like that before, and Lord help, she wanted to hear more. Since graduating college, she'd been drawn to men who she deemed were "safe". She didn't date anyone who wasn't what she'd considered husband material or had a reputation that was as sterling as their career choice.

In college, most of her "fuck buddies" had been law students like herself, not really random so much as convenient—as much friends as actual lovers, as no real love had been made. Sky felt shorted, like she'd missed out and knew this might be her one and only chance to have erotic, raw, unadulterated sex before she settled down with a man who married her more for her brain than her looks or what she could do in the bedroom. Sky was too successful for love, she needed security, valued reality over fantasy. Fate didn't produce Prince Charmings. As much as she wanted to believe the fairy tales she read, she knew they didn't exist, knew destiny had thrown her a bone when it had thrust Travis Redmond back into her life. This was her final chance to act on her feelings before shit got real. And she was going to take that damn bone and gnaw on it until there wasn't anything left, she realized. After all, who was she to look a gift horse in the mouth?

Skyla pulled in a deep breath and stepped up behind Travis. She leaned into his flannel shirt and inhaled him, letting her nose settle between his shoulder blades.

"What has the goddess of love made her lover for breakfast?" he asked, grabbing the wrist she moved to his hip and stroking it with his thumb. "I don't know what turns me on more: that you were mad at me and made me breakfast anyway, or that you can cook."

Skyla smiled as his head turned to give her a sexy grin. "And what if I were trying to poison you, Ares?" Her brow went up.

"Damn, woman, that's not very nice. Sounds like something Athena might do."

Sky laughed heartily. "I told you Aphrodite was the wrong name for me."

"We'll see about that." His eyes roved over her, and she bit into her lip. "You gonna answer me?"

Sky frowned in confusion, racking her brain for the question he'd asked. "Oh, breakfast," she recalled suddenly. "Southwestern omelets."

He grinned again. "Yum."

The tone of his voice made her wonder if he were talking about breakfast or her as his eyes settled at her breasts. If he were trying to unnerve her, he was doing a fantastic job of it. She wasn't used to being scrutinized so.

She moved away from him, garnering every ounce of her courage, to the fridge where she grabbed a carton of eggs. She focused on the task at hand, cracking eggs into a bowl, whisking them, and adding seasonings. Travis continued to stir the contents of the small frying pan, humming and Sky relaxed some, confident he wasn't gonna bend her over the table and have his way with her...well, not right that second anyway.

As alluring as the prospect of finally being with him was, there was that nervous schoolgirl in her that dreaded having him see her naked, dreaded what his eyes would think of her imperfect form and the scars that ran across her lower abdomen. She was still that insecure fat girl and knew she didn't come anywhere close to comparing with the gorgeous models and celebs he'd taken to bed over the years.

Her unease returned, souring her stomach, and when he took a step toward her, she came within inches of dumping their eggs onto the floor before grabbing the bowl and gasping, grateful she'd not been wasteful due to clumsy hands.

Travis thought it was humorous and laughed. "Your nervousness around me is adorable."

She scoffed. "I'm not nervous, I just...I haven't had enough coffee yet," she stammered.

"Right." He was unconvinced, and Sky felt her cheeks flame in embarrassment. She was never gonna get used to his presence. She was hopeless. How in the name of God was she gonna pull this off? She wasn't gonna be able to do it sober. "Here. I'll pour you some more coffee." He winked, and she came close to swooning before moving back to the fridge to grab cheese and salsa for the omelets.

She calmed her heart rate and moved the veggies off the frying pan, dumping them and some cold milk into the eggs before adding a pad of butter back to the pan and lowering the knob of the stove eye.

Travis began to sing aloud as he added more coffee to her mug, using the pumpkin spice creamer for a microphone. Sky joined in, singing "Come And Get Your Love" by Redbone. She lost herself to this moment, to the feeling of happiness being so close to him, connecting with him as she had back in high school before their lives had become intertwined by a tragedy neither of them could have ever fathomed. It was as if no bad thing had ever transpired, as if they weren't running from bad guys, as if this was a normal morning after breakfast between two lovers.

Sky poured half the egg mixture into the pan and watched and waited a couple minutes before folding one side up over the other. She'd been making omelets for a long time. It was one of the few breakfast foods she liked. After another couple minutes, Skyla turned the whole thing over and added a healthy serving of cheese to the top. She popped a lid on to steam and melt the cheese before removing it after another minute and shaking it onto a plate. She then added a dollop of salsa to it and handed it over to Travis. "Bon appétit, Ares." Her brow went up in challenge.

"Well, well, Ms. Larson, this looks great. But how dumb would I be to eat mine first, after you stated your intentions to poison me?"

She rolled her eyes and grinned at him. She then took one of the forks she'd laid out and used it to scoop a bite of the omelet. She brought it to her mouth and shoved it in. Travis watched her chew with amusement. "See? There. No poison. Now eat it, you dope."

"Swallow first," he challenged. She did and he smirked. "You'll be doing a lot of that soon enough… Aphrodite." He bobbed his brows before taking the plate from Sky.

Her jaw hung open as he chuckled and moved to the table. She returned to the pan to make herself an omelet. She was pleasantly surprised when she finished and brought her own plate to the table a few minutes later to see that Travis had waited for her.

"I thought you were starved."

"I'm a patient man when it comes to what I want," he answered, and she wasn't sure he was actually talking about food. She guzzled her coffee down even as she looked down at her plate to keep her eyes off his. "Thanks for making breakfast, Sky." Her stomach quaked as she waited for him to eat his food, but she found herself soaring as he said, "Damn, this is delicious."

"Thank you." Sky blushed and took a bite of her own and agreed —it was delicious.

"If I remember correctly, you owe me a bite," he said after half of his was gone. He didn't hesitate as he scooped up a bite of hers and brought it to his mouth.

"Hey!" she feigned shock and pointed her fork at him. "Stop spreading your germs."

"My germs aren't the only thing I'm gonna be spreading here soon."

The heat coming off his blue eyes held her captive and her entire body shivered, his sexual intent not missed on her. She tried to hold his gaze, but he was the first to break it.

"Hey, you know what? Let's go outside and play."

"Play?" How old were they? Five?

"Yeah, like build a fucking snowman or have a snowball fight or somethin'."

"Alright, Elsa."

"C'mon. When was the last time we *saw* snow, let alone got to go out and enjoy it?"

Skyla thought back and couldn't even answer that question. Georgia didn't get a lot of snow and neither did Texas for that matter. She'd been young the last time she got to actually play out in it. She smiled back at Travis, and he chucked her chin before taking another bite of his omelet.

"I'll do the dishes, since you cooked." He winked. "I gotta get a good workout in today. Don't wanna get soft from all this junk food I've eaten lately."

Skyla could only imagine the rigorous workouts he was used to and his diet. He was probably having so many more cheat meals than he normally got; she was surprised he wasn't sick at this point. He seemed nonplussed though as he took her plate and moved off.

She took that time to finish her coffee and stepped over to the window to look out at the white snow covering the ground and trees. It was fluffy and magical as the sun peeked through the clouds to highlight the ice crystals that sparkled back at her. She smiled, hearing a bird chirp to her from a nearby branch. She looked up to see it was a red cardinal, a sign of a loved one watching out for her.

The danger they'd been in at this point seemed almost like a distant memory; although at any moment, they were bound to be caught by one of the most notorious crime rings in Atlanta.

Sky remembered Jeffers words and shivered. They both were going to be taken and she hadn't bothered to tell Travis—and what difference did it make if he knew? Better to have the element of surprise on his side so that his reaction was genuine. The overwhelming fear paralyzed her suddenly. She worried about what Geraci would do when he caught them. How bad the punishment for them both would be, especially since he more than likely suspected Travis of "disobedience." She'd seen the results of those who'd defied Giovanni Geraci. Skyla prayed that Travis's brother, Tucker, was alright and hoping their inside guy could stay incognito for a little while longer.

For now, she was going to soak up this beautiful day and this beautiful man whom she planned to succumb to before the night was up.

She chanced a glance back over at him and his blue eyes caught hers. So blue, like the waters of a glacier. Damn. She was in some serious trouble.

"Do NOT put a carrot there."

"Oh, why not? It's not like anyone's gonna see it, party pooper." Travis stuck his tongue out at her as he did exactly what she'd just told him not to. "Besides, it's funny." Travis grinned and looked back at the snowman they'd built, with rocks for eyes, a stick for a mouth, and a carrot as a raging boner.

Skyla crossed her arms over her chest and scowled up at him.

"Lighten up, Sky. You can't say that you don't think it's just a little funny…"

Again, Sky looked at him as if he were a misbehaving child. She dropped her arms and took a second glance at their snowman, evaluating the job they'd done. Then a big grin lit her face and she giggled. "Ok, maybe it's a little funny." She nodded back up at him, her copper-gold locks covered mostly by an ugly brown knitted beanie. "But it would be funnier if we built a female one to go beside him with a set of big boobs."

Travis bent double with laughter, his big gloved hands hitting his thighs. "Oh, we're so fucking doin' it."

They set about the task of gathering and rolling enough snow for yet another life-sized snowman—snow*woman*, to be exact—making her leaner and curvier than her male counterpart. It was fun, working together with Skyla, having her loosen up a bit and get the wedgie out of her granny panties. She was patient and easy-going when she wasn't so annoyed with him.

The morning went by quickly as they finished their sculpturing, finding pine needles for eyelashes and a red rock for lips.

When they stepped back to admire their work, Sky even laughed this time. "Now *that's* funny."

"I tend to agree, my pervy compadre," Travis stepped up alongside her and threw his arm around her neck, pulling her into him. "Reminds me of two others I know."

Sky grinned then pulled away, quickly shoving at his chest and taking him off guard, knocking him down into the shin-deep snow. He fell with a splat as the big, fluffy cold stuff surrounded him and gaped up at a laughing Skyla. "Gotcha."

"Hey!" Travis protested and attempted to sit up, but was once again blind-sided as he felt a snowball hit him square in his jaw. The whoosh startled him before the cold splattered his face. He gasped and wiped the snow off his cheek, hearing Skyla run off, laughing loudly. "Why, you..." He didn't finish as adrenaline coursed through his veins. He stood; the snowball fight had commenced. He lowered his hand and grabbed a massive handful of snow, packing it tightly and rounding it out. He prowled slowly as he closed in on a rock wall out front of a grove of Aspen trees, where he presumed his attacker was hiding out.

When he rounded the corner and saw her, he lunged, getting a scream out of her as he made contact and gripped her arm. He crashed the snowball into her hip, getting a squeal out of her. "Travis!"

"All is fair in love and war, Fireball. You launched the first volley."

She somehow slipped out of his grasp, the slick glove losing her as she turned and planted a snowball into his chest. "Ah," he gasped as the cold hit him. "Damn, that's cold." Even through the sweater and jacket he'd found, he could still feel the ice seep through.

"C'mon, wimp, come and get me."

"Wimp? Ha! You're in for it, little girl. Once I catch you, I'm showing you no mercy." He chased her, amped up by the thrill of it all and how unexpected this was of her character. He laughed as his bigger, longer legs ate up the snow banks and the distance between them shortened.

She protested, panicked by his gain. When he was almost on her, she stumbled on a slick rock. He was too close to catch himself and crashed into her, sending them both sprawling down a small hill and into a shallow ditch. He landed atop her, practically in a tackle, unable to stop the momentum of his large body. She hooted with laughter even as he looked her over to make sure he hadn't hurt her; she was so much smaller than him, after all.

"Jeez, I'm sorry. Are you ok?"

Skyla cackled as she smashed another snowball into his face, and he practically growled. He grabbed at the snow covering him and tossed it back onto Skyla's face. She gasped as the cold ice hit her and sputtered. "Uh, Travis."

"Remember, I'm bigger. Don't make me scoop it all over you because I will." He teased. "Do you surrender?"

"Never!" she called out and attempted to fight him off even as he grabbed her wrists and held them over her head. He chuckled as she frowned. *Man, that was easy*, he thought as his head descended and he kissed her lightly, gently at first, before his tongue moved into her opening mouth.

He moaned as his other hand moved to cup her cheek and she gasped. He immediately pulled back.

"Cold," she murmured as she looked into his eyes, her forehead covered by the beanie cap. He grinned at how good he felt in that instant. Butterflies were filling his stomach, and he longed to take her on the cold ground, to love her with an urgency he'd never quite felt before.

Just then a loud reverberation sounded throughout the valley—not unlike a shotgun blast—and Sky inhaled sharply. Travis's hold on her wrists let up as he moved that hand to her mouth and hushed her, listening hard for footsteps, another shot, anything. "Shhh," he whispered and watched Skyla's eyes dart around. He could almost feel her heart pounding in her chest, *or was that his?*

Minutes passed and nothing but quiet surrounded them. Travis held fast though, listening hard, waiting until he was sure they weren't being hunted. Finally, fear evaporated as he looked into Skyla's blue eyes. He pulled his hand away and couldn't help the smile that came to his lips as he looked her over. She was so utterly beautiful.

He was the first to move, he pulled himself off her and stood, extending his hand to assist her up.

"Well, that was scary," Sky said and looked around again. "What do you think it was?"

"An animal. A tree branch breaking. Who knows?"

"Can we go inside now?" Her smile pulled to the side, her cheek ticking with worry.

Travis nodded and extended his hand. She took it and together they walked back up the hill and to the cabin.

CHAPTER SEVEN

"This is the good stuff right here." Sky smiled as she pulled the old Scotch bottle up and out of the bar cabinet in the living room.

They'd come in from their scare in the woods and sat quietly for a time after shucking their jackets and boots, waiting for the raid from Geraci that never came.

After about an hour, Travis had said, "Fuck this," and began to disrobe to only his jeans. He started a vigorous HIIT workout using gallon jugs of water he'd found beneath the sink, a chair from the dining room, and books stacked up. He was good at improv, and Sky soon found herself following his lead as he "coached" her through a heart-pumping routine that had them both drenched in sweat before all was said and done. Her muscles ached and places she'd never felt burned from being made to move in positions she wasn't used to.

Afterward, they'd showered—separately, of course—and took naps after a lunch of sandwiches and chips. When Sky had awoken a time later, she'd found Travis reading *White Fang* and smiled at him as she'd entered the living room. She hadn't wanted to interrupt him, as she felt he didn't get to spend a lot of time "bored" and reading, so she'd moved to the packed bookshelf and selected the crumbling copy of John Berendt's *Midnight in the Garden of Good and Evil*. They'd read in silence for a time before their tummies had begun to rumble and it was time to start dinner.

Tonight, Skyla had made chicken and dumplings—a hearty and indulgent recipe that had been handed down to her from generations past. She and Travis joked and worked amicably together, mutually complacent, and Sky began to realize how much she enjoyed his company. When he wasn't being a cocky bastard, he was kind, thoughtful and considerate—a true shock to her.

But not long after dinner, his eyes had changed as they sat watching the fire, the night closing in on them quickly, blanketing them between the veil of darkness and sunrise. The time where temptation lurked, weaknesses surfaced, and men and women, who weren't before, became lovers. The day had been safe and sure, but the night was full of uncertainties, desires, and itching impulses to do sinful things not considered during daylight. Where his advances had been playful in the light of the sun, now they were more promising, sharper, and harder to ignore. And God, he was so hard to ignore.

Sky knew she needed help as his face turned toward hers and his jaw ticked. She found herself wondering how the stubble there would feel moving over her naked flesh. She popped up off the couch quickly and moved to the cabinet next to the fireplace, remembering her "Uncle Terry" had a secret stash.

"*Good* stuff, huh?" Travis asked, eyeing the bottle of 20-year-old Scotch whisky in her hands.

Sky plopped back down beside him and twisted the cork off the top, smelling the sweet, peaty scent of the libation.

"Yum," she cooed before turning it up and taking a big swig of it.

Travis's sexy brows went up. "Wait. I thought you didn't drink... You like Scotch?"

Sky smacked her lips and savored the burn across her palette and down her throat as she nodded.

She swiped the back of her hand across her lips and smiled over at Travis, handing him the bottle. "I just told you that at the bar because I was afraid you'd get me hammered and take advantage of me."

He gave her a thoughtful look before shrugging. He took the bottle from her and reciprocated, then exhaled an approving sigh after chugging a swig too. "That's a fine year." He winked. "Good call, Aphrodite."

Uh oh, she thought. Ares must be wanting to come out and play. She needed to distract him; she needed more booze before she was ready to acquiesce.

"So, Trav, why aren't you married yet?"

"Oh, hell, let me take another swig or two before I answer that," he snarled and did just that.

"Oh, c'mon, it's a legitimate question."

"I could ask you the same damn thing," he smarted, but realized his mistake as Sky looked down with a frown. "Damn, Sky. I'm sorry, I didn't—"

"It's ok." She sighed heavily, not sure how she was going to handle things when she got back to Atlanta. She was sure the media would expect a public statement from her on the matter, then she would have to actually deal with Sam too. "Pass that back over, would ya?" she asked and motioned to the bottle, of which Travis handed back to her.

"I guess I could simply say I haven't found the right one. That's a true enough statement." Travis shrugged after several minutes of silence. "But then again, I could answer with the fact that I haven't really been lookin' either. And why should I? I got pussy coming at me left and right." He smirked but Sky didn't reply. She'd never had men throw themselves at her, and, although the prospect sounded alluring, Travis's frown said otherwise. "As great as that can be when you're younger and horny with all this fame and talent and energy, after a time, it starts to get old. You wonder if you'll ever find someone who enjoys you for more than your image and your money."

When he looked back up at her, his blue eyes sparkled with regret and sadness.

She gulped. "I imagine that *would* be hard." She looked down again, fiddling with her fingers around the amber bottle. "I would love to know what that feels like though, just for a day."

"Genuine women are hard to find," he said almost randomly.

"Men too...apparently." Sky sighed.

"Hey, you can't beat yourself up about it, you know?"

"You haven't even heard his side of the story. There are always two sides."

Travis shook his head as if she were being ridiculous. "Don't need to."

Sky took another swig from the bottle, her senses starting to numb. "I guess I'll either get one of two things: a poorly-executed public apology or a correspondence of some kind. Maybe an NDA from a lawyer, which washes his hands of me and demands the ring back." She laughed humorlessly.

"He doesn't deserve your forgiveness."

"Ah, who am I kidding? What did I expect, a happily ever after? Those don't exist."

"They do for some people."

"Not me." Sky felt the effects of the alcohol warring within her system- emotion vs. numbness.

"Sky, you'll find it. Just not with a douchebag like him. You don't want some old ass MF-er anyway, do you?" Travis grimaced.

"He was safe."

"He cheated on you! He wasn't safe at all."

"And *you'd* be safer?" she asked, conviction in her eyes.

"Look, I may be a *playboy*, but I don't cheat when I'm in a committed relationship."

"And when was the last time you were in a 'committed' relationship? High school?"

122

"Because," he continued as if she hadn't spoken, "cheating is cheating, it doesn't matter what the excuse is. I know you think you personally did something wrong here, but I blame *him*. If he had an issue with you, he could've talked to you about it first, broken things off before he went and stuck his dick in somebody else."

Travis had a good point; she hadn't even thought about it that way. Sam could have come to her and told her he needed more or less of something, and she would have been receptive...maybe. Hell, who was she kidding, the man did her a favor by cheating on her; it gave her an excuse to be done with a loveless relationship.

"I've accepted that I probably won't be in love with the man I marry," Sky said, feeling hopeless.

"*What*? Did you really just say that?" Travis furrowed his brows, confused.

She had his full attention now. He sat up and turned his body toward her.

Sky looked at him for a moment before dropping her head and taking another swig of the whiskey bottle. Travis jerked it from her grasp. "Answer me," he demanded. "Why in hell won't you love the man you marry? Is it martyrdom or marriage, fuck?"

Sky swallowed hard, tears coming to her eyes. She shrugged, trying to understand her feelings enough to explain how she felt to a man who didn't know her. "I'm not... I'm not..." She pulled a breath in. "I'll have to settle."

"Skyla." Travis's whisper of her name made her shiver. "You don't have to settle, baby. Why in God's name do you think that's even an option?"

"Because I don't look like Brittany!" she cried loudly, anger seizing her once more.

"So fuckin' what. You don't *need* to look like Brittany. You're you."

"I know, and I'm ok with that. I'm not a prize wife. I know that if I *do* marry, whoever I marry won't be doing it for my looks."

"Jesus, Skyla." Travis covered his face with his hands briefly before dropping them. "You're absolutely stunning. Why would you think something so ludicrous?"

She gaped up at him, again astounded by his words. "You—you think I'm *stunning*?"

"Yes. Why do you *not* think so?"

"Because you haven't seen all of me. You haven't seen me *naked*. You…"

"Wow, easy now. Just breathe, Sky." Travis gripped her shoulders.

Had she forgotten to breathe? Fuck, why was she suddenly hysterical? He pulled her into his arms and cradled her head to his chest. Dammit! Was she having a panic attack again? God, he was going to think she was a loon, in need of a psych eval before this was all over. But as much as she tried, the inner damaged teen would not be dampened down.

"Shh, it's ok, baby doll. I got you. Skyla. Just breathe, baby. I got you." His words pulled on heartstrings she hadn't felt in so long, the soft even tone of his deep voice making her heart skip a beat and her panties dampen.

Then kisses covered her cheeks, her forehead, her eyebrows. Her body hummed, her sex clenched, and her numb face began to tingle, coming to life by his butterfly-like beats across her hungry skin. Soon, she was moaning instead of hyperventilating and turning her face up to his grinning one.

"There you are. You were falling into a pit of despair. I think I might've just pulled you out." He winked. God, he was so gorgeous. Far more gorgeous than she could ever be. Far more gorgeous than she deserved. He must have sensed her darkening thoughts for he cupped her cheek. "Skyla. You gotta tell me, darlin', why do you think so little of yourself?"

"You haven't seen me," she repeated.

"Then take your fuckin' clothes off so I can."

She vigorously shook her head, pulling her arms across her chest.

"You're afraid?" Travis's brow went up again. "Of me? I thought ADA Larson wasn't afraid of anyone. Not even Giovanni Geraci."

Travis was fishing, but she wasn't taking the bait, not with this. It was too important. "Tell me."

"It's… it's better if I just show you."

"You can show me, Skyla. Your secrets are safe with me."

Travis's eyes held hers, and she pulled in a deep breath. A part of her was just as eager to share the burden she'd hidden most her life as she was anxious to reveal the secret.

She laid back and began to unbutton her pants, peeling them down to her thighs. Her palms gripped her panties and slid them down with graceful ease. They began to come down her hips and shame, pain, and remorse filled her veins. "Look," her plea was a whisper.

She closed her eyes as he moved toward her and her stomach dropped as she heard his sharp intake of breath. Now he'd seen them. Her shame. Her scars. Her ugliness. The secret she could never truly conceal, only keep at bay.

"Sky…you were a cutter?"

She nodded tearfully and grabbed for her panties, only to come up short as Travis seized both her wrists in his big palm. She pulled, attempting to escape his grasp, but wasn't strong enough to do so. He leaned down, examining the cuts she'd given herself twelve years ago, cuts that helped to ease the pain then but only added to it now, as she hated herself for the marks she would never be able to erase. Tears fell down the sides of her face, and she closed her eyes in deep regret as she felt Travis trace the long scars with his index finger.

"Oh, Skyla. Baby," he murmured and his head lowered. She felt his hot breath on the tender skin of her abdomen and his lips cover the marks. His kiss was gentle, sweet, forgiving, and she felt the love she'd always had for him swell inside her heart, threatening to burst it. She knew that if she died right this very second, she would die happy because he was acknowledging all the things she'd hated about herself for far too long, and he was accepting her for who she was, who she'd been, what she'd been freed from. Travis's head came up and he looked at her. Not in pity, not in sadness, but in understanding, and if she hadn't been in love with him a decade ago, she definitely was now—*God help her.*

"This is why?" he asked. "This is why you think you're ugly?" Skyla nodded. "Oh, my beautiful Aphrodite, scars don't make you ugly. Scars are proof that we survived."

"I gave these to myself...when I hated who I was. It's my reminder that I'll never be beautiful."

"But you *are* beautiful. This is a reminder that you rose above what you thought were your shortcomings. Proof of how amazing you really are."

"Easy for you to say, you don't have ugly marks covering your entire lower abdomen," Sky retorted.

"No. I don't." Travis rose up then moved off the couch to stand in front of her. "Mine aren't on my torso."

Sky furrowed her brows in confusion and sat up as Travis began to unbutton his jeans. He unzipped himself, and Sky gawked as he peeled his pants down. Seeing him naked for the second day in a row was wreaking havoc on her womanhood, especially when his not-quite-flaccid penis was still incredibly impressive. But it was the marks he was pointing to on his upper left thigh that gave her pause. How had she missed seeing them last night? Oh, she'd been distracted by his ridiculously noteworthy cock!

"These are from my old man. He was a violent drunk and took his aggressions out on me quite frequently. I got these when I pissed him off one night trying to defend my mom, and he decided I'd make a good ashtray. He purposely tried to burn me in the balls one night. That was the night he realized I was getting to be just as strong as he was." Travis's lips tightened in anger, reproach, and hate.

Skyla moved quickly, gently fingering the scars he loathed as equally as she loathed her own. Travis's breath hissed through his teeth and at first, she was sure he would push her away and ask her to stop touching him there. This seemed too private, something about him she'd never known, never would've guessed. He seemed even more uncomfortable with his marks than she did hers, the wound still as raw as the day he'd received them. Hers had been self-inflicted, his were from someone who was supposed to love him unconditionally, someone who was supposed to have been protecting him, someone who'd broken his trust and his spirit at the same time. But it was utterly endearing that Travis had chosen to share this secret side of himself. It made Skyla love him all the more.

Travis moaned softly as Sky leaned in and kissed the circular cigarette burns scarring his muscular thigh. He licked his lips as Skyla's eyes looked up at his when she pulled back slightly.

The desire within her to look at his growing shaft, which lay inches from her nose, was almost too much to resist. She longed to lick the head of him, taste him, get lost in the moment and let him take her as he'd intended to since the night in the bar; but something held her back, and she rose on her knees. He came back to the couch and moved toward her, inches from touching her.

"This is why you wanted this," he said as he motioned to the bottle of scotch in his hand. "You needed liquid courage tonight because you were hesitant for me to make love to you. Afraid for me to see the scars."

"I'd hoped to hide them from you… as long as I could."

His eyes narrowed and he looked hard into her eyes as if he were seeing her for the very first time. "You have no need to hide *anything* from me, Skyla. After tonight, there'll be no more hiding."

CHAPTER EIGHT

S ky had never been more nervous in all her life, she wasn't sure if it was the way Travis's eyes turned stormy, that he'd said that he would *make love* to her, or that there'd be no more hiding. She audibly gulped as he looked her over, acutely aware that her pants were at her knees, her panties were precariously hanging off, and that her entire body shivered and not because she was cold.

"I'm sorry that you hated your body so much that you cut yourself," he said as his hand came up to cup her cheek. His chest hit hers and his growing erection hit her belly, making her sex hum.

"And I'm sorry that your father beat you and burned you." She rested her forehead on his and he sighed. "It's different when it's not done by your own hand."

"It's harder, more personal when it is," Travis insisted.

Sky looked up into his eyes. She'd wanted this moment her whole life. Imagined it to be as sensual and erotic as sex could possibly be with a lover. Would it be as amazing as her mind had dreamt up? Or would it disappoint her once more? And was she willing to chance it? As his other hand came up to cup her other cheek, she realized that she would, she could, she must.

"Travis," she practically pleaded, hearing the fire pop in the background.

"Skyla." He kissed her nose softly. "I'm sorry her words made you do this." His finger moved to trace her scars again, and she felt tears threaten her eyes. "I'm sorry that you wanted me so much, and I had no idea. I'm sorry you never thought you were good enough, because you are, Sky. You're *too* good...for everyone!"

Sky closed her eyes against the emotion building inside her. She didn't want to cry again. She wanted to beg him to love her like she'd always wanted, to take away some of the stigma she still felt, but as she opened her eyes, she knew she wouldn't need to be begging.

"I never felt good enough either... especially for my hard-ass, abusive father who drank himself to death years ago. I realize now that I've still been trying to be good enough for him, prove myself, protect my brother who he scarred too, only in a different way. But dammit... I'm done proving myself. This is me. Me standing here before you, asking if tonight, you'll let me be good enough for you."

Skyla smiled and nodded. She moaned aloud when he tilted her face up with his big palm and kissed her, allowing the outpouring of emotions to transform into passion. A passion she'd never unleashed until that moment. A passion to be overcome by the one and only man who'd ever held her heart—Travis Redmond.

She realized it was true. He'd always held her heart in his hands even if he hadn't been aware of it. She'd given it years ago without truly knowing she'd done so. It was evident as she kissed him back with unrelenting fervor. His lips were hungry yet giving at the same time, tender yet furious, soft and hard. His kiss held her captive and set her free, gave her life and took it from her all at once. She moaned again, letting his tongue invade her mouth and stroke across hers, seducing her even more, for that's what Ares had done... or had it been she, Aphrodite, who'd seduced him? She wasn't sure for he seemed to be as captive as she was in those moments, overwhelmed by the burning desire between them as he, too, moaned and rubbed at her belly with his hard, hungry sex.

His palm on her face moved into her hair and his fingers interlocked with her strands, gripping her scalp as he turned her head to feast on her mouth. His other hand moved down her bicep, brushing the knuckles down her bare arm. When had she lost her flannel? She didn't know and didn't care because all she wanted was to feel her naked skin against his hard, muscular body. She began to pull at the shirt covering his frame in a futile attempt; when she didn't succeed, her hands went underneath to grip his pecs and caress his enticing washboard abs. She had no idea his muscles could have her so aroused, but it was happening.

He chuckled when she, once more, attempted to rid him of his shirt and pulled back. "Alright, Fireball, I'll shuck it." In one motion, he peeled the shirt over his head and slung it aside. "Better?" he asked, raising a brow.

"Mmm," Sky responded, feeling fully awake and alive as she looked his gorgeous body over. Sinewy muscle wrapped every inch of his shoulders, chest, arms, and abs. He was truly a "God of the Gridiron," as the fans were beginning to call their Atlanta Gladiators. "God, you're so sexy." She ran her hand over the expansive black tribal tattoo that covered his left pec, shoulder, and bicep.

"Me? No, you are. I'm ready to see my Aphrodite in all her naked splendor."

Sky was momentarily taken off guard as she looked up into Travis's unwavering eyes. She didn't protest as the thin tank top was pulled over her head and his large palms moved to unhook her bra. When it fell from her frame, she held her breath as his eyes roved over her now naked torso.

He grinned as his fingertips touched her chest. "I could trace all the constellations with these enticing little freckles of yours, Sky."

She shivered as his fingertips moved down her cleavage, eager to feel him touching her breasts.

"I hate my freckles."

"And I adore them." He leaned in—to prove it she assumed—and touched them with his tongue individually before swirling it around to play connect the dots with the generous spattering of brown spots marking almost every inch of her porcelain flesh.

Skyla's womanhood was literally humming and she could feel her core moistening before his tongue finally found her nipple and began to swipe it back and forth. She gasped as his mouth covered her peaked flesh and he suckled her, his other hand gripping the other breast, kneading it greedily. She was literally quaking as his mouth and tongue had her center dripping with desire before he popped off and smiled up at her.

"I love tits—I should've mentioned—and yours, baby, yours," he groaned and took them both in his palms, "are exquisite." He leaned down again to love the opposite breast and had Sky moaning and reaching for his manhood before she was upended onto her back on the couch.

She gave an "ummph," as Travis pulled off the jeans that hung from her legs and his frame settled over hers. He kissed her once more, slow, sensual, and almost torturing as a hand moved unhurriedly down her breast, her belly, and to the delta of her thighs which were splayed to accommodate his massive legs between them.

"Oh fuck, Sky, you're so wet for me, baby." He practically growled as his thick finger moved into her folds and entered her. She gasped and arched her hips. "Mmm, my greedy little kitten." His mouth moved back to her breast and suckled her again as his finger began to fuck her. She became a greedy little kitten, hungry for the orgasm her lion was building inside her. She gripped his shoulders, running her hands down his chest as she moaned and arched.

Sky was far too close when Travis moved, his entire frame dropping down. His face hovered over her lower body and he grinned big, the grin of the cat with the canary in his mouth. "Aphrodite, my exquisite goddess, I worship at your altar."

Before she could even respond, Travis's mouth was at her womanhood and his palms were cupping her ass as he began to feast, the feast of a starved man. His tongue and lips and teeth assaulted her and she almost lost her mind, whining and bending and begging as she rubbed herself against him. His fingers entered her as he sucked at the swollen bud between her thighs. She screamed out and threw her head back, her sudden orgasm coming in splintering beauty. She felt tears fall down her temples as she sputtered and moaned and came back to earth to see her god of war waiting eagerly, a mischievous look on his handsome face.

"Mmm," he moaned and licked his lips. "I don't know what's hotter, Fireball, your moans or your taste, or your pussy squeezing me so tight I could get off without even being inside you yet." He growled once more as he came back to his knees, his prominent erection looking as fierce as the rest of him. Sky licked her lips, wanting to taste him too, and touch him and feel him buried deep inside her. "*See*, fuckin' Aphrodite. I told you." Her eyes came back to his; they'd darkened even more now. How was that even possible? "Come here, woman, before I die from anticipation."

Sky giggled even as he pulled her hips toward him and jerked her up and off the couch. She gasped as he moved them to the floor, to the big bear-skin rug in front of the fireplace. She cupped Travis's cheek with one hand and blindly grabbed for his cock with the other as he aligned their bodies.

He scolded, "No, no, darlin'. I'm an impatient god. I can't wait. I need to be inside you now." His fingers came back to her drenched sex as she spread her legs wide.

Just as he guided the head of his member to the entrance of her body, she gasped sharply. He stopped and looked up at her apprehensively.

"Travis, I—"

"What? Oh! Shit." He frantically moved back to his jeans and fished a condom out of his pocket. In lightning speed, he had it unwrapped and sliding down his shaft. He returned to come back in between her legs but before he entered her, he stilled and rubbed a hand on her belly, seeing her uncertain eyes. "What is it, baby? Tell me."

Sky was somewhat embarrassed that she was almost thirty years old and had never had an internal orgasm or an orgasm *ever* with a man inside her. Perhaps something was wrong with her, but she wanted Travis to know. She didn't know why, but she wanted him to know. "I—I've never orgasmed during—"

His eyes burned as bright as the fire before them and his hand came up to cup her breast again before his finger stroked her chin. "No worries, Fireball. When I said I was going to make love to you, I wasn't exaggerating."

With a wink, he slid into her and she gasped, from the incredible feeling of being filled by his thickness and the awe of it too. She was getting everything she'd ever dreamed; Travis Redmond was having sex with her. And as he leaned down to cover her body with his, the emotion became too much; she felt the tears run down her cheeks as he pulled back and thrust again, shivering and moaning.

"Fuck, Sky, you feel amazing, baby girl." His lips returned to hers as her hands gripped his brawny biceps, the muscles twitching as he made her his. She moaned back into his mouth and tangled her tongue with his as his rhythm increased and her thighs gripped him tightly. "Shit, Skyla, I never— God." He growled and pulled up on his haunches. He lifted her hips in his hands, moving his palms to her ass, and dipped his hips, the angle of his length hitting a spot she never knew existed and she climbed as he began to move quicker inside her.

"Oh my God, Travis, holy…" she trailed off before literally screaming as her orgasm crashed into her. Her body was ravaged by spasms she couldn't contain and her mind soared as tears continued to gush from her eyes in rivulets.

Her body was set back down as Travis moved them both, turning her onto her side and laying behind her. One arm moved beneath her to grab her breast as the other opened her thigh and tucked it behind his. She felt him penetrate her from behind and moaned again. His hand moved from her leg to the delta of her thighs and he stroked her wet folds as she sighed wantonly. God, his cock and fingers and mouth sucking at her neck was destroying everything she'd ever known of sex. It could be as amazing as she dreamt—it *was* amazing—as Travis brought her to yet another earth-shattering orgasm.

"Yes, my sexy Aphrodite, come for me. Fuck, baby. I can't hold back. I—" An unhuman roar came from his lips as he bit into her shoulder and thrust hard into her. A battle-cry of old, the melding of lovers, as he emptied himself inside her. His grip on her was possessive and sexy as he came, and it made her self-esteem soar that she could reduce this massive man to a quivering bundle of nerves as she just had. When his breathing finally returned, his lips moved over her flesh and made her shudder. "Damn, Skyla. That was incredible." He moved the hair off her neck and kissed her shoulder, his fingers continued to torture her swollen flesh and taut nipple.

Emotion soared through her again, and she was disappointed that she hadn't touched his penis at all. "I—I didn't even get to..." she trailed off.

"Get to what, Fireball?" He pulled out and turned her in his arms.

He was even more beautiful in a post-coital state, his eyes now back to their soft blue, the storm within him calmed. He stroked her cheek with his finger and kissed her nose.

"I didn't get to touch you," she blurted out finally, trying to hold in a sob.

"Baby, you can touch me anytime you want." His eyebrows bobbed.

"But..." She looked down, unable to explain to him what she'd meant.

Another log cracked on the fire, it was dying, and Sky shivered as the cold nipped her skin.

Travis jumped up, his gloriously naked body so impressive. An athlete trained for battle, built to forge through the line of the enemy, a true powerhouse.

"Damn, you're droolin', darlin'." He winked. And she realized she'd ogled him while he threw more wood onto the fire. "Stick your tongue back in before I find a place for you to put it." The sexual promise in Travis's voice was inescapable as he came back to her side, propping his head up on his bent arm. "Now what were you sayin' about wanting to touch me?" His tone turned playful, and Sky realized once again that she was clueless when it came to the opposite sex.

She breathed heavily as Travis's free hand came to hers and he guided it to his condom-less crotch; he must have shucked the prophylactic when he'd gotten up to attend to the fire. She realized as her fingers touched him that his member wasn't flaccid—*was it ever completely flaccid?* She cupped it and squeezed lightly, getting a groan out of him. She became fascinated by the length and girth that grew harder and longer in her hands the more she stroked it, the veins that popped up, and how it jerked when her thumb moved over the tip. She'd never really gotten to be so personal with an erect male sex organ before, her inexperience had always stymied her from doing so.

"Baby, mmm, damn, look what you did," Travis scolded. "I'm hard again. What on earth are we gonna do about this?"

Sky couldn't help but smile at his enthusiasm and bit into her lip, another wave of confidence washing over her. She wasn't sure where it'd come from, but she felt as sure as Aphrodite, a wanton woman of seduction, love, and passion at that moment.

"I know what I'd like to do. I'd like to worship my Ares, as the god of war *should* be worshipped."

The dark eyes that stared into hers would have frightened her if she'd not been so turned on herself. She gulped again and worried her lip, fearful that now she'd promised something she wasn't sure she could give. She looked down at the generous erection she was stroking, frightened that she couldn't take him down her throat, that she would embarrass herself when she puked on him due to her overexaggerated gag reflex. What had she done? What had she gotten herself into?

As if she'd spoken the words aloud, Travis moved and stood before her. Sky hit her knees, looking up at him, his raging boner so prominent and enticing and she did the unthinkable even as his palm came to her cheek. "Sky, if you—"

"No, I want to," she murmured up at him and gripped his shaft in her hand again. She looked back at his cock, the cock that had haunted her dreams for as long as she could remember, the cock that had just given her multiple orgasms. She intended to try and return the favor, even if she couldn't finish him as he was used to being finished off.

A blush took her cheeks as she pulled his member to her lips and kissed the head of him, getting another deep moan from his throat. His reaction spurred her on and she opened her mouth to take him in. Slowly and with a pounding heart, she guided his girthy sex into her mouth and down her throat, inch by rock-hard inch. She adjusted and was able to take him further in than she ever thought possible. Then something happened. An instinct, a drive, a womanly characteristic she wasn't familiar with took hold of her and kicked in.

Travis moaned as she moved her mouth over him, slowly and with calculated precision. Her hand came up to cup his scrotum and the other moved from the base of his member she was gripping up his belly to his chiseled abs. His fingers interlocked with hers there and he groaned again. "Yes, baby, fuck, that mouth…so fuckin' hot."

Once more, his words propelled her onward and her speed increased as his grip on her hair tightened and his hips began to rock into her. Having him be putty in her hands did incredible things to her own body, and she moaned too as her hand moved from his abs to her wet folds, stroking herself as he'd done earlier. "Yeah baby, make yourself come. Damn, you're so fuckin' sexy." Sky's grip tightened on his scrotum and her speed increased once again. Her grip returned to the base of him as she sucked him hard and popped off, licking the head of him before shoving him back down her throat. "Jesus, Sky, you suck my cock so good."

Sky moaned around him as she shoved her finger inside herself and went to town. Her head bobbed even as she grinded on her finger. "Fuckin-A, you're the hottest thing I've ever seen. Come, baby, come for your Ares while you worship him." And she did, moaning and coming undone as she continued to gobble down his cock like a pro. "Aww, fuck, Sky. Oh God, I'm gonna come."

"Yes, baby, do it. Down my throat." She grated out before returning her mouth to him and went crazy, fisting his member with one hand as she sucked and stroked his scrotum with the other.

The snarl that came from him this time was as terrifying as it was alluring. She took the load he shot down her throat as he thrust against her, gripping her hair with a force that made her sex clench.

"Fuck, Skyla. Sonovabitch." He whined as his movements slowed and he stroked her cheek. "That was the best fuckin' blowjob I've ever had, baby doll. You really know how to worship your god." Sky looked up into his surprised face and grinned, pulling her lips from his sex even as her tongue licked the tip and made him shiver.

"Well, I'm not called Aphrodite for no reason," she quipped with a shrug and got a laugh out of her Ares, his waning erection bobbing in front of her as she tickled his thigh.

"Told you." His brow raised and he came to his knees, aligning their bodies. "I hope you know that I'm not finished with you tonight. Ares has more battles to wage still."

Sky giggled, hopeful for more moments that blew both their minds. "I'm all yours, Ares."

And at that, she gasped as her gridiron god flipped her onto her back.

CHAPTER NINE

Travis groaned in delight as he awoke to the feel of Skyla's naked chest pressed against his. He looked down to her cinnamon and sugar swirls of hair splayed across him and immediately he grew hard. Fuck! What was it about this woman that he simply couldn't get enough of? They'd fucked enough last night to last a lifetime, but apparently his dick disagreed. The greedy sonovabitch wanted her again...and again...and again.

Travis had never had this happen before. Sure, he'd bedded beautiful women with ravenous sexual appetites, but none that had his mind and body fully engulfed, like Skyla had. There was something about her that fueled every male instinct within him. He longed to possess her as he'd never possessed any woman before her, and that thought thrilled and frightened him.

She moaned suddenly and her nose tickled his nipple. Her hand moved down his belly to rest on his cock, and he growled aloud. "Careful, love, you're about to awaken The Ram."

The blue eyes that sought his electrified him, and he was stunned by how much he wanted her once more. "My Ares, you fail to realize I'm not afraid of The Ram."

His eyes narrowed and he moved fast, pulling her atop him as if she weighed nothing.

"How dare you tempt a god, blasphemer! Now you must atone for your sins. Hop up here and pay your penance like a good worshipper."

Sky grinned naughtily, and Travis's dick jumped in anticipation. How he had any seed left to spew was anyone's guess. He'd never been so sexed up and didn't know when or if this would end. And God help him, he didn't want it to.

At some point in the night, they'd moved here into the bed and once more fucked like a bunch of rabbits. Skyla had been passionate, giving, and generous, and he'd eaten up everything she'd offered him. They'd fallen to sleep at some point, finally giving into exhaustion.

Now, she was gripping his cock like she owned it, and his head was falling back in submission as he moaned. If she wanted him splayed before her, she'd have him that way. He was hers to conquer, hers to control, hers to have as she pleased. And he was loving every second. He palmed her breasts and squeezed as she gingerly mounted him, biting her lips as she slowly impaled herself. "Easy, love. Can you take it?" he asked, concerned he might hurt her.

"Mmm, Ares, your cock it..."

"Fits like a fuckin' glove," he grunted and stilled her hips as his scrotum threatened to unload their burden. "Jesus, Sky, I've never..." he grimaced, and begged himself not to prematurely ejaculate, for this seductress deserved hers too. *My God, what is this woman doing to me?* he thought for the second time in two days. She was pulling him into a pit of undeniable pleasure and feelings he couldn't ignore.

She moved on him, far sooner than he was ready, and he gasped as the feel of her around him threatened to destroy him. "Sky..." he protested, even as her hips lifted and lowered on him.

"It's ok," her lips oozed silk as she moaned and rode his cock.

His hands moved from her hips to her ass and gripped hard. "Oh, fuck, baby, you feel so good."

"Mmm, you do too. Your body. I love your body, Travis," she cooed as her hands moved from his chest to his abs and back again, caressing him with her fingertips. He shivered as he fought the urge to hammer her. She must have sensed his reserve as her hands stilled on his belly. "Travis, fuck me."

"Mmm, baby, I—"

"It's ok. You made love to me last night. I want you to fuck me now."

He scoffed and looked into her serious eyes. Why would she want that? Didn't most women want it sensual, not frenzied? Travis prided himself on being an unselfish lover. But even women wanted it fast and hard sometimes too, right? When the occasion called for it.

Without hesitation, he let his body be his guide as he pistoned into her, meeting her lunges with hard thrusts that shook them both and Skyla's mouth fell into an O as he fucked her like his life depended on it. He sat up and cupped her breast, pulling her nipple to his mouth as he continued to pound her relentlessly. The other hand moved to the back of her head and gripped her hair lightly as he watched her eyes. He loved her breast and popped off, watching her come as she cried out and her head flew back. He wanted to fall with her, but he was too damned greedy and when her release faded, he pulled her from his lap and flipped her over on all fours.

She grunted even as he covered her and thrust into her from behind, moving his hand down her bottom and smacking it hard as he hammered into her. "Mmm, Ares," she cried as she bent her upper body down, jutting her ass out.

"That's right, baby, bow before your god. You wanted The Ram, now you got him."

"Oh, shit," Sky muttered as his hand moved to stroke between her legs. "Fuck me, baby, fuck me hard."

"Oh, naughty girl now, huh? You want it. Tell me how much you want it."

"Oh," she cried again as he smacked her plump ass once more. "I want it, God, I want it. Give it to me."

"No, not until," Travis grated out, fucking her so hard his thighs burned, "*you* give it to me, sweetheart." His fingertips rapidly stroked her sensitive folds as his hips hit hers violently, her sex milking him into oblivion.

Soon, she screamed out, burying her face into a pillow as her body succumbed to his ministrations and without warning, Travis pulled out and exploded on Skyla's tight little ass, gasping and sputtering as his seed squirted halfway up her back.

"Sky, shit, baby. Fuck, you're so damn sexy."

After several moments of attempting to gain his breath, Travis finally moved and ran to the bathroom to grab a towel. He cleaned his semen off Sky's ass and back and turned her over to make sure she was alright. Her face was red but she was smiling, so he took that as a good sign. He kissed her lips softly before falling to the bed and bringing her to rest on his chest, tucking her head into his shoulder. "Fuck, Sky, I haven't ever had this much sex. I swear."

He looked up to see a blushing Skyla. "I—I never knew that..." She looked down. "I thought men only came once."

Travis looked around, raising his brows as Sky's head came up. "I mean, as you've noticed, guys can come more than once during sex. Not like women can, but it's not unusual to ejaculate more than twice, I guess." Travis shrugged.

"What were you gonna say before? This morning and last night, you had just gotten inside me and you started to say something but then stopped. You said, 'I never—' then stopped."

Travis tried to remember, but being inside her literally blew his mind and made him forget everything but her silky heat swallowing him whole. "Oh! I remember. I've never been so close to coming in my life than when I slide into you."

"Really?" Her brows furrowed in surprise.

"Yeah really. You're so tight and hot and...fuck, I'm getting hard thinking about it again."

Skyla giggled, and Trav literally felt his cock jerk in response. "Keep it up and you're gonna be so raw, I'll have to fuck your ass next."

Sky gasped in surprise and shook her head, getting a laugh out of Travis. "I—I've never. No. Just no."

"Oh, c'mon. Don't knock it 'til you try it."

"Anal is gross!" She protested. "There's so much bacteria. Eww." Clearly, she'd never tried anal or she wouldn't be so opposed, but he wouldn't push it...not today, anyway. "We forgot to use a condom again."

Dammit, that made the *second* time. Travis frowned, displeased that he'd let his desires override his rationale. "I'm sorry about that. I'm clean just so you know. I get tested frequently."

"I mean...I'm clean too. It's just—" she lowered her head, bashfully.

"What, don't tell me you're a major germ-a-phob now and don't want me jizzing in you?"

"No, I just, I'm not on the pill or anything."

"Oh fuck!" Travis grunted but remembered that he'd pulled out last time too, thank goodness. The last thing this fling needed was an illegitimate child while they were running for their lives. But then he laughed, sensing Sky's shift in moods. "We'll just have to name the little bastard Minotaur or some shit."

"Not funny, Trav," she elbowed him even as she kissed his pec and fingered his nipples, getting a hiss out of him. "Everyone knows that Ares and Aphrodite had at least four children and they were winged, of which, none were Minotaur."

Travis knew nothing of the sort. He did good to remember his routes. Greek mythology was cool as shit but he could barely pronounce the names of the gods, let alone remember their children. "Thus, why you're smarter than me. I'm just a dumb jock, remember?" He winked and got a giggle out of his Aphrodite even as she leaned in to kiss his lips. He loved her soft lips and her firm tits and ass and...

"Mmm, Travis," she said breathlessly as his hands roved over her and their kiss deepened.

"Mmm, yes, I know. I don't need to father anymore winged children but damn, woman, I know now why Ares couldn't stop himself from having affairs with the goddess of beauty."

Aphrodite laughed heartily. "Oh, just chill, god of war. I don't know if I'm physically capable of anymore sexual relations with you right now."

Travis moved on top of her and cupped her face, admiring her natural beauty: no makeup, no mascara, nothing but rosy, post-sex bliss smeared her cheeks. "Fine. I'll give you a break. For now," he smirked. "I mean, I guess we could eat and go play in the snow again. I wouldn't mind sledding."

Her lips lifted in a smile. "Sledding, huh? And more workouts?"

"Definitely more workouts. I need to bench press you so I don't get soft." He winked.

"The likelihood of you getting soft around me is gonna be slim, stud."

"Oooh, I love this new confident Skyla. She's sexy as fuck."

He kissed her lips again and cupped her breast, bringing it back to his mouth to love. After a moment, she wriggled beneath him and he felt his dick getting hard again.

"Travis," she sighed, in equal parts want and exhaustion.

"I know, I'm sorry."

"No, you're not." Sky giggled in response.

"Ok, I'm not," he confessed. "I gotta ask though, was it everything you'd dreamed of?"

"You *would* ask me that, you cocky jerk," she hissed. "But it was more...so much more."

Travis smiled and leaned his forehead against hers. "It was for me too, Sky." He felt his heart flip as she cupped his jaw, running her fingers over the thick scruff there.

"I'll never forget this time I've had with you, no matter what happens. I'm…I'm really glad I ran into you, even if we do die. I want you to know that."

"Well, that's comforting." But he understood why she'd said it. They could still die. Geraci could still find them before the cavalry came. "I think it's time we fed the beast," Travis motioned to his growling belly, and Skyla laughed again.

"I thought we'd already fed him." Her blue eyes sparkled in amusement.

"Oh, he'll feed again. He likes wanton maidens best, ya know."

LATER THAT DAY, they went sledding after they'd eaten, finding a sled in the shed out back. Then they worked out, another sweat-scorching, high-intensity routine. After working his neck and legs, Travis had literally bench-pressed Skyla for a total of forty reps, before he'd finally called it quits.

"How many pounds can you bench?" she asked once he'd set her down beside him on the floor.

"I mean, I can press close to three hundred, but usually I don't lift more than two-thirty. I'm not a power lifter, so our focus is technique and working fast twitch muscles, not necessarily bulking up."

"You lost me there, stud." Sky laughed. "But whatever you're doing, it's workin'." She winked and squeezed his bicep.

"You mean, I know stuff you don't know?" he scoffed.

"It's technical. I'm sure your workouts are very specific to you; you have coaches and dieticians and such."

"Yeah, my dietician and coaches would eat me alive right now, but what can I do? Just waiting on Wyatt Earp to come rescue us, right?"

Sky smiled and nodded then frowned. "You're getting a cut in pay and have fines too, right? For your suspension."

"Yeah." He shrugged. He didn't keep up with the money side of it. That's what his lawyer was for.

"Right, I forgot, twenty-five thousand dollars is a trip to Walmart for you. Why get all up in arms about it?"

Travis didn't miss her tone. "Hey, c'mon. It's not like I can go back and change anything. I fucked up, okay? I own that. I'm missing out too, though. I miss my teammates and football. I'm being punished here."

"You look so punished," she pouted and leaned in to kiss him.

"I am. Tortured beyond words by this sultry little sex goddess I'm cooped up with. It's straight damn torment, something out of the underworld. Hades would be downright jealous."

Skyla giggled again and let him jerk her up and into his lap, where she settled easily against him and ran her fingers through his hair as he made love to her mouth. He gripped her back and lost himself to her ways, loving her moans and taste and soft curves pressing into him.

"Mmm," he moaned and pulled back. "My Aphrodite knows how to handle a horny ram." He looked down at his growing hard-on and got another laugh out of Skyla. God, she was gorgeous when she was happy.

"Gah, you're such a perv. We should shower and make dinner, Ares."

"I'll make *something*, naughty girl. Make you scream my name like you have been. That's enough to satisfy me."

And so the night went, with them wrapped in each other's arms, loving one another like there was no tomorrow. Going through the box of condoms like it was their freaking honeymoon and they had not a care in the world but to please and be pleased. Travis gave himself fully to this enticing love goddess of ancient Greece who stirred his sex and heart in ways he hadn't known were possible.

As he buried himself inside her for the umpteenth time and still didn't feel fully satiated, he came to the conclusion that when they got through this and life was back to normal, he was going to take her out on a real date, invite her to his big mansion in Buckhead, and even bring her to meet the guys—Brett, Linc, TJ, Paxton and the others. As he made her his tonight, he realized he wanted her to be his long after this night was over. He wanted her to be with him, tomorrow and the next day and the next.

"WHERE THE *FUCK* ARE THEY?" Geraci growled into the phone.

"We've found them, sir. They've been spotted just outside of Estes Park, Colorado," Mathers answered, knowing he had to give in.

"Colorado, huh? Interesting."

"It would seem Ms. Larson has a hideout there. We're digging now. It's just a matter of…"

"Time is something that is wearing my patience *thin*, Kane. And we all know what happens when I get angry, so you find them and you bring them here. That's a direct order, do you understand? I want them unharmed, but in your custody in the next twenty-four hours. Is that clear?"

"Crystal, sir. They will be ours by nightfall tomorrow. I'll call you when it's done."

"Good. I expect you won't disappoint me. You haven't thus far, Kane."

And Casey hoped he wouldn't; he needed Geraci's trust for this all to come to fruition.

"I'll make you proud, Gio."

"Good man. Safe travels."

Giovanni hung up the phone, and Mathers took in a deep breath.

Travis and Skyla had the night then hell was coming for them. He prayed they were ready to face it.

SKY LAUGHED AGAIN and smiled at her lover as the bubbles encompassed them.

"I heard this can give you a yeast infection," Travis said, grunting even as Sky moved atop of him and guided his erection to her entrance. "Mmm, fuck, you feel so good."

"If I don't have one yet, I'm bound to never get one," she retorted and moaned along with him as he gripped her waist.

He kissed her passionately as he matched her thrusts. "Mmm, I'm just sayin' we can do this outside of the water. I know it's your first time but this, mmm, isn't easy on..." he trailed off as Sky's walls clenched him and her eyes sought his as she came closer to the edge. "Damn Sky," he chuckled, "you're so easy."

"Can it and give me my O, muscle head," she grunted on a moan.

"You should be careful how you speak to your god, Aphrodite."

"Mmm, what'd you have in mind, Ares?"

She gasped as he scooped her up and out of the water. He threw her over his shoulder as he got out of the bathtub, smacking her butt and getting a squeal from her as he walked them to the bedroom. She enjoyed the view of his firm-as-hell glutes and hamstrings before she was thrown onto the bed and a ferocious-looking Ares growled down at her. He threw his hands on his hips and snarled. "I think it's time to bend you to my will, Fireball."

"Oh Ares, you frighten me with your wrath," Sky teased and tickled her fingertips down his washboard stomach.

Travis almost laughed but caught himself as he gripped her wrist. "You'll rue the day you chose to smite— Ok seriously, did they *really* talk like this?"

Sky laughed even as her hands fell to his hard member and squeezed him in her hand, getting a gasp out of him in response. "Now Ares, you're breaking character. The mighty Aphrodite was shaking in her sandals."

"Right. I'm sure she was." He stroked her hair. "Mmm. I love it when you cup my balls like that."

"Ugh, Trav. I hate when you say balls...and tits."

"What's wrong with that?" he asked and frowned down at her.

"It's childish, to be honest."

"Childish?" His brows rose, and Sky stifled another giggle.

"I mean let's use more adult-like words, less porn-star vocab."

"That's it, I'm hog-tying you."

Skyla squealed again as Travis grabbed for her and cupped a hand over her mouth. She attempted to bite him and he chuckled. "Down, girl. Damn. That might be all kinds of new fun right there."

Her mouth flew open, and he used that moment to tickle her and pull her arms behind her back. He kissed her lips and had her quivering as his mouth moved to her neck; he sucked, licked, and nibbled…and had her wetness oozing down her thighs. He moved them up in the bed and had her place her arms back above her head as he positioned himself between her legs, running his hands up and down them, making her moan in anticipation. "I'm gonna bend you now, flexible girl." He winked and she nodded, eager for something new and exciting with him.

Travis pulled her legs up to rest on his muscular chest as he leaned down, folding her in half, her knees touching her breasts. His finger entered her and she moaned as he began to finger her, preparing her for his sex.

Sky had never known lovers could have so many sexual encounters and still want and be able to have so many more. It was as if her body simply couldn't get its fill of Travis "Ares" Redmond and needed multiple daily doses to function.

Travis groaned as he entered her and leaned down upon her as he thrust, caging her thighs on either side of her as his forehead came to touch hers. "Oh, oh my God, Trav," Sky whimpered as her calves rested on his shoulders, her feet touching as they came close to interlocking around the back of his neck. Her hands came to grip his biceps as he rocked inside her.

"Right? That feels fucking fantastic, doesn't it?"

"Mmm," was all Sky could get out as his sex hit somewhere deep inside that she never knew existed. He moved stealthy, with precision as her orgasm began to build within, higher and higher as his speed increased. "Oh Travis. Oh God." His name was torn from her lips as her body gave into his caresses once more and she tumbled head over heels into sexual ecstasy.

Travis followed soon after with a beastly groan of his own and chuckled as he came down from his high. "I fuckin' own you, Fireball. Don't you forget it." He winked and kissed her forehead even as she squeezed him, using her pelvic muscles. He grunted and gave her a self-satisfied grin.

"Keep tellin' yourself that, hothead, whatever works for ya."

"I see you haven't had enough of the god of war just yet."

"Fire on the head…"

"Right. I don't know why I'm surprised." He feigned exasperation as he pulled out of her and helped her legs down, for they were like Jell-O.

"You'd get bored with me if I was subservient." She kissed his cheek and he pulled her tightly into his muscular embrace.

"You wouldn't be. You're Aphrodite, a goddess in her own right."

She wasn't, not until he'd awakened the sleeping sex goddess. Skyla wasn't sure she'd be able to exorcise the bitch now that she'd been invoked. It was like trying to stuff a genie back into a bottle or a can of biscuit dough back into the tube once it was broken; it wasn't freaking happening.

"Ah my sweet, I think you've finally worn me out." Travis yawned and tucked her head into his chest, resting his chin against her hairline. "Sky?"

"Yeah?"

"I…" he paused and Skyla's heart fluttered as she looked up at him. He searched her eyes before blushing. "I'm really glad you aren't marrying the mayor."

As thrilled as that statement should make her, it didn't; she swallowed down the disappointment his words brought her. She gave him a weak grin and held back her tears. What had she been expecting? A confession of love? In a few days' time? Negative. He was just having fun fucking her. That was all. This wasn't love. Not for him. As much as she knew that, it still hurt.

She tried to tuck it down as her mind relaxed and her body absorbed his seed. Once more they hadn't used a freaking condom, and he'd come inside her this time. Great! Her body was reveling in his love-making, seeing it for more than what it was. Her heart was breaking apart and bleeding, and her mind was rationalizing it all into compartments of all the stupid things she'd done in the last four days. It had a board and a tally and it was pissed!

"Hey," Travis stated as he pulled her chin up to look at him. "You ok?"

How could she genuinely answer that question? No. She'd finally gone and had the best sex of her life with the man she'd been in love with as a teenager, she was cervix-full of his cum, and worried about getting pregnant, worried about being killed by a gangster, and wanted him to tell her he loved her. No, she was indeed *not* okay.

"Sky? When we get home, I…"

"Please, don't. Ok? I don't want you to feel obligated or anything. I mean this is just a little fling, right? No need for us to make it more than what it is." It took every ounce of her willpower to look up into his surprised eyes and not waver, but she did.

Travis frowned but nodded. "Right." He gave her a weak grin and kissed her forehead. Skyla felt her heart shatter in two even as his arms cradled her.

She'd wanted to be wrong. She'd wanted him to say something to make her doubt the nagging in her gut. She'd wanted an admission of feelings, but she should've known better. Travis Redmond was a professional athlete with a reputation and an image to uphold and none of that would change now that they'd been intimate. He wasn't any different than he'd been before they'd stepped into the cabin, and he wouldn't be any different when they left. He didn't love her. He didn't want her. She wasn't good enough.

Her heart tried to tell her she was wrong, but her brain wasn't listening. It told her to soak up these last few moments with him because they would be the last.

She tucked her legs into her chest and listened to the steady thumping of his heart beat in her ear as she surrendered to the exhaustion their union had induced.

Hours later, Sky awoke with a start. Some sound had woken her and her heart beat rapidly as she rose in the bed. Something was wrong. It was too quiet. It was too dark. She was still naked, she realized, and reached for Travis only to find an empty bed.

"Shit," she groaned, fearfully.

She pulled herself from the comforter, feeling her skin chill as she moved to the bathroom, remembering where her clothes were last. She opened the door slowly, acutely aware of the loud creak of the hinges as she did so. She moved with purpose, feeling for her jeans on the counter and her bra and tank top, pulling them on quickly as she searched for the missing flannel top. She began to panic when she heard a loud thump. It sounded like flesh hitting flesh but she couldn't be sure. Her mind raced with other options she didn't want to consider. She had to find Travis.

She moved back into the bedroom and slowly tip-toed to the door. When she opened it, her eyes fell on the empty den, fire dying in the stove and scarce lighting to guide her to the kitchen. She crept there and opened the fridge to give her light. She froze when the light revealed two large men in suits standing in the corner and a kneeling Travis, shirtless with a gag in his mouth, his arms tied behind his back. She gasped and heard Travis groan, mumbling to her despite the gag.

"There you are, ADA Larson. Someone of great importance has requested your presence, my dear. He's eager to meet you."

"Of course. Just let me grab a shirt and some shoes for Travis, and finish dressing myself."

"Naturally. We're happy to accommodate you." The taller man of the two nodded.

"Make it quick," the bulkier man snapped roughly.

Skyla nodded and moved to turn the lamp in the living room on, feeling a large presence behind her that made her shiver. She balked at his closeness but prayed for her backbone to hold out. This was going to get worse before it got better, she knew. She moved into the bedroom and found her flannel quickly, pulling it over her shoulders before donning the boots she'd found in the closet two days ago. She grabbed the thick coat off the rack, grabbing one for Travis too, and a flannel for him then nodded to the hulking giant scowling at her.

They moved back to the kitchen, and she motioned to Travis as she spoke to the taller, more civilized-looking man of the two. "You'll have to untie his hands if I'm to put a shirt on him."

"Only if Mr. Redmond can agree to shelve his hostility."

"I'm sure we can agree to that, right, Trav?" she asked and looked into his eyes. His brows drew but he grated a, "Yes," through the gag, and she looked expectantly to their captors.

The tall man stepped forth, untied Travis's wrists, and stepped back. Travis shook the rope off and pulled the gag from his mouth. "What the *fuck?*" he growled and took a step forward only for Skyla to put a hand to his chest, stopping him.

"Travis," she implored. "Here, put your shirt and coat on." She motioned to the clothes in her hands.

"Assholes jumped me while I was getting a water from the fridge."

"He's not called Ares, the god of war, for nothing," Sky cooed to the men who looked ready to have a reason to knock him down a peg or two.

"Mr. Redmond, if you could please finish dressing. My boss is not a patient man. He's eager to see you both."

"You mean fuckin' kill us. Why the hell should I be eager for that?"

"We have direct orders to bring you in 'unharmed,' but that term has been loosely defined before," the bulkier man of the two jeered.

Travis took another step forward. "If you so much as *look* at her the wrong way, I'll—"

"Mr. Redmond, I won't ask you again to kindly put your fuckin' shirt on." The tall man pulled a pistol from his back and cocked it. "Perhaps I didn't make myself clear enough."

"Travis, please?" Sky begged and handed Travis the shirt. He threw it over his shoulders, and the coat she'd grabbed, and shoved his feet in the boots that sat next to the front door. He then took Sky's hand and nodded for the men to take them away.

Sky didn't know where they were going and didn't know precisely what would happen when they got there, but she could say with certainty that she was scared shitless of Giovanni Geraci.

As they were herded into a stark white van parked in the snowy drive, she prayed as Travis pulled her into his side, prayed that they lived to be able to tell their grandchildren about this.

CHAPTER TEN

Two days and several hours later, the van finally parked one final time.

They'd been permitted to use the restroom when they'd stopped for gas. Remote gas stations had been chosen—with facilities that hadn't been the cleanest either—but Travis was grateful that they'd at least been allowed to evacuate their bladders. They'd also been given food to eat and water to drink, so the treatment was far better than he'd anticipated. He'd attempted to stay as calm as he could, for Skyla's sake, although she looked far more reserved than he felt. He'd been less nervous at his last Super Bowl than he was today, meeting Geraci for the first time. Although, he feared more for Skyla and his brother than he did for himself.

"Travis," Sky whispered when the two men got out of the vehicle. "I love you."

Her sapphire blue eyes called to his soul as he looked back into them and lost himself to their depths. Like the fisherman of ancient Greece, summoned to their deaths by the alluring voices of the sirens, he was helpless. He leaned in to kiss her, knowing his words would simply screw it up, and let his lips do the talking for him.

When Sky pulled back, she said, "I know I already told you, but that was *before*. Before I knew you. Before I'd given myself to you. It's truer now than it's ever been."

Travis gave her a smile and cupped her face before pulling her into his arms, tightly. "Sky, when this is all over—"

Travis never got to finish. The side panel opened quickly, and he was grabbed by four rough hands gripping his shoulders and torso. He saw Sky gasp, attempting to hold back a scream. He beckoned to her with his eyes, pleading with her to hear the words he'd not said.

When he was turned around, the tall dude from the van looked him over.

"Geraci would like to see you now."

"Great, he spottin' the drinks?"

Travis turned his head to look at Skyla who was being assisted out of the van. He started to question where she was going but, much to his relief, she was following him, trailed by the bulky dude.

They entered what looked to be a warehouse, smelling like wood shavings, and went up a metal staircase to a glass enclosed office of good size. It smelled like booze, sex, and dirty money. When they were made to sit on the black velvet sofa, Travis cringed a little. This felt like something out of far too many gangster movies he'd watched; he wanted to flee as fast as possible.

Sky rested her hand on his thigh and watched the two henchmen back up against the wall. They all waited with bated breath while Geraci took his sweet-ass time; inside, Travis was quaking. He wondered what Giovanni planned to do with them, mostly what he planned to do to Sky. Would he hurt her, rape her, kill her to make a public statement? Travis knew the man probably wouldn't push his luck, since Sky was the assistant district attorney, or would he? These men were above the law, right? Travis had seen that himself in the way Geraci's crony had roped him into losing football games. Was Tucker even alive?

Travis would soon find out as the door ahead of them opened and a plump, middle-aged Italian man entered the room, decked out in a mauve pin-striped Versace suit. The dark hair on his head, graying at the temples, was slicked back and he had a cigar tucked in the corner of his thin lips. His straight teeth emerged in a wide smile as he saw them.

"Well, well, look who we have here!" His exuberance was unnerving. "Roll out the red carpet, we have celebrities in the house tonight."

Travis couldn't tell if the man was usually this jovial, if he'd been drinking, or was simply putting on a show. Whatever the case, this didn't bode well for Travis and Sky.

"You two have taken me on a wild goose chase for the last week. I'm so glad you're back...and well, as I'd asked."

"Mr. Geraci, I—"

"You've traveled a long way. Could I interest you in a drink, dear? Travis? Or should I say, Mr. Redmond. It's good to finally meet you face-to-face."

"Two scotches, please," Travis said, his eyes lifting to Geraci's. If he wanted fear, he wouldn't get it from Travis.

"Of course, of course." Geraci motioned to the tall man who moved to the bar to pour their drinks.

"Where's my brother?" Travis got straight to the point.

Geraci held up his hand as he moved to sit in the red straight-back chair adjacent to them. "Drinks first. Then business. As always." His smile, again, was unnerving. He was gonna draw the suspense out for as long as he could. "How was your ride? You both look well rested."

That motherfucker. Travis attempted to rein in his temper which was growing shorter by the minute; he couldn't help himself, he was a hothead by nature. Patience was not something he was known for. But he knew anger wouldn't get them anywhere, so he gripped Sky's hand on his thigh, letting her touch soothe him some.

Geraci's eyes flickered to the contact before he smiled at them again. Tall dude set their drinks down, and Travis literally inhaled the two ounces before slamming his glass down onto the coffee table, eyes narrowing at Geraci again.

Geraci chuckled heartily, like he'd just been told a funny joke, and Travis felt Skyla shiver beside him. "Travis Redmond, you really are the 'god of war,' huh? Look at you, you're ready to run me down. All that adrenaline. How do you get it out stuck in a cabin for days on end?" Geraci's brows rose and his eyes roved over Skyla, Travis growled. "Oh, I forgot. You were cooped up in a cabin with *this* beauty. I'll bet you got out more than adrenaline, didn't you?"

Travis looked away before he said something that might hurt them, counting to ten before looking back at Geraci.

"Since you've finished your drink, I guess we can get right down to business."

Here we go, Travis thought and squeezed Skyla's fingers lightly.

"I didn't like being shown up in that bar in San Antonio. I don't appreciate being deceived. You of all people should know that, ADA Larson."

"Mr. Geraci, I can assure you—" Skyla began.

Geraci held his hand up once again, silencing her. "Please save the commentary for after I finish, dear." Of which, Sky nodded and bowed her head. Travis held in another growl. "Then you run from me."

"With all due respect, *sir*, we didn't run until we were being chased. After your boy here blew a man's head off!" Travis interceded.

"Man, you *are* an impressive specimen," Geraci said to Travis then lifted his chin. "Kane?"

The tall man—apparently named Kane—stepped forward.

"Gag him." Geraci spat, and Travis flinched even as he stood. He knew that if he fought these men, he wouldn't win; they had guns and he didn't. He wasn't going to get Sky or Tucker or himself killed over his smart mouth, so he acquiesced; he was bound and gagged, and thrown roughly back onto the couch.

Sky shivered, and Travis hated himself in that moment. She was the only one left to defend them. He was now helpless, thanks to his short fuse. Sky remained calm though, her inner attorney taking over. "Mr. Geraci…"

"Why were you in San Antonio, Ms. Larson?"

"I was sent to investigate some cases believed to be tied to you."

"How convenient."

"I assure you, I had no idea that my former classmate, Travis Redmond, was going to be in the bar that night."

"He's not your informant?"

"No, sir. Until that night, I'd not seen him for a decade."

Geraci laughed heartily. "Right. And I double as Mary fuckin' Poppins. Tell me the truth or things are gonna get bloody." Geraci's smile faded, the bull was stomping his hoof.

Fuck, Travis cursed his damn mouth as he watched Sky's frightened face.

"Are you, or are you not, Travis's lover, Ms. Larson?"

"I—" Sky hesitated, and Geraci's eyes narrowed. *Shit.* They were gonna die. Right fucking here and now. "Mr. Geraci, I swear, I wasn't…until the cabin."

Geraci belted out into another fit of laughter, bending double before he righted himself and wiped his eyes. Travis was slowly starting to despise the sound of his nasally laugh.

"Lovers by convenience. What a coincidence! So, you knew *nothing* about me blackmailing him to lose his football games?"

Sky simply shook her head.

"I'm sure he told you that I have his brother."

"Yes. Is he alive?" Sky's eyes held Geraci's, and Travis's heart stood still.

"He's a bit banged up but he'll live…probably," Geraci dismissed.

Travis breathed a sigh of relief.

Sky continued, "I heard you've been laundering money, extorting others like Travis. You're part of an underground sex-trafficking ring, among other things."

"I'm a business man, Ms. Larson."

"Right. And *I* double as Mary fuckin' Poppins."

"Ooh, wee! We got a live one here, boys." Geraci chuckled and looked Sky over like she was a decadent treat. Travis felt his anger surge. "Those redheads." Geraci's eyes came to Travis's, and Trav narrowed his in return. "You know, don't you? You greedy bastard." Geraci pointed to Travis. "Well, perhaps, she's worth sharing."

Fuck! No, not that. Dammit. And now he was tied down and could do nothing.

"Mr. Geraci, why did you kill that trucker? Were you aiming for Travis?" Sky interceded, the lawyer in her taking charge of the witness.

"Of course not! Travis can't die. He's our star attraction. He's gonna continue to be my pawn and lose or win games as I see fit. That is, if he wants his brother to live…"

"And how is he supposed to do that?" Sky smarted. "When he's wanted for the questioning of a murder?"

Geraci smiled. "You are such a clever girl. No worries. His record will be expunged. You'll make sure of that, won't you, ADA Larson?" He winked. "Your lover didn't do anything wrong, after all."

"And why did you kill him to begin with? Travis's record wouldn't need to be *expunged* if you hadn't killed an innocent man for no fucking reason other than a scare tactic."

"Ms. Larson, you try my patience. I'm sure you've heard of the term 'collateral damage.' The trucker was just that. Nothing more."

"*Collateral* damage means the trucker *wasn't* the target. So, you admit you were aiming for your golden boy?" Sky's brows went up. "Let me guess: you thought he'd planned to meet me in the bar and decided his number was up before he spilled the beans to me?"

Geraci stilled for a moment then removed his cigar and put it on the coffee table. He stood and began to applaud. "Well done, Ms. Larson. And that's why you'll make DA soon enough. I can help with that too, if you'd like."

Sky gasped then frowned. "Murder isn't the answer to everything, Geraci."

"It is when you're counted on to do whatever it takes to keep the business running."

"So, you admit to murdering five people?" Sky rattled off their names rapidly. "All because they, like Travis, were going to 'rat you out'." She lifted her hands to air quote her words.

Geraci's eyes narrowed once more. "I admit to doing what's necessary to keep the order. Murder, extortion, fraud, I've done it all. And there's been *far* more than five. But who's counting?"

A look of victory crossed Skyla's face; it was so fast and fleeting that one would've missed it had they not known her as well as Travis did. She cleared her throat and looked down though, as if she were disappointed. "Did that trucker have a family?"

"Who the fuck knows?" Geraci shrugged. "Now, how do I plan to punish my mouthy star athlete here? What can I possibly do to make him understand that I won't tolerate insubordination?" Geraci put his fat hand to his double chin, in thought. "I mean, I can't harm him physically, I need him healthy. And I can't kill my ADA, not when I can extort her, too. What a conundrum."

Travis gulped; he didn't like where this was leading.

Sure enough, Geraci's smirk made Travis's stomach drop as he eyed Skyla and licked his lips. "Come to me, my dear." He opened his hand, and Sky eyed it wearily but didn't move.

Kane, the tall man, approached then bowed his head obediently. "Uh, Gio, I don't ask for much, but…"

Geraci laughed. "Kane, my loyal subject, I forgot! You like redheads, don't you? Does this decadent little morsel interest you?"

Travis yelled behind his gag, scooting forward.

"She does, indeed." Kane moaned as his eyes moved over Sky with open interest. He adjusted himself in his pants, and Travis full out growled, leaning across a cowering Skyla in a futile attempt to shield her.

"Alright then. I guess you can test her out before I have my turn. You've got thirty minutes. See, Mr. Redmond, loyalty is rewarded." Geraci scowled, and Travis yelled again as Kane drew nearer. Travis out-bulked him by much, but was helpless with his arms pinned behind his back.

He pushed up off the couch and rammed at Kane's middle, planting his trunk-like legs. Kane was able to shuck him off after long moments of struggling. After all, Travis was a powerful running back; pushing through and breaking tackles was his forte. Kane flipped him back onto the couch, onto his belly, and dug a knee into his ass cheek. It hurt, but nothing hurt as much as the thought of another man touching Skyla, probing her, violating her body. It made Travis insane with rage. He continued to fight until the bulky dude jerked him up and held him fast, making him watch as Kane took Skyla's hand. She stood, looking up at her soon-to-be-violator as tears ran down her cheeks. She wasn't fighting. She was and had always been smarter than him. She knew if she fought, it would only be more painful for her.

Travis's anger peaked as Kane drew nearer to her and fingered a tear on Skyla's cheek. "Don't worry, *angel*. I'm gonna make this all worth your while." He leaned in and kissed her, and Sky froze. She looked up at him; it didn't seem like fear or reproach or dread...it looked like...*recognition?* Did she know this guy? What the hell was happening? As soon as the moment happened, it was over. Kane gripped the back of her neck and turned them. "Thanks, boss. I'm gonna enjoy the hell out of this sexy ginger."

With the slam of the door, Travis's fight left him and his heart broke into a million pieces. The woman he loved—he suddenly realized—was going to be raped, taken, and there wasn't a damn thing he could do about it. He fell, heavy onto the couch as the sheer magnitude of his hopelessness ate him like a cancer. They were here because of him, because he'd been too afraid to go to the authorities in the first place. They'd ran because he'd told them to.

He lowered his head, knowing that with everything that had happened, the biggest regret he had was not admitting, after she told him she loved him in the van, that he felt the same exact damn way about her.

Skyla sniffled and tried to dampen the panic rising in her throat as she was led down the stairs and into a dark room beneath the staircase.

She had to play it cool and disarm him at just the right time, using the self-defense moves she'd learned years ago. She tried to remember where on his back he kept his gun holstered. She flinched when the light came on and heard Kane close the door behind them, fighting the need to evacuate the bile threatening her throat.

Stay calm, she told herself. *Wait for the right moment. Don't blow it.*

But the hair on the back of her neck stood on end as she felt his presence behind her. Before she could stop and think, she was whirling around, knee up, ready to shove his balls into his throat. His hands blocked her motion, and she protested with a battle cry as her right fist shot out towards his jaw. He blocked that, too. Dammit!

"Skyla, stop." Kane gripped her hand and spun her around, pulling her arm to her back and disabling her. She cried out again, terror ripping through her chest as his hand came to her throat and held her still as her back hit his chest. "Shh, calm down. It's me. Agent Mathers," he whispered into her ear.

Agent Mathers! Agent Mathers? He was FBI! Oh, thank God! The relief she felt was bone deep, for although she'd never met the man, she'd heard his name many times from Jeffers in the past. "Mathers, oh my—" her sigh came out on a strangled sob.

"Shh, not too loud. Everything's gonna be fine. We got what we needed." When he turned her around, Skyla looked up at him, confused. He pointed to his chest. "I'm wired." He put his index finger to his lips and gave her a smile.

Again, she blew out her breath. Everything Geraci had said, everything he'd confessed to, had been recorded; someone was on the other end of the line, hearing them right now. She covered her mouth, overcome with overwhelming emotion. They were gonna be saved. She wasn't going to die. She wasn't going to be raped. Travis wasn't going to die. They were gonna get out of this!

"I love you, DA Jeffers," she whispered into the mic. "I can't wait to see you again." The happy tears ran down her face and she let them, for once not ashamed of her emotional side. But as she looked up at Mathers she knew they still had roles to play before the cavalry came. "Tucker?" she asked.

"In bad shape, but alive. I did the best I could."

Oh, God, what did that mean? Skyla fearfully looked around at the sorry excuse for a "bedroom" to the bed in the corner of the concrete store room. The cracked wooden frame looked as if it'd seen better days. She almost gagged at the thoughts of who and what had gone on atop the stained cream comforter. She looked away and rubbed her arms.

"How long do we have before they're here?" she asked.

"ETA is a half hour."

She nodded. "Alright." She took a deep breath in. "What do I need to do?"

GERACI HAD TRIED to make small talk while Travis waited for the earth to split open and swallow him whole. The entire time he'd thought of nothing but the sheer horror Skyla was experiencing, his stomach threatening to unload its contents, straining against the gag in his mouth. Tears stung his eyes, and he hated himself for every wrong he'd ever done; but he'd never hated himself as much as he did at this moment. The two people he loved most were being held against their will, being hurt because of him. He'd never felt more miserable.

Just when he thought he couldn't take another second of the despair within him and was complacent to let Geraci's steroid-filled crony blow his head right off, the door opened and his gut jerked at the dishevelment that Skyla was in.

Travis fell to his knees, his legs giving out as she was shoved inside the office, head lowered, her clothes hanging off her frame. He couldn't see her face but he heard her sniffles, saw the tears in her jeans and the rips in her shirt, and swore to God above he was gonna kill the smug bastard behind her for ever laying a hand on her.

"Ah, there you are. I was starting to wonder if you'd ran off with her," Geraci remarked, looking back at Travis with a self-satisfied grin.

"Sorry, boss," the man called Kane chuckled cynically. "She put up a good fight. I might've got a little carried away." He adjusted himself in his slacks, and Travis roared, ready to kill him.

"Uh uh," bulky boy gritted his teeth and pointed the gun at Travis, who shook with the rage that overtook him. "Control your-self or your little girlfriend's gonna get to see me plaster your face all over that sofa."

"Now now, Biggs, easy. Put the gun away. Our 'god of war' here is just letting out his frustrations, seeing as he's been dethroned." Geraci chuckled again, and Travis growled over at him.

If it weren't for the horror that Skyla had already been through, Travis would've sprinted over to Geraci, tackled him to the floor, and beaten his fat nose into his skull, using only his forehead as a weapon. Hell, he was The Ram after all.

"A king doesn't like sharing his queen, am I wrong?" Geraci smirked and stood. "Looks like it's my turn now." His gray eyes burned into Travis's, and that's when he made his move. He would be damned if he simply stood by and watched while yet another man took the woman he loved out that damn door again; he would die before he watched it happen twice.

He shoved with all his might to lift his big frame off the floor, engaging every muscle in his core, thankful he was strong enough to do so.

He heard Skyla's scream and the blast of a gun behind him as he launched himself at Geraci and knocked him to the ground.

That's when absolute chaos erupted all around him: glass splintered, metal clashed, shouts echoed, fog blanketed, and darkness followed. Gunshots ricocheted, the sounds of footfalls thundered around his head. He closed his eyes, waiting for death to take him.

Travis wasn't aware of how long the struggle lasted or exactly what the hell was happening. He only knew when silence followed and he was jerked roughly up, his restraints and gag were removed simultaneously.

"Mr. Redmond? Travis! Are you ok?" It was Kane who was asking. And Travis growled, balling his fists. "Easy there, Ares. I'm Special Agent Casey Mathers, FBI. It's over. We got him."

"What?" Travis was dumbfounded. This minion of Geraci's wasn't his minion? He was an FBI agent? "Skyla?" was his next thought. "Skyla!" he called, needing to see her.

"She's fine. She's right here. Took a graze from a bullet, but she's gonna be okay."

"Travis," he heard her soft voice from the floor in the corner. Flashlights and SWAT team members came into view as Travis looked around. He hit his knees as he fell before her and scooped her into his arms, despite that she had medics tending her, gauze covering her right bicep. He needed to feel her against him, needed to know she was safe, needed to show her what she meant to him. The relief that she hadn't really been raped or beaten was palpable, and he felt a heavy burden lift from his heart.

"Sky, I—" he began.

"I know," she said with a smile and cupped his cheek. "It was all a show. I'm ok."

"Your arm." Travis frowned and looked at the bleeding wound covered with gauze and tape.

"'Tis a scratch." She winked and kissed his lips quickly.

"ADA Larson, I have DA Jeffers on the phone. He wants you on the first helicopter out of here."

"Ok, what about—?"

"Mr. Redmond needs to come with us. We've got questions—"

"Where's my brother?" Travis grated and turned, shooting up from his squat. *"Where* is my brother, Agent Mathers?" He came close to pulling the man's shirt-collar before he realized if he did so that would be a federal offense.

"He's being medevacked, as we speak." Mathers tone was grim. Travis felt sick to his stomach once again, as if he'd suddenly been punched.

"I need to be with him, please? I'll answer any questions you have but... I need to go and be with him. And call my mother." Travis looked down, then felt a soft hand take his.

He looked into Skyla's solemn face. God, he loved her so much that it hurt. He'd spent less than a week in a cabin with her and was now head over freaking heels for this woman. That's all it took apparently. A little playful banter, some mind-blowing sex, a traumatic event, and he'd found the woman of his dreams.

"I'll do everything in my power, Travis," she said. And he knew she meant it: his brother's care, getting them both exonerated, and taking care of the sleaze-ball Geraci. She *would* do everything in her power to make things right, he knew for a fact.

He nodded and squeezed her hand, pulling her to him as he wrapped an arm around her waist and leaned his forehead against hers. He took that moment to absorb her essence, the calm and peace she'd brought into his life, the certainty. She renewed and refreshed him. She was the balance he'd always needed. As much as they butted heads, he'd never felt more alive than he did when he was with her.

Just as he was about to tell her so, another agent in SWAT gear came up with a phone and motioned for Skyla to answer it. "Sorry, ADA Larson, it's the mayor. He says it's urgent."

Travis's eyes narrowed even as Skyla nodded, took the phone, and looked up at Travis. A million emotions crossed her face, but the one that she left him with was remorse. Plain and simple. It was as if she said, "It was fun. Don't call me, I'll call you."

Instead, she covered the mouthpiece of the phone in her hands and replied with, "Take care, Travis." She smiled and took the call, walking away from him.

Mathers came up at that time and patted Travis's back. "Alright, we're gonna follow your brother to Grady. You ready?"

Travis nodded but not before looking back at Skyla one last time in regret.

For the second time that day, his heart broke.

CHAPTER ELEVEN

"Hi, Trav," Madison Thomas said as she strolled up to the ice bath Travis was plopped in.

"Hey, Mad. What's up?" Travis smiled at the gorgeous blonde, who happened to be both the wife of his teammate, Hunter Thomas, as well as their CEO, and the daughter of Jerry Taylor, owner of the Gladiators.

She was dressed to kill in a navy-blue dress that accentuated her curves and tan skin with matching heels. Her golden blonde hair, curled in swirling ribbons, framed her heart-shaped face, and her lips were painted coral. Blue-green eyes stared into his as she pulled up a chair and sat down beside him, resting her hand on the back of his.

He was grateful for her presence for he'd felt off the last two weeks since he'd been back and enjoyed the company she provided. She frequented the locker rooms and attended their practices and games—hell, she worked at the complex. She was their CEO and VP, and she was super involved with the team and its players.

Travis had taken the helicopter along with Agent Mathers to be with his brother. Once Tuck was deemed stable, Trav had called their mother, Fiona, in San Antonio, and Mathers had coordinated her travel to get to Atlanta. She'd arrived the next morning and together they'd waited for Tuck, who was intubated and being fed nutrients through a nasogastric tube, to awaken from his emaciated and beaten state.

Mathers had questioned him about the entire ordeal that had started months back while Trav was still playing for the Stallions. Travis had explained his involvement and terms of the agreement with Geraci, how Tucker had been threatened if he didn't comply to throw the games in San Antonio. When he'd been traded to Atlanta, Geraci had expected the same from him; and so it had gone until he'd gotten suspended for taunting. Mathers took all the information down, told him not to worry, and explained that—if asked—he'd been involved in the FBI investigation from the beginning. His record had been immediately expunged, and from what Travis had gathered, Geraci was being indicted for a list of charges longer than the ink-sleeve that ran down Travis's arm.

Travis had gone back to Atlanta, to the Gladiators complex, labeled a hero once Tucker had woken from his medically-induced coma last week. Tuck, too, had been questioned and his record was also being cleared. Travis wasn't sure how she'd done it or why, but Skyla had set them both free. If Tucker's demeanor was any indication, this had been a life-changing event for him. He'd lost a toe and came very close to dying. Perhaps that had finally been enough to open his eyes once and for all. He was enrolling in a local college once he was fully healed, much to Travis and his mother's shock. He wanted to work in forensics.

Travis had been happy to see his teammates, his friends, and fellow football players, but his heart was still broken and continued to be despite that his suspension had been lifted and he'd started practicing right away when he'd returned. He hadn't heard from Skyla and, last he'd seen, she'd been on the news speaking about Geraci's arrest along with other members of his organization. She planned to shut the entire ring down, claiming it was just a matter of time before the other crime bosses were discovered, called out, and charged for the crimes they'd been getting away with for far too long. "We *will* clean up Atlanta," she'd promised, getting a standing ovation from the crowd.

She looked healthy, determined, and more beautiful than ever, he thought as he watched her make her proclamation. She'd been seen with the mayor, much to Travis's disappointment. He couldn't believe she would go back to that bastard after what he'd done to her. Travis was devastated, heartbroken, and felt taken advantage of —not for the first time in his life. He knew that Sky hadn't intentionally used him, quite the contrary. It had been an affair of convenience, high emotions, and overwhelming curiosity. A fling with intensity and passion unlike he'd ever known and he was reeling. And had *been* reeling since she'd chosen that asshole Samson Steinberger over him.

"I swear I didn't throw the game," Travis admitted finally, feeling Madi's eyes evaluating him.

"I know," she answered.

"The guys probably think I did," he muttered and kicked his feet out, grateful for the ice that numbed his body.

"No, they don't. I know them, better than you do."

Trav opened his eyes and scowled at her. She grinned. Fuck, she was stunning. Not Skyla stunning but equally as radiant in her own right. Hunter was a damn lucky man.

Travis huffed again and looked down. "I'm sorry."

"Don't be. You ran for almost two-hundred fifty yards. That's incredible! And you had *three* touchdowns. No one is mad at you. I promise."

He did have a stellar game tonight. He'd been proud to come back and serve his team until he got tackled in the fourth quarter and hurt his thigh pretty badly. He'd been pissed about having to leave the game, but, after attempting to walk it off, it was evident the injury was more severe than he'd originally thought.

Madi patted his hand. "Travis, this goes deeper than the injury though. You've not been yourself since you came back."

"Well, Mad, not to be a smart-ass or anything, but I *was* running for my life from a mafia crime boss and all." Travis shrugged and watched Madison's face lift in triumph. *Fuck!* He'd walked right into that one. He pulled his lips in.

"That's right. You were...and with a very attractive woman named Skyla Larson, the assistant district attorney. I heard you were in a cabin with her for a few days." Madi's blonde brow lifted in implication.

Not that the news had covered the ordeal in great detail, other than to state that Travis and ADA Larson had been working together in conjunction when the shooting occurred outside the bar in San Anton, went into hiding in Colorado, and Geraci had been apprehended following a raid in an Atlanta furniture warehouse. Travis knew Madi wasn't the gossip type and wouldn't overstep, despite that he'd only known her such a short time.

"Not like it matters..." Travis grumbled. "She's apparently back with the fuck she was engaged to who cheated on her."

"The mayor cheated on her?"

"Yup! And what the hell does a woman her age want with an old fart like him, anyway?" Trav huffed.

"You fell in love with her, didn't you?"

Travis looked up at Madi's surprised face. "I knew her back in high school. We never dated but..."

"You rekindled the old flame?" The sophisticated blonde grinned again.

"Something like that." Travis looked off, not really understanding why he was telling his CEO all this. But she had a way about her that made it easy to talk about this kinda stuff. She had the girl next door vibe going on. Beautiful, fuckable, but easy for a man to be himself around. She was like one of the guys—she loved football, horror movies, and poker—only with tits and an affinity for sexy shoes. And she reminded Travis of Skyla; she had no idea how enticing she was.

"Have you tried calling her?"

Travis shook his head. He'd spent the better part of a week at the hospital waiting for Tucker to wake up and when he hadn't been there, he'd been on the phone with his lawyer, Vernon Carnegie, or at the complex at practice. His exoneration came two days following the raid. Madi herself had gotten the call from ADA Larson personally explaining Travis's involvement in the case and pardoning him for his behaviors and reactions during that time frame, stating it had all been an FBI operation and he'd simply been playing his part to capture Geraci. The NFL hadn't known what to do with this situation, as nothing had ever occurred like it before. Travis had publicly apologized to Pollux Reed, he'd been fined by the NFL for his unsportsmanlike conduct, and was allowed to return to his team, his suspension lifted immediately. Travis also had his lawyer track down the trucker's family and donate money into a fund for his kids; he wanted to make sure they'd be taken care of.

"Look, I don't know what happened, and it's none of my business, but I've seen a change in you. If she was the one who did it, then maybe you *should* go after her. True love doesn't come around often, you know?"

Ah, what did she know? She was happily married to the goofiest, most reckless asshole around. Hunter was the most likeable guy on the team, a true class clown, and Travis had officially titled him Hermes. "Easy for you to say, *Mrs.* Thomas."

"You know what I mean. Don't let it slip past you. She obviously wasn't in love with Steinberger or *whatever* happened in the cabin wouldn't have happened."

Madi had a point, but it would appear that Skyla was still planning to marry the S.O.B—or at least, they had the media believing it to be so. "Hey, Mad, tell me somethin'. Would you marry a man you weren't in love with simply because you considered him 'safe'?"

Madi's brows went up again. "Safe?"

"Yeah like stable, steady…"

"Oh, you mean boring?" Madi giggled. "No. no, I wouldn't."

"I'm not husband material, I get that. Maybe that's what she thinks."

"A man who cheats isn't husband material either." She shrugged. "Or safe."

"I said the same freakin' thing." Travis let his head fall back hard onto the bunched-up towel behind him. "The sex we had though. Gah, it was fucking incredible. I mean, I haven't fucked that much since..." he trailed off, realizing Madison was blushing. "Shit, sorry. I just—"

"No, it's alright. Amazing sex, who doesn't want that?" She looked like she might be swooning. Damn, all women were such romantics.

"Right? And I know that she'd never experienced those things before. It felt different, you know? You're right, something like that doesn't come along every day. It was special. It was—"

"Hey," a deep voice interrupted. "Good game tonight, Ares. I'm headed home to crash. See you tomorrow. Take it easy on those tree trunks of yours." Brett "Brickhouse" McFadden came up and gave Travis a fist bump and a wink. Travis thanked him. "Call me later, Madi." He leaned down, kissed her cheek, and gripped her shoulder before heading out.

Now, there was another story in and of itself. Those two had known each other since they were like seven. They'd gone to grade school together, then college, and now they worked together. Although Brett—aka Zeus—was a gunslinger of a quarterback, he'd been hand-selected by Madi and her dad, Travis was sure. He was their golden child. Despite that he and Madi stated that they were like brother and sister, Travis was sure he'd never looked at his sister like that before...well, if he had a sister, he wouldn't. It was obvious that Brett was the victim of major unrequited love. It made his colossal, tough outer exterior even more understandable. Brett was the epitome of serious. Sure, he laughed at jokes, but he was their leader; a bigger Captain America with more frown. Which was why he'd been deemed Zeus, king of the gods, by Linc—plus Brett had a knack for throwing "thunderbolts" with ridiculous speed and accuracy.

Speaking of Linc, he and Paxton popped their heads in to check on Travis too. "There's our Ares. You hanging in, my man?" Linc smiled and Travis nodded. "You killed that record tonight, brother. Get some rest. I'll see you in the morning."

"You too, bro, kiss Val for me...and the twins." Trav waved.

Linc scolded him with a pointing finger, laughed and nodded. Pax gave him a shaka sign—his signature hand gesture—then followed after Lincoln, leaving Travis and Madi alone again.

They'd named their linebacker, Paxton Guthrie, Poseidon, for the guy was a California boy; a former surfer with long blonde hair and a flair for "releasing the Kraken" when it came to taking down the opposing teams QBs. He'd even gone as far as to slam down his invisible "trident" and cross his arms over his chest following a QB sack—a gesture that the fans utterly ate up.

"Trav, call her. Ok? At least get some closure. I don't feel you got it. Or, at least, from an unbiased observer you didn't seem to." She gave him another big grin, and he returned it.

"Hey thanks, Mad, for sitting with me."

"Any time, *Ares*. After the way you played tonight, you deserve some accolades."

"And a good rub down," the trainer, Kit, said with a smile. "Shower and I'll get you in bay 2."

"Thanks." Travis said as Kit walked past to check on their offensive lineman TJ Rawlins, who'd also been injured pretty badly tonight. Travis motioned to rise from the tub, still clothed in a pair of shorts and socks. He moved to a towel rack and stepped behind a curtain to undress just as Hunter rounded the corner.

"Jeez, everyone is always wanting to get naked around my wife," Hunter joked when Travis stepped out in a robe, towel draped over his arm.

"Can you blame us?" Trav cajoled and slugged at Hunter's half-naked middle.

Hunter shrugged and grabbed a laughing Madi, pulling her to his freshly showered frame, clad in only a towel. "No, I can't. She's gorgeous." He wrapped Madi tightly in his arms and kissed her passionately, dipped her, and pulled her back up, giving her a sound smack on her bottom.

"Hunt," she protested bashfully and apologetically over at Travis.

"What? I can't resist. Besides the game's over, time to finish the 3 day no-sex streak." Hunter's brows went up.

Travis rolled his eyes. "Dude, you seriously do that?"

Madi scoffed and ran her fingers through her husband's hair. "He has since college."

"Science has proven that it only pertains to a couple hours before a game, you know?"

"Don't care. Not changing it now."

Travis didn't need to respond; he understood how superstitious his fellow players could be, himself included. His game-day ritual consisted of a hearty breakfast of ham and eggs and always putting his left sock on before the right.

He watched Hunter and Madi, feeling envy and want fill his chest. He wanted to have that with Skyla. He missed her so much. The feel of her body against his, the taste of her lips, the smell of her hair.

Madi was right. He had to call her. He had to get closure. If she preferred Sampson over him then he needed to know, but the not knowing was what was killing him. And there was a part of him that was too afraid to find out the truth.

CHAPTER TWELVE

Another two days passed before Travis worked up the courage to pick up the phone to call Skyla—his off day, which he spent the better part of binge-watching sappy shit on Netflix and napping, followed by a rigorous practice day. He didn't have her direct number, but he had connections and his lawyer always came through, good ol' Vern.

Travis's heart sped up as he dialed it, sitting nervously on his leather couch in the mansion that suddenly felt too big for one person. Then his heart stopped as a man answered the phone.

"Larson residence." At first, Travis thought it might be a butler, then reality kicked in... it was *him*. He recognized the voice. Her ex-fiancé now turned fiancé again.

Travis's heart plunged. It was fate. His answer to the unspoken question he'd asked. He wanted to be wrong. But now he had proof; proof that Skyla didn't want him.

"Uh, I'm sorry, I have the wrong number."

"Good day," the older man said and the phone clicked.

Well, it'd been fun, but now it was over, truly over.

Only, Travis Redmond wasn't sure how to move on. But he had to, indeed, move on.

"RUN IT AGAIN," Coach Haskins, their offensive coordinator, shouted from the sidelines as Travis attempted to catch his breath.

Fuck, he was tired and running this play, trips right, toss right, for the fourth time in a row was getting old.

He looked over at Brett and rolled his eyes, getting a crooked grin out of his mountain for a QB. Brett stood at six foot five inches and was two-fifty, one of the biggest in the league; but the man could run and hustle incredibly easily. He had a barrel chest and once more reminded Travis why they'd christened him Zeus after he did a chest bump with the man on the last play and he knocked Travis down. Linc had gotten tickled from the sidelines and pointed over at him, getting a finger from Travis.

"Alright, let's do this!" came Hunter's exuberant voice. Where the man got his energy was unbeknownst to Travis; he had to have ADHD.

Brett pulled them in for a quick huddle with a smirk on his face. "Trav, trips left, toss left." Travis grinned, realizing Brett was having him run the exact same play, only to the opposite side this time. Haskins was gonna be pissed. He nodded and they all slammed their hands together when Brett said, "Break."

"Draco 80, Draco 80," Brett chanted. "Set, hut."

Brett turned to the right, tossed the ball, and Travis caught it, tucking it into his chest with his right arm and ran to the left. He evaded two defenders and was wide open, running the ball thirty yards into the end zone for a touchdown.

His teammates came in behind him and began clapping him on the back, excited for his quick moves and score. He smiled and pointed at Brett, even as Haskins threw his hat down and turned purple. Brett could deal with that shit. Trav was only doing as his QB told him to.

Travis was walking back toward Brett as their head coach, Greg Cavanaugh said, "Hell, lighten up, Haskins. It's Thanksgiving. Besides, our ram here scored so I don't care if he didn't run the exact play you wanted."

Coach Cavanaugh gave Trav's helmet a smack and laughed. "Well done, Redmond."

"Thanks, Coach."

"Alright boys, let's call it a day. Hit the showers and enjoy the rest of your day. Eat some dessert for me, alright?" Cavanaugh patted his belly and whined. After being recently diagnosed with type II diabetes, his wife had him on a strict diet. No pumpkin pie for him. Although, Travis liked pecan the best personally. "Just don't get too stuffed that you can't practice tomorrow."

Friday was gonna be brutal, he knew.

He'd just moved into the locker room and pulled his pads off when Hunter came up behind him, grinning. "Hey man, you coming?"

Hunter was referring to the invite Madi had extended to him and the other players, a Friends-giving she was having at their house. "Yeah, I'd like to. Thanks for inviting me, Hunt."

"Of course, buddy. We're glad to have you."

Travis showered and moved back to his locker, where he'd hung a pair of khakis and a light sweater. He was eager to hang out with his teammates outside of the complex. They'd been practicing and working hard these last couple weeks and needed a day to let loose. Travis felt he had much to prove after all that had happened. He'd wanted to show he was an asset, and loyal, to this team he was starting to love being a part of.

The Gladiators organization was different from the Stallions— different even than the team he'd played for before that, the Amarillo Renegades. The Gladiators were more family oriented it seemed, less about the money. Perhaps that was Jerry Taylor's doing; he'd owned this team for the last thirty years. A lot of the money that the organization garnered went back into the community. Jerry encouraged the players to donate to charities, stating that just a portion as small as ten percent helped a lot.

Travis felt that Jerry hadn't come from wealth, or maybe he'd fallen on hard times before getting what he had. Madi and Brett didn't act like money dominated their lives. They were more focused on the team's reputation as a whole, not how much money they brought in. Hunter, however, was more show-boaty, which Travis picked up on immediately as he pulled up to the estate's circular drive and parked.

He hadn't known what he'd been expecting, but it hadn't been this.

The wrought-iron gates out front should have forewarned him, but the huge white-pillared, Georgian-style manor was more extravagant than he could've ever seen Madison living in. She seemed like she would've wanted something homier, more Victorian or even farmhouse, this was... well, excessive to say the least.

Travis expected butlers and maids to come popping out of the door to welcome him. But he smiled and followed Brett and Pax into the front door.

"Welcome to my humble abode," Hunt said with pride.

And he *should* be proud, the "abode" was ridiculous. A huge—and probably outrageously expensive—crystal chandelier hung from the massive ceiling and two winding staircases with intricate wooden patterns made the entryway a work of art.

Travis continued into the marble-floored foyer, listening to their footfalls echo into the kitchen that could've probably fit their entire team, and comfortably, too. It had white cabinets, black granite, and a backsplash that screamed elegant.

Hunter brought them to the bar where he offered them drinks.

Lincoln and Valeria came over then with the boys—the most gorgeous twins God ever blew breath into—dressed adorably in vests, button-ups, and khakis. Trav smiled as both Lennox and

Lofton reached for him—their bright green eyes, brown curly locks, and the most beautiful mocha-colored skin he'd ever seen.

"Hey, my little buddies." Trav scooped them up, Lennox giving him a smooch on the cheek as Lofton fingered his chin. "I missed you mini future lady-killers."

"They've been such rascals," Val confessed. "I almost stayed home with them, but Linc said we could pawn them off on someone and run off to the car for a quick root."

Trav laughed and looked up to Linc who just shrugged like his words were justified.

"I can imagine it's not easy at times."

"Nothing is easy when these two are still fighting over my norks. I can't wait to have 'em back to myself." Valeria smirked even as she ran a hand down Lofton's little back when he whimpered. "God, but I love these two brats so much though." Val's beautiful golden-tanned face wrinkled up, and Trav's heart shuddered. "To think, how Marly would've adored them. She'd always begged for a little brother."

Lincoln pulled her into his arms then, tucking her head under his chin. "You promised, Val."

"I know. I know. It's a happy day. I can't ruin it with my blabbering."

"Oh, c'mon you guys. It's still a happy day. You have every right to mourn your daughter, no matter how much time goes by."

They'd lost Marly a year and seven months ago. It had been the worst day Trav could ever remember; seeing that precious angel in a coffin would haunt him forever. He couldn't even fathom what Linc and Val had gone through. Linc had tried to kill himself the November after she'd passed, but somehow, unbeknownst to medical professionals, he'd lived to tell a supernatural tale. Linc and Val had gotten their shit straightened out shortly after and now had two beautiful boys.

Lennox laughed at Travis as he played peek-a-boo with him

while Lofton cried and reached back to Val, who looked lovely today in a blue silk dress that flattered her skin tone.

"Oh, little mamma's boy right here," she cooed to Lofton, who laid his head down on her shoulder.

Travis smiled and continued to get baby cackles out of Len as he tickled his little belly.

Madison came over then, dressed in her usual sophisticated and flattering red cocktail dress, her lips the same color. "Mad, you look stunning as always," Travis quipped.

"And you look swoony holding a baby, Travis. Be still, my ovaries."

Travis laughed big and rolled his eyes. "Don't be getting any ideas now, Mad. Hunter might freak on you."

"Oh, I have actually. I got Val and Linc working on another one just for me." She winked over at Val, who almost choked on the champagne she was sipping. Both women laughed then Madi pouted, "But, aren't they just *angels*?"

"Angels with little red horns hiding in their hair," Val retorted, patting Lofton's bottom as he fussed again. "I think this one is teething."

"Oh, poor baby. Want some whiskey?"

"Yes!" Linc stated with a laugh before Val shoved an elbow into his side. He frowned and blushed. "She means for the babies. Their gums. Right, Madi?"

"Right. Or so I'm told." Madi shrugged, unsure what she'd started.

"My mother would approve, but I think I'll go feed him and see if he'll lay down so that I might actually get a hot meal today," Val sighed and patted Lofton's bottom in comfort once again.

"Of course, the guest room is just down the hall. Make yourself at home, Valeria," Madi stated, patting Val's arm as they walked out of the kitchen.

Linc bowed his head. "I swear I haven't had a drink since..." he trailed off.

"She knows, buddy. We all know."

"Yeah, but she's always gonna wonder."

"Hey," Trav gripped Linc's arm and looked up into his deep brown eyes. "Listen. One day at a time, remember? You're stronger than your addiction. You own it, it doesn't own you. Besides, you have a lot to live on for, she knows that. She's just tired—buggered, as she'd say."

Linc nodded and smiled, feeling a little better, Trav could tell.

Paxton came up then and tried to steal Lennox away but the little tyke wouldn't go to him, much to Pax's dismay. Trav felt a sense of "uncle" pride knowing his nephew loved him.

What Travis wouldn't do for those two toddlers; they had him wrapped around their little fingers. Linc moved over to talk to TJ, while Travis moved over to the appetizers Lennox pointed to, searching for something he could give the six-month old.

Jerry Taylor and Brett McFadden approached him then.

"Howdy, Travis." Jerry extended his hand and Travis took it and shook it.

"Sir."

"Just Jerry. No 'sirs' here, son. Today, we're family." Jerry winked and gripped his shoulder.

Brett slugged Trav's arm softly and grinned at him. "Who's this little dude you got here?" he asked and tickled at Lennox's belly, getting a laugh out of him.

This was really the first time the guys had all been out with their families in tow. Yeah, they'd all gone out together and even met the wives, but not the kids.

"This is one of Linc's twins. Brett, meet Lennox. Lennox, Brett McFadden, your next hall-of-fame QB, buddy."

Brett smiled and extended his finger to the baby who took it and gripped hard.

"Ouch. A future corner for sure. Nice to meet you, kiddo." Brett laughed, a good hearty laugh that Trav wasn't used to. It was surprising to see his serious-ass quarterback lighten up a little.

"So, you got a girl, man?" Trav asked and watched a flicker of sadness pass in Brett's emerald eyes before he shook his head. He'd known he didn't but still wondered about the story there between Brett, Madi, and Hunter. One day, he'd get it, he was sure. Probably after several rounds of Jose Cuervo.

"You not hanging out with your family today, Trav?" Brett asked.

Travis had planned to fly his mom and Tuck out yesterday, but she'd gotten sick with the flu and Tuck had stayed home to take care of her. She'd told him they'd make it up the following week or two when she was feeling better. He'd sent his best and told them he'd miss them. Trav relayed all this to Brett, who nodded and told him he hoped she felt better soon.

Linc came back over then to grab Lennox, who cried when Linc took him from Travis. Travis insisted he didn't mind, having a baby in tow might help him score some chicks; but Travis knew he was only kidding himself. The only chick he wanted, the only chick he could think of, was probably feasting with her fiancé without a care in the world, without thinking about him at all.

He'd told himself he could move on, but he hadn't been able to. Her words, her voice, her moans, even her scars were embedded deep in his head. The sounds and feels of her falling apart while he plunged himself inside her were still so sharp in his memory. He'd tried to tell himself that it had been all in the moment—the fear, the uncertainty that they were gonna live had propelled them into feelings they would have felt otherwise; that the heightened emotions simply stemmed from the intensity of the trouble they'd been in. But Travis knew that simply wasn't true. He didn't just miss having sex with Skyla; he missed their arguments, her smart mouth, her sass and most of all her face, her touch, how complete he felt in her presence. He'd felt out of sorts since his return and knew without her, he simply wouldn't be whole.

They had a feast fit for a kingdom—or a football team, as it were —complete with a beautiful golden turkey (three, actually) decadent sides of every kind including the Thanksgiving classics of dressing, cranberry sauce, green beans, mashed potatoes and gravy.

Casseroles, rolls, salads, and pies of various kinds. They all sat around the luxurious and enormous dining room table, eating and conversing, having a great time socializing and enjoying their comradery.

Hunter and Madi thanked them for coming, and Jerry made a speech about how proud he was of the team, how hard they worked, and how they were a family and not just an organization. It made Travis proud and glad to have been traded to Atlanta, despite how angry he'd originally been with Fred Nolan and Rhett Henry for dismissing him so easily. He hoped they were eating their hearts out and ruing the day they let Linc and Trav go. Rumor had it that Tyron Smith was a free agent at the end of the year. He hadn't been living up to the hype that San Antonio had expected, which made Travis internally jump for joy.

It was well after five when all the guys ambled into the huge media room to catch the Dallas vs. Giants game while most the ladies, save for Val and Madi, went to another room. Madi sat in Hunter's lap sipping a Corona, kissing his cheek when the Giants scored.

"Fuck yes!" Hunt high-fived Travis. "They're killing it today."

"About fuckin' time," Brett retorted. "Eli needs to get his head out of his ass."

"You'd know all about that wouldn't you, Brett?" Hunter smirked.

Brett looked back at him, his eyes narrowing, but let it go. Again, something was stewing here, just beneath the surface. Brett sat silently for a time before he popped up, claiming to go grab another beer. Madi stood to follow, only to have Hunter pull her roughly back into his lap.

"Oww, easy..."

"Sit the fuck down, baby. We're about to score again." He pulled her face to his and kissed her hard. It was a possessive kiss and, after about a minute, she pushed at his chest and pulled back.

"You mean *they're* about to score, Hunt, not you." She grunted as she extricated herself from his grasp and stood, adjusting her dress. He smacked her bottom as she moved off.

"Grab me a Bud Light, woman." He laughed and elbowed Travis who sat next to him. "Women." Hunter rolled his eyes, but Trav didn't laugh. He didn't understand this. Surely Madi and Brett weren't having an affair, were they? No, they both valued their ethical code too much. And despite Hunter's brutish behavior on occasion, he and Madi appeared to love each other.

Travis would soon find out as the afternoon turned into evening. The game got exciting, and Hunter passed shots around, getting them all good and sloshed.

"Fuck love, I say," Pax muttered in reply to Travis's rambling about Skyla before he threw his next shot back.

It was only a matter of time—booze and pent up emotions went hand in hand.

"I just don't get it," Trav slurred again. "The man fuckin' cheated on her. Why would she wanna go back to him?"

"Because women get comfortable with what they know," TJ threw out.

"Old wrinkly balls?" Trav wrinkled his nose. "Gross! I gave her some high-quality cock, dammit, does that account for nothin'?" he snarled and threw back another shot.

"Sex isn't everything." Brett offered with a shrug.

"What the fuck do *you* know? You haven't had sex in so long your balls have shriveled up," Hunter grumbled.

"And you'd fuckin' know, wouldn't you? Since you've had so many partners."

The two men squared off, both sets of brows drawn. Fists were coming out soon, Trav just knew it.

"I just thought we had something special," Trav whined.

"It takes more than a weekend to know that, brother," Linc said solemnly.

"I dunno, I believe in love at first sight," TJ countered and all the men laughed at him. "What? Call me a sap, I don't care. I do!" he defended, making Hunter laugh so hard that he was rolling on the floor.

"Love at first sight? That's ridiculous. *Lust* at first sight, definitely," Hunt replied.

"Not *every* man sees a woman and wants to immediately fuck her, Hunt." Brett's brows drew again.

"Coming from the man who's in love with his best friend's *wife*." At that, both men stood, toe to toe, nose to nose. They all stood then, ready to break up the fight. The last thing they needed was anymore injuries.

"You need to shut your fuckin' mouth," Zeus growled.

"This is my damn house, asshole. I ain't *gotta* do shit."

"Guys," Langley Richards, one of their tight-ends warned. "Let's not be hasty."

"You don't fuckin' deserve her," Brett said, almost inaudibly, as he turned on his heel and walked off.

That was enlightening, Trav thought and looked over at Hunter, who stumbled and muttered, "Fuckin' dick," under his breath.

"C'mon now, you guys cut it out. You're best friends," Pax said and stopped Hunter from following after Brett.

"Best friends don't go around wanting to bone the other's wife," Hunter grated.

"He doesn't."

"Just because he don't say it out loud, doesn't mean he doesn't want to. You don't know, Paxton, you weren't there." Hunter huffed. "Dammit."

Travis could see that they'd all had too much to drink.

"Dude, let's be honest, there ain't a lot of men in this room who *don't* wanna bone your wife, Hunt," Langley stated with a laugh, even if he was treading on thin ice.

TJ and Pax shrugged. Hunter's drunk gaze fell to Travis, who, too, shrugged apologetically. "I mean, she loves football and hates shoppin'. I'm just sayin', Hermes," Trav suggested.

Hunter busted out laughing then. "Fuck all of you. Teammates, my ass."

The mood seemed lighter then, and Travis was grateful as they continued to watch the game.

A short time later, his brother called and he walked outside to take it, making sure Tuck and his mom were ok. He talked to his little bro for a few minutes before ending the call and staring up at the moon, enjoying the calm and clear night. It was cold and it felt good.

Just then the door opened, and Travis found himself greeted by the hostess with the most, Madi Thomas.

"Hi," she cooed and leaned against the column opposite him. "Beautiful night, huh?"

"It really is." Trav smiled up at the sound of an owl hooting in the distance. "Hunt ok?"

"Yeah, he's fine, in bed now." Madi wrung her hands uncomfortably. "He can get mouthy when he's drinking. It's not the first time he's gone at Brett like that. Brett knows when to let it go."

But does he and should he have 'let it go'? Travis wanted to ask but knew it wasn't the time or place.

"Tomorrow it'll be like nothing ever happened. That's how those two are. They're like brothers, they fight, they love. It'll be alright. I hope they didn't upset you."

"Nah, I'm used to our team banter. Just noticed some tension between them as of late." That was as close to probing as Travis Redmond would do.

"They just need to duke it out, I guess." She giggled, but Travis could read between the lines and she looked tired of their "fighting." "Did you ever get your closure? I didn't wanna ask in front of everyone else."

"I, uh," Travis paused and looked down. "I tried to call, but...*he* answered the phone."

"Oh, wow. I'm sorry, Travis."

"That makes two of us. But thanks."

They both stared off into the night sky, listening to the sounds of crickets in the distance, both absorbed in their own issues for a time before Madi finally spoke again.

"So that's it then, huh?" Madison blushed and looked down, fiddling with her hands, "I figured you actually would go and see her. Look her in the eyes and demand she tell you that it's really over."

"I dunno. I thought about that, but... It seems so forward and..."

"So, you can truly live the rest of your life not knowing whether she feels the same way you do? She's going to marry another man, Travis. You're not gonna fight for what you want? After how amazing you told me things were between you two, I'm surprised you're allowing that to happen... You can honestly just walk away and leave so much unsaid?"

No, no he couldn't. He wasn't ok with any of it... not at all. He was going *fucking* insane.

He frowned over at her. Wondering if that's what had happened to her and Hunter. Had she married him, loving Brett instead? Had Brett been in Travis's position but never told Madi how he felt, so she'd gone and married Hunter? He didn't want to ask, but he knew there was much she wasn't saying.

"Don't let your fear stand in the way of being with who you love. Love conquers all. I won't say any more about it. It's your life, after all." Madison blushed again, but he was riveted on every word she said.

She was right. Dammit, of course she was. Nothing was greater than love. Nothing. And he had to know the truth. He simply had to. He was going to go to Skyla. He was going to look her in the eyes and hear from the "horse's mouth" that she didn't want him. He would be able to see the truth in her eyes with him right in front of her; she wouldn't be able to lie about it. Sky had told him she loved him. So now he had to make her see that love was worth fighting for.

Because dammit, he was Ares, the god of war, and he wasn't going down without a fight.

CHAPTER THIRTEEN

"Coming," Skyla called to the door as she dried her tears and checked herself in the entryway mirror. She looked aghast, her face red, hair greasy and up in a bun, donning yoga pants, a thin camisole top, and a cardigan.

She'd ordered Chinese food and was grateful she had nowhere to go and nothing to do this Black Friday after the drama she'd experienced these past couple weeks; especially after she'd broken things off with Sam once and for all yesterday.

She opened the door and gasped in shock. "T-Travis, wh-what are you doing here?"

"Sky, wow, you look—"

"Horrible, I know. Oh my God," she whimpered and wanted to die of shame. Travis Redmond, the love of her life, was here at her door, all sexy as hell in a tight, black muscle shirt and red shorts... and she looked like absolute crap. Of all the days she had to be without makeup and decided not to wash her hair.

"No," he recovered, "I was gonna say, you look amazing."

"Travis, no I don't. I—" Sky shook her head. "What are you doing here?"

"I, uh..." He stammered. "I wanted to thank you...for everything you did, for me and Tucker. Saying that I helped in the investigation. Getting our names cleared."

So, that's why he was there? To thank her. Not to confess his undying love for her. Of course!

"Well, you played your part in the case." Sky brought her chin up. "And the city of Atlanta thanks you for your service, Mr. Redmond."

Travis blushed, and it was the sexiest expression he'd ever had. She could have melted onto the floor but held her ground. And suddenly, she remembered her manners.

"Oh, uh, would you like to come in? I, uh, I have some Chinese food coming. I could grab you something to drink, I—"

"No, I'm not really hungry. But thank you."

"Oh, of course."

"I mean, I just finished practice so..."

"Oh." God, this was so freakin' awkward. "Well, uh—"

"But I *would* like to come in."

"*Really*? I mean sure, please come in?" Sky stepped back and motioned for him to enter her townhome. Oh, God. *He's coming into my house.* "I'm sure you're thirsty. Want some water?"

"Yeah, I would actually. Thank you," Travis answered as she closed the door behind him. She lead and he followed her into the kitchen. "This is nice."

"Oh, thanks. It's not quite as nice as your home, I'm sure. It's fairly small."

"Nothing wrong with that."

Skyla took a breath in and opened the fridge, trying to still her shaky hands and frazzled nerves. "Water, you said?"

"Yes please."

Dammit, you need a glass, Sky, jeez. She needed to get a grip on herself.

She turned towards the cabinet to retrieve one and froze as she nearly ran headlong into him. "Oh, my. I'm sorry."

"How was your Thanksgiving?" he whispered as if they weren't almost nose to nose.

"It, uh, it was fine. And yours?"

"Good…but it was missing something."

"Oh?" Her heart leapt into her chest as his hand raised to cup her cheek, and he separated the distance between them.

"You can't marry that asshole, Skyla."

Her mind ran, unable to still on a single thought. She couldn't move. She couldn't breathe. "W—why?"

"Because you don't love him. You love me."

She gasped; it was true. It was why she'd finally told Sampson yesterday to pack up the few things he had there and leave. She wasn't going to marry him; she didn't want him back. She wanted him gone, for good. She wasn't going to wed a man who didn't care enough about her to stay faithful. She wanted fidelity. She wanted love. She wanted passion. She wanted Travis Lamar Redmond.

She gulped, unable to speak.

"Say it isn't true, Sky. Tell me you don't love me, and I'll leave. But you know what we had in the cabin was real. It was…" he trailed off and looked at her lips, making her lower belly tingle in yearning.

All she'd wanted since she'd come home was to feel it again, feel *him* again, inside her, on top of her, behind her—*everywhere*. She'd not felt alive again until now. His touch had her flesh quivering with desire. But her brain had other plans.

"Lust. It was lust. We scratched the itch, that's all." Logic won out over emotion.

"Oh, that's all it was, huh?" he asked and began backing her toward the wall. She went, an obedient dog on a leash, helpless to stop her body from reacting to him as his big arm wrapped around her waist and pulled her into his chest. "Answer me this, then? If that's all it was then why do I know, for a fact, that I can take you right now, against this wall and fuck your gorgeous brains out and still wanna do it again and again and again, even after I come harder than I ever have in my life?"

"I-I don't—"

"No, you don't know because you can't explain it either. Fuck, Sky. I've missed you so much, baby." He leaned his head down and kissed her, his lips crashing into hers breaking her resolve like a wave crashing into the shore, beating the sand down and leveling it out. She was fully awake, fully alive, fully incapacitated. She moaned as she kissed him back and wrapped her arms around his neck, reveling in the feel of his solid frame against hers. He cupped the back of her head and gripped her hair, growling as he took what was his, what had always been his.

"Mmm, Travis," she mumbled as he pulled back to breathe.

"I want you, darlin'. I want you so much. I'm dyin' without you." He cupped her breast and moved his mouth to her neck, getting a whimper out of her as she felt his length hardening between them.

"Oh, yes, oh God." Sky gripped his shirt in her fists, the pull of their bodies too much to resist. Like magnets, they were helplessly drawn to one another. "Take me, Travis. Take me right here. Right now."

Travis chuckled, as if pleased she'd acquiesced, and lifted her. She wrapped her legs around his waist and her back hit the wall as he pulled her hands above her head, capturing her wrists. "My naughty little Fireball." He pulled her camisole down roughly and her breasts popped out of the top. He grinned up at her then looked down at them, his eyes appreciating their vulnerable state, his for the taking. His mouth lowered and pulled a nipple in, and Sky cried out wantonly, feeling as if she'd just died and gone to Heaven, for he was loving her body once more. She arched her pelvis against his and got a growl. "Umm, baby, you want it? I'm gonna make you come as many times as I've dreamt of you since you walked away from me weeks ago. I hope you're ready. Ready to be exhausted. Ready for this." He cupped himself suggestively and thrust against her. She gasped.

Just then the doorbell rang, and they both froze. Travis looked up into her eyes, his blue orbs questioning.

"It's—it's the takeout. I ordered takeout," she stammered, her thoughts muddled.

He gave her a crooked grin and released her, stepping back. He ran a hand through his hair before moving out of the kitchen. Sky pulled her shirt up and readjusted her clothes, following him. He opened the door and the young Asian man, her usual takeout driver, Ling, waved to her from behind a bag of food.

"Hi, Ms. Larson."

"Hi, Ling. Thank you."

"Dude, you're—you're Travis Redmond. Holy crap. I'm a huge fan!"

"Uh, thanks. I'll uh, I'll give you an autograph next time, huh, buddy?" Travis winked and took the bag from him.

Whatever he was communicating, Ling got it and stammered, "Of—of course, Mr. Redmond. Thanks, man."

"See ya, kid," Travis said and closed the door behind Ling as he turned. "Fuckin' shit," he mumbled and adjusted himself in his shorts. "Sit this shit down. I can't wait for you to eat. My balls are turning blue."

"Jesus, Travis. Hold up a second," Sky said, taking the bag from him and walking back into the kitchen.

"Why?"

"Because we should talk before this," she motioned between them, "happens again."

"We *were* talking. Our bodies were doing it all for us."

"Just. Stop, please?" She shoved at his chest even as he pulled her to him.

"Why? Are you expecting company?" he grated out, angrily.

"No. I broke up with him."

"Again?"

"No, not *again*. I never let him back in in the first place."

"Right, tell that to the news."

"Oh c'mon Travis! You know the media are blood-suckers, they take a story and—"

"I tried calling you." He scowled and stepped back, turning from her. "He answered the fucking phone; so that means he was here, in your house."

Sky inhaled sharply, hating she'd missed his call. It touched her that he'd tried though.

Travis turned, crossing his arms over his muscular chest. He was waiting for an explanation.

Sky sighed and sat down at the small table in the breakfast nook. She looked out the window at the big, shady oak tree in the back-yard. "He *was* here. He attempted to get me back—several times, in fact. Apologized. Sent flowers. It was rather pathetic, really."

"Did you sleep with him?"

"No," Sky sneered.

Travis seemed to relax some and stepped forward. "So, he left?"

"Yes, I told him to pack his things and get out of my life. I can't be with someone who can't stay true to me."

"Good, that's the least a man can give you."

"I guess so."

"You deserve honesty, trust, and love."

"Sure, I guess."

"Stop saying that you *guess*, Skyla. You do! You're an amazing woman. You're perfectly lovable in every way."

"If you say so."

"I do, dammit. Now stand up."

"Why?" She furrowed her brows.

"Because I said so."

"Travis, I—"

"I said to stand up, woman. Don't disobey your god of war. You'll awaken The Ram." He growled and the sound of it thrilled her even as her heart quivered in uncertainty.

"Travis, I'm being serious right now."

"So am I."

Skyla rolled her eyes and stood.

"Now, take your clothes off. I wanna watch you strip."

She eyed him, feeling vulnerable in that moment, possibly more vulnerable than she'd been in the cabin with him their first time. Her heart was on the line here. She gnawed her lip.

"If you don't take your clothes off, I'll tear them from your body, Aphrodite. A god needs his goddess."

She whimpered as he came closer. "Travis..."

"My beautiful Skyla, you still don't think you're good enough, do you?"

She shook her head. "I'm not a supermodel or a celebrity. I don't know that I have what it takes to keep you satisfied. You're... Well, look at you. You *are* a walking sex god. And I—I'm..."

He gave her another sexy grin, that delectable dimple popping up. "Baby doll, you're everything a man could ever want. You're everything this man wants." He pressed his fingertips into his chest. "You may not be a celebrity, but you're ADA Larson and that's pretty damn close." His brow went up.

She shook her head, tears threatening her eyes even as her lips quivered. She stepped forward, his open arms beckoning her to him even as she surrendered. She inhaled his scent, the fragrance that was him: manly, sexy, musky, woodsy.

"Oh Aphrodite, I guess I'm simply gonna have to prove to you how much I love you."

Sky gasped and looked up, shock stilling her.

"Yes, I said it. I love you, Skyla Larson. I did the minute I made you mine. I knew something had changed and I'd never be the same. And I haven't been the same, not since you walked—very sassily— back into my life. You're here, in my soul now, and that's where you're gonna stay."

Sky gaped, flabbergasted. "But, you haven't even been on a date with me or..."

"Sky," he rolled his eyes, "we went to prom together, remember?"

Skyla laughed even as he leaned down to kiss her again. His lips pulled every emotion from her, drowning her doubts and heightening her self-esteem, making her sail across a football field of reassurance.

When he pulled her clothes off and shucked his own, she could see the vulnerability surface just beneath his beautifully tanned skin. "I won't disappoint you, Skyla, not ever. I just can't be without you. I don't wanna be. Say you'll let me prove my worth."

Skyla grinned. "Prove your worth to me, Ares. And do so, against that wall there." She pointed, and he growled as he lifted her once again.

"As you wish, my Aphrodite."

Travis began to love her body again, turning her into a quivering bundle of nerves and making her sex drip with desire. He roughly backed her against the wall and thrust inside her in one smooth motion, taking her lips like a man starved. She gasped, loving the feel of his shaft buried within her once again. As she wrapped her legs and arms around him, she knew she would never stop wanting to hear this man call her his Aphrodite—not in a million years.

SKYLA AWOKE to the feel of Travis's big palm gripping an ass cheek.

"Mmm, Trav."

"That's Ares to you, Fireball," he insisted, sliding a finger between her crack and sex and dipping it into the entrance of her body.

"Oh, my..." she trailed off on a moan, unsure how she could possibly be so turned on still after the many times they'd done it last night.

Soon, he was moving and on top of her, entering her from behind as he sighed heavily, a sigh of a man fully fulfilled and still unsatisfied at the same time. He moved his hands beneath her and cupped her breast, his mouth coming to her shoulder and neck as his chest rested on her back. Travis sunk his teeth into her flesh, making shivers run up and down her spine as he made love to her once more. His speed increased as the passion seized them both, and his hand moved to her aching womanhood. With rapid succession, his fingers stroked her folds as his pelvis thrust, keeping the same pace. Skyla buried her face in her pillow as her orgasm hit her hard and felt Travis pull out, releasing his seed onto her ass and back.

"Fuck, fuck, fuck," he groaned then rested his hips against her, spent once more.

After he'd taken her against the wall last night, they'd had sex again in the shower beneath the spray. He'd turned her and pressed her into the cold, stone wall, his mouth moving over her skin, languidly pulling her desire to the surface again as his lips moved from her neck to her shoulders, her back, her hips, her ass. He'd kissed her in places she'd never been kissed and had her begging for him before he'd turned her around to face him and taken her against the shower wall with a sensuality that thrilled her. She'd never been so loved, her body so adored, never been ravished like that before. And she was loving every second of it.

She was glad she'd been wrong about them simply scratching an itch. That itch hadn't gone away and by the looks of it, it wasn't going to...at least not for a time.

Travis ran to grab a towel and cleaned her off as her body continued to revel in the release he'd just given her. When he finished, he crouched down in front of her, took her hand and pulled it to his lips. "As much as this god of war would love to do this all day, maybe even take you to a very late breakfast, lunch, dinner and have you for dessert, I gotta go get packed and head out to Cleveland. I got a game tomorrow."

"Oh, well, I..." Skyla blushed.

"I want you to come, too. Come see me play. Meet my teammates."

"Really? Are you sure it's not too soon? I don't wanna—"

"Sky. Please? I want you there."

His sexy blue eyes made her heart dance in her chest and she smiled. "Of course. I would love to."

He grinned and turned her over, his big body coming down on

hers as he kissed her breathlessly. When he pulled back, there were stars shining in his eyes as if he were the happiest man alive. "I'll have my PA, Trent, arrange everything. I'll have you flown in tomorrow morning, first thing, and brought to the stadium so I can have a good luck kiss before the game." Sky blushed. "I would fly you in tonight, but we have a curfew and all that and we can't have overnight guests." He winked.

"Oh, okay. Well, I *do* have to go into the office later today, so…"

"Say the word and I will. I don't wanna be without you any longer than I have to. I'm sure Madi can arrange something."

"Who's Madi?"

"She's our CEO, future owner of the team. She's great, you'll love her. She's half the reason I came here yesterday; she kept pushing me to fight for you."

"Oh?"

"Yeah, she believes in the power of love." He winked again, and Skyla pulled him back to her for a kiss. "Mmm, baby, I want that mouth on other parts of me, but if I don't go now, I'm gonna be fined a shit ton of money, and I know you don't like wasting money. I'll call you as soon as I can."

Skyla pouted and admired his firm, naked ass as he moved away to throw his clothes back on.

"I'm snapping a mental shot of you right now, just like this," he said, his glacier-like eyes roving her body, before blowing her a kiss and walking out her bedroom door.

She closed her eyes, listening for the front door to close behind him. Internally she was swooning; he loved her, he wanted her, and now they were going to go public.

The media was going to have a field day.

"Skyla Larson, welcome. I'm Madi Thomas, CEO and VP of the Atlanta Gladiators. It's a pleasure."

"Mrs. Thomas, the pleasure is all mine." Skyla shook the hand of the tall, drop-dead gorgeous, blonde bombshell before her. Travis had failed to mention how beautiful Madison Thomas was—Damn him! She towered over Skyla by several inches; if she had to guess, the woman was five-eight without the heels. She wore a crimson dress, the same color as the team's, and matching pumps with a thick black leather trench coat and a gold scarf. Sky felt underdressed in a form-fitted black dress and red wool pea coat.

"So, we have about thirty minutes before we can see the guys. Would you like a drink?"

Skyla nodded; she was going to need a little liquid courage to get her through the day, meeting all the players. Madi must have sensed her enthusiasm, for she smiled big and nodded to the bar of the huge luxury box suite overlooking the stadium. "Wow, this view is incredible."

"Right? Great view, all warm and toasty with comfy leather seats. Almost as good as being on the sidelines…" Madi's brow went up.

"We—we're gonna be on the sidelines?" she asked.

"One of the perks of owning a team," Madi replied with a wink.

Holy shit!

"But just for a little while, then we'll be up here. You'll get to meet most the guys, the coaches, my father, our GM, and some of the other wives."

Wow, this was almost like Christmas. Sky had originally become a fan because of Travis. But over the years, she'd gotten to where she enjoyed the sport of football despite that it had the most injuries in sports—in the top five, anyway—and took three to four hours for a game to be played.

"What'll you have?" Madi asked and looked over at Sky, who perused the full bar before her. Sky hesitated far too long, and Madi grinned again. "Bob, two peach bellinis, please."

Sky blushed and nodded.

"They're light and don't have too many calories, either." Madi gave her another wink and turned to greet someone who came in.

A gorgeous, golden-tan blonde hugged her, and Sky heard an Australian accent as she took the drink Bob handed her with a smile.

"Skyla meet Valeria Porter, Lincoln's wife. Valeria, this is Skyla Larson, Travis's girl."

Wow, *Travis's girl*. That sounded so good.

Skyla gave her a smile and took in yet another stunning woman, she wondered how many she would meet today, feeling incredibly self-conscious again.

"Skyla? Oh, you're the woman he was in the cabin with."

"Valeria!" Madi scolded.

"Sorry! I'm a mother of two six-month-olds, who are both still breastfeeding at the moment, and I tend to have diarrhea of the mouth when I get around adults for a change. Forgive my manners," Valeria apologized and shook Sky's hand. "I have no filter, and I know I can't believe everything I hear on the news. My apologies."

"No worries. But yes, it was me." Sky blushed.

"I hate to state the obvious here, Skyla, but be prepared. The media's gonna go nuts when they see you. You and Travis are gonna be the new power couple. Especially since he was helping out with your investigation. It's like something out of a steamy romance novel." Madi looked all dreamy, and Sky couldn't help but smile at her.

"Yes, sexy as hell, if I can be so bold," Val said and approached the bar, ordering shots of Grey Goose. "Trav could give Linc a few lessons in the romance department, that would be fine by me. We've not got to root without a baby being right beside us."

"Val, jeez, it's only noon." Madi motioned to the drinks Val had ordered.

"I know! I gotta get them in so I can pump 'em out of me before I feed the boys tonight." She grinned as Bob sat the shots down and pounded them back with ease. "Ah, much better."

Madi shook her head and took Sky's elbow. "I'll give you fair warning, you won't want to sit next to her later. She'll be yelling your ears off," she whispered. "Let's go on down."

Skyla's heart leapt into her chest as Madi led her out of the box and into an elevator adorned with brown and orange, the colors of the Browns.

They entered a concrete tunnel, passed the training area, and were in the locker rooms in no time. Sky and Madi stopped behind a glass door, watching the coaches talking to the players who were already dressed for the game. Madi told her about what they were probably discussing, how long it would be, and Sky found herself intrigued by all the rules, regulations, and strict policies that the NFL had. She'd had no idea.

Madi was a wealth of information, explaining that she'd been in this life since she was seven years old when her father had bought the Gladiators. She'd fallen in love with the sport and gotten mad when she wasn't allowed to play. She'd decided to go into the business aspect of it; numbers had always been her forte, and couldn't be more pleased when her father had named her CEO several years ago after she'd graduated with a master's in business and marketing. She seemed to have a great attitude and genuinely cared for the team and its success. The Gladiators were lucky to have her.

Sky watched as the team dispersed, and Madi moved suddenly through the door. All eyes moved to them, and Sky swore that her heart stopped as Travis's eyes fell on her. Some of the players moved off, attending to their phones, others headed out to the field, and a few stopped to watch, but Sky's eyes never left Travis's as his beaming smile took up his whole face.

"Hey there, gorgeous," he said and moved to stop in front of her.

Holy hell, he was so much bigger in his uniform, pads covering him, the big white and gold number 21 centered on his jersey-covered torso. "Wow," was all Sky could manage to get out.

"Thanks for taking care of my girl, Mad."

"Of course." Madi shoved at Travis, then squealed as number 83 picked her up and spun her around. "Hunt!" she protested before she was lifted to a tall frame and ardently kissed.

Sky knew she was gaping, but she couldn't help it.

"I need my game-day kiss, baby. Stop squirming," Hunter Thomas said as Madi giggled and wrapped her arms around his neck in compliance. Skyla realized Madi was Hunter's wife; she'd known the last name, Thomas, had rang a bell. She watched football, but she wasn't that knowledgeable about the players personal lives.

Sky smiled even as Travis leaned in. "Do *I* get a good luck game-day kiss, too, Aphrodite?"

"Do you want one, Ares?"

"Is that a trick question?" he asked even as he, too, lifted Sky and pulled her to his bulky frame. His lips touched hers, and she was engulfed in fire as desire spread through her core. It might be the situation, the sexy, uniformed football player pressed tightly against her, or the fact that she hadn't kissed him in twenty-four hours. Whatever the case, she indulged in every delectable second of the intimate touch before he finally pulled back and set her down. He grinned goofily before turning to Hunter.

"*This* is Skyla."

"Hey, Skyla. Hunter Thomas, aka Hermes. Best WR in the league. Good to meet ya." Hunt extended his hand, and Sky took it.

"Fuck *me*, you did *not* just say that, asshat!" came a deep voice from number 52, linebacker Paxton Guthrie as he slammed his palm into Hunter's shoulder pads. "Dammit, go do some Hail Mary's or some shit. You're gonna give us bad juju." He turned to Sky then. "Sup, pretty lady? I'm Pax, Poseidon as Ares here likes to call me." The long-haired Hawaiian beamed brightly and gave her a shaka sign. She smiled and returned it, taking in his massive frame and shoulder-length, flaxen-blonde hair.

"Hunter, I swear to God," came another booming voice. It was "Zeus" himself, number 14, Brett "Brickhouse" McFadden. "If we lose today, you're running routes until you puke afterwards. I mean it, you arrogant SOB!" Skyla took in the team captain that was twice the size of most, as broad in stature as Paxton was. He was far too big to be as agile and shifty as he was and far more handsome than he was on television with his light brown hair and deep green eyes.

"You freakin' know it, Brett, don't even play. You don't believe in all that nonsense about jinxes, anyhow." Hunter shoved Brett light-heartedly, but the deadpan quarterback didn't crack a smile.

"Brett McFadden." Brett finally acknowledged Sky with a firm handshake, after turning his gaze from Hunter. "It's a pleasure, Ms. Larson."

Sky smiled. "Likewise, Mr. McFadden."

"Anyone seen my husband?" Valeria came through the circle then with a hiccup.

"Val, wow, already hitting the Goose?"

Val winked at Hunter and nodded. "I'm childless for a few hours, I'm going to enjoy it."

"Last I saw, he was sitting in the meditation room talking to God. You know how he gets," Trav answered Val, who took off in that direction.

"Alright guys, let's hit it. Time to warm up." Brett motioned to the others to follow him, the no-nonsense QB taking his stance.

"Almighty Zeus has spoken," Trav stated with a laugh and took Sky's hand. "I'm glad you're here, sexy lady." He pulled it to his lips and kissed her knuckles, making ribbons of licking lust pool between her thighs. "I'll come meet up with you after the game."

Sky could do nothing but nod; her heart was melting in her chest.

Madi gave Brett a kiss on the cheek and took Sky's elbow again. She blew kisses to her husband and the rest of the guys and wished them all good luck. "You hungry?"

"Sure. I could go for a hotdog or somethin…" Sky trailed off when Madi stopped and looked at her with a smirk on her face. "What?"

"I mean, I could probably score you a hot dog if you really want one…but…well, you might like what we have in the box a little more than a simple hot dog." Madi gave her a wink.

CHAPTER FOURTEEN

Travis took to the field; it was third and long in the second quarter. He was more nervous today than he'd ever been, knowing Skyla watched him from the box seats. But he felt amped up and raring to go despite that. He wanted to prove himself to her, be worthy of the nickname he'd been given...worthy of her.

He sneered at the defensive line as he took his stance to Brett's right, waiting for the snap. When he heard his QB chanting, he braced his legs; at the snap, he came running to the left for the pitch. Brett tossed the ball smoothly and Travis caught it with ease, tucking it into the crook of his right arm. With his left hand, he stiff-armed the lineman coming at him. He spun and juked right then left, eyes on the prize. He hurdled a cornerback and saw an open field straight ahead, save for his TE, Richards, blocking for him. *Fuck yeah, get him, Lang*, he thought and dug in, hearing the deafening roar of the crowd as he closed in on the red zone. Fifteen, ten, five yards.

Almost there.

He felt a jerk on his thigh, but it was too little too late, he was passing the line. He slowed and turned as he entered the end zone, raising the ball like a trophy over his head. He'd just scored his

SHANNA SWENSON

second touchdown in the last two possessions, and he felt unstoppable. The score was now 17-10 Gladiators.

His team came to pick him up and pat his helmet, praising him for his victory. Travis relished it, loving that he was back in their good graces and grateful, thanks to Skyla, that all had been forgiven.

He looked up to the box she sat in, despite that he couldn't directly see her from his viewpoint and pointed; even as his offensive lineman, Berkley White, lifted him onto his shoulder.

Once he was set back down on the ground, he slapped Brett's outstretched hand, giving him a high-five, and ran with him back to the sidelines. His heart soared as his coaches and other teammates patted his jersey and helmet and gave him acclaim. He ate it up. He was on fire today. The Ram had come to play ball.

"Great play, Ares!" Hunter moved next to him and smacked him hard on the ass.

"Thanks, man. I saw green and just went for it," Travis replied, out of breath.

"Gotta go for the gold, brother."

"Every time."

Travis moved to sit on the bench, removing his helmet and opening his mouth for the Gatorade that was squirted in compliments of a water boy. "Thanks," he murmured and shook the hand of his offensive coordinator, Haskins.

Brett came back by and hit his shoulder, sitting next to him for a breather. Travis scooted over to make room as Brett took his helmet off and grinned down at him.

"You're on fuckin' fire today, Trav."

"They don't call me Ares for nothin', Zeus,"

Brett shook his head. "You *do* realize we're technically Gladiators not Gods, right?"

"Yeah, yeah, but the fans are eating this shit up."

"It's true. Hear that?"

Travis heard the crowd chanting, "Ares, Ares, Ares," even as their special teams took the field to kick the extra point.

208

"This year may not be our year, but next year looks promising… for all of us." Brett gave him a smile, teeth and everything, which was rare for the hard-ass that Brett was. It was good to see him come out of his shell a little bit. Travis punched at his shoulder, getting a laugh. "Keep up the good work, Redmond."

"Yes, sir." He saluted his QB.

Hunter came to sit down on the other side of Brett and gave them both a silly grin. "You gonna share the ball, Trav?"

"Shut the hell up, Hunt, you jealous baby," Brett countered and pounded a fist on the top of Hunter's helmet.

"Ah, I'm only kiddin.'" Hunt smiled like the big jokester he was. "It was one hell of a play, man, seriously."

"Get open, and I'll throw you another one," Brett said and elbowed his best friend playfully.

Trav smiled at them before looking back to the field to watch the ball being punted to the opposing team. He wondered how these two opposites ever even became friends in the first place. More than likely it was the love of football…and a certain woman, if he had a bet to place on the matter. They'd played in college together, after all. Although it was only for a season and a half. Hunter had been a Bronco for a short time before coming to Atlanta to once again be by his bestie's side. They worked well together, read each other seamlessly, as in sync as a quarterback and his receiver could be. Despite the fight they'd had days ago, Madi was right; it was as if nothing had ever happened.

Travis wondered, again, what deep-seated resentments had caused it.

He wouldn't get a chance to ponder any further, though, as Pax made a tackle and caused a fumble. They all jumped to their feet to watch as he grabbed the ball up, ran five yards, and got tackled. Their linebacker had made an interception. *Holy crap!*

Brett laughed, "Well, I'll be damned. Gods, let's do this thing. Hunt, get open. You're getting the next touchdown. I can do this all afternoon."

With a chuckle, they donned their helmets and took the field again.

THE GLADIATORS—AKA Gods of the Gridiron, as everyone was calling them now—won by four touchdowns. After Travis's score in the second quarter, they went on to score four more for a team record at most consecutive unanswered points in a game. The crowd was going wild, the guys were in high spirits, and even the media was buzzing.

Travis couldn't hide his bright smile as the mics and cameras were shoved into his face following the game.

The slim brunette he knew from ESPN got to him first. "Mr. Redmond, you were killing it today with one-hundred and forty yards rushing and three touchdowns. It would appear that The Ram is back. Where do you think this surge of self-confidence has come from?"

"Ya know, our morale is high right now. It was hard fought and hard won. We got a great team."

"You definitely appear to have your conviction back. That doesn't happen to have anything to do with a certain assistant DA, would it?"

Travis grinned and felt a blush cross his cheeks. "Uh, I'm not going to discredit Ms. Larson for having a positive effect on me."

"Could that be because you two had ample time together in a cabin in Colorado?"

Travis swallowed hard. They were throwing her reputation down the toilet, and he couldn't have that. "ADA Larson is as professional as they come, Ms. Swartz. Our investigation was strictly that and nothing more. Rumors are what destroy reputations. As you *well* know," he warned.

"So, you're denying your relationship with ADA Larson, Mr.

Redmond? After all, she's *here* tonight, isn't she? And you were seen at her home just yesterday, were you not?"

This bitch! "I deny nothing. As a matter of fact: yes, ADA Larson and I are dating, and I can publicly acknowledge that now that the investigation is over."

Cameras flashed in his face again and he blinked, blinded by them.

"Travis, are you confident that Giovanni Geraci will indeed serve time for the allegations against him?"

"I'm not at liberty to comment on that, but may the scales of justice serve our beautiful city of Atlanta as they always have. Go Gladiators."

He thanked her and moved away, pulling his lips tight as he ran to the locker room.

He tried to calm his anger even as his coach pulled them in for a victory speech then dismissed them. Travis showered quickly, eager to see his girl and inform her that now they were officially dating, if she had any doubts whatsoever.

SKY SAT WATCHING the clean-up crew and drinking the remnants of a peach Bellini, happy for Travis and the team as the owner, GM, and other administrators celebrated behind her. She was still in the box with the lovely and kind Madison Thomas, waiting on Travis to come up and see her following his shower, before the team flew back out to Atlanta.

Madi had graciously invited Skyla to fly back with her on her private jet, and Sky had gratefully accepted.

"It's much quicker than commercial. I only wish Travis had called me sooner, and you could have flown in with me," Madi stated with an apology.

"Oh, it's fine, really. I appreciate the offer."

"Hey, I'm grateful for the company. It gets boring being the only girl." Madi took her hand then and smiled big.

Sky had watched an exchange between a cheerleader who'd run over to Travis at one point before the game was over; she'd been frowning at the interaction when Madi assured her.

"Oh, don't worry. We have a strict no fraternization policy between the cheerleaders and players. Besides, she'll be in some serious trouble for that little stunt, I assure you." Madi had then whispered over to a man in a suit who'd left the room in a hurry.

The entire incident had left Sky rattled, so much so that Madi had gone and gotten her another Bellini, the one of which she was just finishing off now.

"Well, well, there's our MVP for the evening," Jerry Taylor's voice brought Sky from her reverie and she turned to see Travis looking mouthwatering in a khaki-colored suit and crimson tie, beard neatly trimmed, his hair styled with gel. She felt her panties dampen and gulped as his eyes held hers.

"Jerry," Travis said with a smile and shook the owner of the Gladiators' hand.

"Job well done, son. We're glad to have you."

"Pleasure's all mine, I assure you."

"Dad, let's not hog our champ's celebration," Madi said with a giggle and took her father's elbow, giving Sky a wink as they moved off.

Sky's knees shook as Travis separated the distance between them. "You dress up nice, Mr. Redmond." Her eyes moved down his chest, his torso, his legs and back up.

"Really? Because I feel like your eyes are saying something more," he smirked.

She bit her lip and leaned in. "You look sexy as hell."

"You're only saying that because I won the game."

Sky shook her head and looked down, getting a chuckle out of Travis. "It was a great game."

"Right? I thought so, too." He cupped her cheek. "I wish I could fly back with you, but it's only two hours, right? And I'm sure they wouldn't mind but…"

"No, it's fine. Celebrate with your team. Madi's taking me back. On her private jet."

"Ah, traveling in style, I see." He winked playfully.

Sky blushed and smiled even as he leaned in to kiss her softly. "Get used to it, Ms. Larson. You're my girlfriend now."

"Oh?" she asked, gripping his lapel and pulling him to her for another kiss.

"Yeah, I went public about thirty minutes ago. Hope you're cool with that." He grinned, but Sky knew he was asking.

She answered him back with her eyes. She couldn't wait to have him to herself again and do some "celebrating" of her own.

"I'll walk you out. We'll be leaving shortly. Wanna wait for me back at the airstrip? I'd love to spend the remainder of my night with you. If you're up for it?" His eyes held such promise that she almost moaned aloud.

He took her elbow and motioned to Madi with his eyes, who in turn nodded, and Travis led Skyla out.

"How was the food?" he asked as they walked down a long hallway.

"Are you kidding? It was delicious. I always wondered what they offered in these boxes."

"Better than turkey legs and nachos, huh?"

"Hmm, absolutely. Shrimp cocktail, beef Wellington bites, and crudités."

"Sounds great, I'm starving."

"Oh, I'm sorry."

Travis laughed big and turned her in the direction of the elevator to the tunnels. He pressed the button and stood waiting, wrapping his arm around her waist. "Don't be. I'll eat on the plane."

"Yuck." Sky crinkled her nose.

"Nah, it'll be something good. We have our own private jet too, ya know? With a gourmet chef. I think someone mentioned it was French cuisine tonight."

"Wow. Living in the lap of luxury."

"Doesn't hold a candle to your cooking, Fireball," he confessed before pulling her into the empty elevator.

The minute the doors closed, he literally attacked her, kissing her like she was the feast he'd mentioned. She helplessly melted in his arms as his hands roved over her, cupping her breast with one hand, her ass with the other. She moaned aloud as his mouth settled on her throat and licked down to her collarbone.

"Fuck. Have I told you how much winning turns me on?" Travis murmured in her ear as he squeezed her ass cheek and pressed her further against the elevator wall, her thighs splaying instinctively. He pressed his growing erection into her belly and she gasped. "Mmm, I could take you right here in this fucking elevator, Sky, I swear to God."

"Mmm, Travis." Sky's breath came out raspy. She attempted to gain her sanity, sensing they were close to their destination. She pulled away just as it leveled out and a ding signaled they were stopping.

Travis moved behind her and adjusted himself as Sky walked out in front of him. He took her elbow again and led her to a white limo behind the buses. Cameras flashed and she heard the media calling her name. She gaped and felt her heart hammer in her chest even as Travis pulled her to his side, ignoring them.

He grinned at her again, his hand stilling on the door handle as he looked into her face. "Wait for me at the airfield. I'll have my driver pick you up. I'll make it worth your while, I promise."

Sky smiled and nodded. "Of course. I'll be there."

"Don't stand me up now." He winked and took her hand, kissing her knuckles. He then opened the door and saw her in before turning and moving to the buses with his teammates who were filing in.

Skyla inhaled sharply and let her tummy settle. This was like a dream come true. Only it was real. It was really happening. She was Travis's *girl*. It was all she'd ever wanted. All she'd ever dreamed about. But the nagging insecurities inside her began to build. She'd seen the cheerleader talking to him. Wondered what the hell that had been about. Could she do this? Could she live this extravagant life? As much as she'd always wanted him, Sky wondered if she, indeed, would be enough for Travis Redmond. If she could make him happy. And what if she couldn't keep him entertained, couldn't keep him satisfied, couldn't keep him faithful to her? She'd already had a man cheat on her once before. Could she go through the stigma of infidelity again? She closed her eyes and let her doubts take hold of her.

When Madison Thomas moved into the limo, Sky tried to keep her muted tears at bay, but they wouldn't be silenced.

"Skyla. Are you ok?" Madison asked and scooted next to her. "What's wrong?"

That's when Skyla proceeded to tell Madi everything.

"TRAV'S GOT A GIRLFRIEND," Hunter playfully sang behind Travis as their private jet took them home to Atlanta.

"Hell yeah he does, and she's a little red fox," Paxton teased next to him, getting a scowl out of Travis.

"Can it, *Point Break*, before I rearrange your face."

"Ooh," a roar of voices sounded around him, and Travis playfully rolled his eyes at his teammates.

Linc patted his shoulder and gave him a wink. "She *is* really pretty, Trav."

"Ouch, touched a nerve. Sorry bro." Pax laughed and slugged at him; Travis chuckled.

"She and Madi hit it off pretty good," Brett added in.

"Yeah, and we know Mad doesn't have many chicks for friends," Hunter insisted.

It was true, and Trav would have to remember to thank Madison for her hospitality tonight. She'd taken Sky under her wing, and he was forever grateful for her.

"So, you gonna tell us what happened in that cabin, Ares?" Hunt's brows went up.

"Oh, listen to your Jack Johnson and hush," Trav retorted and motioned to the Beats resting on Hunter's neck.

"Aw, shit. I know he's got it bad now. At any other time, he'd be regaling us with his sex-capades. Guys, this is serious! I think we need an intervention." Hunt put his hands out. TJ and Langley cracked up.

Travis rolled his eyes and looked to Brett. "You call this bozo your best friend."

"Not in large crowds." Brett held his index finger to his lips, getting more laughter out of their teammates.

"Dude, that is *so* not cool." Hunt crossed his arms over his chest in a mock pout.

"Y'all, Brett just made a joke, I think we need a doctor. Trainer! Trainer!" Pax shouted, acting panicked.

Brett chuckled heartily. "Seriously though, guys. Hey!" He whistled to quiet the team of fifty-three players down. After all was silent, he stood and looked around. "Guys. I just wanna say—way to play, way to hustle. All our hard work is payin' off. Hunt. Travis. You guys played like true gods tonight and although we're Gladiators, I'm kinda feeling this whole Greek god vibe Trav and Linc have brought with them to our organization. I think we need to sell it, and if we keep playing like the team we did today, I see big things happening for our future. I know you got the game ball tonight, Redmond, but to you. Thanks, man." Brett gave Trav a fist bump and for the first time in a long time, Travis felt really good about his life, his job, and the family he had made in Atlanta.

He couldn't wait to get home and make love to his woman. Things were truly looking up for him. Life was good. And he couldn't wait to celebrate with the one who'd turned it all around.

"Wow, Travis." Sky looked around the beautiful mansion of Travis's and loved everything about it. It was simple, elegant, and homey with modern furniture, glass and industrial touches.

"You like it?" he asked. "I haven't had it long, just since October."

"It's gorgeous. I love the minimal touches." She looked at the light grey kitchen walls with cream and sea foam blue accents.

"Perks of being a bachelor, babe," he winked and poured her a glass of Pinot Grigio. "Here's to you."

"No, Mr. Redmond, you're the MVP tonight, if I remember correctly."

"Oh, stop, not you too."

"Ha. Like you don't enjoy being the center of attention," she smirked even as he stopped in front of her and looked her over, making her hot beneath her dress.

"Speaking of center, all I've thought about is being balls deep in yours all fucking day."

"Your language—"

"Turns you on and don't pretend like it doesn't." He pulled her glass from her fingertips and set it on the island counter.

It was true, she couldn't deny it. She let him pull her against him as the soothing sounds of piano and saxophone made her body tingle.

"I loved having you at the game today, meeting my people, getting to know my CEO."

"She's great, really."

"Isn't she? But not as great as you." His eyes stared into Skyla's soul, piercing all those doubts she'd confessed to in Madison's limo. Speaking to another woman about her feelings had made her feel good. It had been so long since she'd had someone to talk to, someone with common interests, someone who could understand her. Madi had soothed away her insecurities, saying how she shouldn't worry, that the guys were used to unwanted attention; that it hadn't meant anything.

"I like Madi a lot."

"Uh oh. Do I sense competition?" Travis teased, and Sky laughed aloud.

"Oh, Mr. Redmond, as much as you might enjoy for me to say I'm bisexual, I'm sorry to disappoint you; I only like cock."

"Mmm, say that word again, baby. I love it dripping from those lips of yours."

When she said it again, he moaned aloud and kissed her, thrusting his tongue in to torture her. He deepened their connection and had her breathless in seconds. She gripped his blazer and started to unbutton his shirt. He pulled back and grinned, watching as her desire made her eager. It made her ten times more ravenous as he seemed so unhurried while her sex throbbed painfully between her legs.

"You'll be surprised to know, I'm glad you don't want women...or other men, for that matter. I'll admit the thoughts of anyone else touching you the way I do makes me insane with jealousy."

"Oh?" she asked and ran a fingertip down the line of his chest and abs. "Likewise."

"I love what you've done to me, Sky. I only see you. Only think about you. Only want you. You. You. You. I think you've ruined me, dammit. I close my eyes and see you. Last night, you're all I could think about while I laid there in that hotel room by myself. I finally had to turn my Calm app on and have that dude from *Reading Rainbow* put me to sleep."

Sky laughed and looked up at him sweetly. God, he was so adorable. "Oh, Travis."

She pulled him to her and kissed him gently, loving him with everything inside her. Loving that he was hers and he was here and she could have him again, without the fear of dying, the fear of Geraci and his men coming for them.

Before she knew it, she was untucking his shirt and unzipping his pants, and he was pulling her dress over her head, admiring her silky black bra and panties with his fingers.

"Damn baby, you in this and heels makes my dick ache."

"Mmm, then maybe I should torture you with it more."

"Fuck yeah, you should. Come with me." He took her hand and led her to his bedroom where he shucked his blazer and shirt and jerked his pants and boxers down, revealing his glorious nakedness. She licked her lips, unable to hide her arousal at his prominent shaft, thick and pronounced.

"God, you're so beautiful, Travis."

He grinned and shook his head, pointing at her. "You did this to me. You, that body, scantily clad in those undergarments. They should be illegal."

"Lay down, Ares."

"Oh, baby. Aphrodite calling the shots now?" He cocked his head, and it was all she could do not to throw herself at his enticing body.

Skyla pointed to the bed and waited for Travis to lay down atop it. He settled against the hoard of pillows there and propped his hands behind his head, watching as she sashayed her hips toward him. He licked his lips ever so slowly, and it did amazing things to her womanhood. "You like my fuck-me heels, Ares?"

"Oh yeah, baby. Take everything off but those."

She did as he asked, slowly removing her bra and panties, giving him a little peek show as she watched his dick jerk in response, fighting everything within her not to jump on him and ride him like Seabiscuit.

When she stood before him naked, he groaned and moved his hand to his erection, pumping it slowly as he said, "Touch yourself, baby. I wanna see what you did last night. Show me."

Before they'd had lights out, he'd called her and they'd had phone sex. It had been sexy and erotic, something Skyla had never done before.

She bit into her lip and began to squeeze her breast in one hand, pinching her nipple with her thumb and index finger. He moaned aloud, which spurred her on. She moved her other hand between the delta of her thighs and slid a finger down her folds, smearing the wetness that had pooled there.

"Oh shit, Fireball, look how hard you're making me. Finger yourself. Tell me how much you want my cock inside you."

"Mmm, Travis…God, I love having your cock inside me." Sky sighed as she spread her legs and did as her lover had bequeathed, thrusting her middle finger into the entrance of her body. "Oh, God." She gasped and felt her walls clench as Travis pumped his erection again and again, his eyes making her desire unmanageable. "Travis?" she begged.

"You love it?" he asked with a smirk. Sky nodded hungrily, wanting to fuck him like a wild banshee. As if reading her thoughts, he said, "Then come fuck it, baby. Come fuck it like you own it."

She didn't need any further invitation. She pulled her finger from within herself and scrambled toward the bed, climbing his thighs and mounting him, sliding his rock-hard shaft into her wetness. They both gasped as she settled down on top of him.

"Jesus Christ, Fireball," Travis whined and gripped her hips. "How does it possibly get better each time with you?"

"Mmm," Sky agreed and began to ride him. "Oh, God. You fill me so deeply."

Her speed increased as his moans excited her even more and soon, she was grinding on him like her life depended on it, slamming down on him hard as her body heat rose to a level that made her cheeks flame. She came violently as he sucked her nipples and smacked her ass, riding her orgasm out while he grunted, holding himself back with hisses through his teeth.

Travis flipped Skyla over suddenly and was thrusting hard and deep, gasping as her heels dug into his ass. He pounded into her with a rhythm that rattled her teeth before he was soon roaring his release. "Oh, oh, shit, baby." He shivered and quaked before he stilled inside her. She grinned up at him, running a hand through his tousled brown hair.

"Mmm, Ares, I thought you owned *me*." Sky's brow went up.

"I take it back, my alluring little Aphrodite. I don't own you, it's *you* who owns me."

She giggled even as he kissed her cheeks and fell beside her.

She jerked the blanket from the foot of the bed, covering her chilled body and his as his eyelids began to close. She kissed them, then his forehead and smiled down at his handsome face.

"Sleep now, mighty Ares. Your battle has been won."

"Mmm, I love you, Skyla. My naughty Fireball."

Those words swamped her soul, making her feel as full and complete as she ever had in her life as she fell to sleep, letting them echo in her brain.

SKYLA AWOKE to the stroking of Travis's fingertips up her spine.

"Time to wake, my love. I gotta be at the complex by nine for our team meeting. It's film review day—joy."

Sky grunted and rolled over to face him, smiling into his handsome face. She gazed for a time, still unsure how she'd gotten so lucky. He appeared to be doing the same thing to her and soon, he was pulling her to him for delicious kisses that made her entire body hum with longing.

"Sorry I crashed last night." He looked down at his naked frame beneath the fuzzy blanket.

"You were beat from that incredible game you played. You deserved to get to crash."

"I *was* pretty awesome, wasn't I?" His brow went up, and Sky rolled her eyes at his cockiness. "What?" he asked, already knowing her thoughts. "If you think I'm bad you should hear Hunter. He's ten times worse than me."

"Oh, lord help. How does Madi stand it?"

"At least he's funny too. It kinda balances out...sometimes."

Sky smiled again. Plus, Hunter was handsome too with his light brown hair and eyes; he reminded her of Ryan Reynolds. "You can shower first. I don't have to be to the office 'til later this afternoon. Can you believe Geraci's lawyer is requesting bail?"

"*What?*" Trav asked incredulously as he rose from the bed. "Will he get it?" His brows drew in concern.

"Abso-fuckin'-lutely not. I'll do everything in my power to keep that from happening."

"What about the other guys? You said there were more. Do you know who they are?"

Sky frowned. There were many things she couldn't tell him. He must have sensed it for he looked down. "I'm sorry, Trav. It's just—"

"I know. It's ok." He took her hand and squeezed it. "I just wondered if they were gonna come after us now, too."

"I don't think so. There's another inside guy, and so far, it's been quiet. I think they're laying low for now. Don't want to draw attention to their remaining businesses for fear we'll blow the lid on everything. Now that their muscle is out of commission, they'll have to resort to other resources. I think it's safe to say that we're safe—for now, anyway."

Travis looked away, hoping like hell she was right she was sure. "Wanna shower with me?" The dimple on his left cheek seduced her, but she shook her head.

"If I do, you're gonna be late to work," she smirked and stroked her foot across his vast thigh, teasing with her big toe.

"Fine." He pouted for a second before asking eagerly, "Dinner tonight?"

Sky nodded and laid back down in bed, pulling the blanket to her chin as she watched his firm ass move into the huge bathroom. He turned the shower on and watched her as he got in. She smiled and observed his slow, subtle movements, admiring the span of sinewy muscles covering his large frame. She closed her eyes and imagined she was in there with him, knowing it would have felt amazing. She wondered where they would go for dinner, would he take her out or would they stay in? Either prospect sounded good, so long as she got to see his gorgeous face again.

Skyla grinned as Travis began to sing a U2 song she loved and pulled herself upright. She got up to find her clothes and see if her dress needed to be quick-refreshed in the dryer. She moved to the nightstand where her bra lay thrown across the lamp and grabbed it. As she did so, she heard Travis's phone ding beside her and saw an Instagram notification pop up on the screen. Some blonde chick named CheergirlHeidi had left him a DM that said, "It was great seeing you this weekend, Trav. Great game!"

Bile rose in Sky's throat and she thought she might vomit. She tried to reason this out. He'd been in Cleveland Saturday night. Had he seen this girl then?

No, he wouldn't do that to you, her heart insisted, but her brain said otherwise, *He's a* man, *isn't he?*

She sat down and put a hand to her chest, attempting to keep her heart in her ribcage as tears stung her eyes. Surely this was a misunderstanding. He loved her. He'd said he did. Surely…

They'd moved too fast—gotten too hot and heavy too soon. This wasn't going to work.

Travis stepped out of the bathroom then and grinned over at her, a white towel wrapped around his hips, another drying his hair.

"You wanna hang out here today? I don't mind," he offered.

"Uh, no, I—I can't. I…" she stammered, trying to come up with something believable. "I need to go." She pulled her bra on quickly, covering her nakedness as if she'd been caught in the nude by the damn pope or something. She pulled her panties on and threw her dress over her head, grabbing for her shoes.

"Everything okay? You look like you don't feel well."

She tried to avoid his eyes. "I just got a text. They need me at the office."

"Sky, is something wrong?" he moved toward her suddenly, and she flinched back. He balked, startled by her reaction. "What the hell happened?" he growled, his defensive side kicking in.

"Nothing bad. It's just paperwork I have to fill out." When he didn't appear to take her answer at face value and moved to approach again, she shooed him away and added, "I'll be fine. I just need to eat."

"Alright, give me a sec and I'll call—"

"No, I'll Uber."

"Uber? Fuck that!" he grated. "Let me get dressed. Hang on just a minute."

Sky wanted to curl into a ball and just die. The scared little girl in her wanted to cower, hide in her shell. She knew this was going to happen. Knew he couldn't be committed to her. Knew he would want more than she could offer.

Travis had his teeth brushed, clothes and shoes on, and was pulling on a baseball cap as he grabbed a set of keys from the dresser. "Ready?" he asked.

She wanted to ask where his phone was but saw the outline of it in his shorts pocket. Had he seen the message? She wouldn't ask. She simply nodded and moved to the door, begging her backbone to hold out a little longer.

As they headed toward his cherry red Audi R8, she felt tears sting her eyes. Once she got home, she could break down; but not now, not in front of the man who'd unknowingly destroyed her last shred of self-esteem.

CHAPTER FIFTEEN

"Travis, are you paying attention?" Coach Cavanaugh turned from the white board and laughed over at Travis who blushed suddenly.

He was in a piss-poor mood and it showed. Sky wasn't saying something, and it was bothering the shit out of him. She'd not kissed him when he'd dropped her at her house, saying she didn't want to give him something if she had a bug; he wasn't buying it. She'd acted funny. What the hell had happened in the span of such a short time? Was there something she'd seen on her phone, had the media reported some stupid something about what he'd said at the game and it had upset her?

"Let's take a break, guys. I can see your cumulative short attention spans need a minute," their head coach insisted and turned the lights on, pausing the game film from Sunday's game.

Travis took that time to grab his phone up and swore aloud when he did.

"Fuck my life!"

"What? What happened?" Pax asked, chomping on a bag of

carrots and hummus—hippy boy and his rabbit snacks. How did a man like that get as big as he did eating all veggies and no meat?

"Fuckin' Instagram happened?" Travis scoffed and threw his phone down on the conference table, showing Paxton, Brett, Langley and Hunter his DM from some bimbo named Heidi. "No wonder Sky was acting weird this morning. She probably saw this shit and came to all kinds of conclusions. Jesus. What am I gonna do?"

"Heidi, huh? She's kinda hot." Lang shrugged.

"Dude. You're *so* in the doghouse now." Hunt busted out laughing, getting a shove from Brett.

"Who is she?" Brett asked.

"I don't have the first clue. But she sure made it sound like I did, huh?" Trav sighed, feeling like Atlas—the weight of the world on his shoulders suddenly. "Dammit."

"Ok, now let's just be rational about this," Pax suggested. "You did nothing wrong, right? This girl just randomly DM'd you. It happens all the time. We're public figures."

"Try telling that to my ridiculously self-conscious girlfriend," Travis grumbled and crossed his arms over his chest, knowing how bad Sky already felt about herself.

"Hey guys, what's up?" Madi's sweet voice called from the door. "I got checks for you all coming tomorrow. Whoo hoo, payday."

"Hey, sexy," Hunter cooed and moved from his seat to embrace his wife. He tickled her, and she playfully swatted him off but kissed him back after he grabbed her and planted one on her. Travis couldn't help but smile at them even as he pondered the predicament he was in with Skyla.

"Hey, maybe Madi can help," Brett offered.

"What did y'all do now?" Madi feigned exasperation as Hunter led her over to the table. "Who do I need to pretend to be this time?" She approached and put her hand on Trav's shoulder, making him relax a little. She was referring to the last time she'd come to the rescue. She had to call Travis, pretending to be his angry girlfriend when he got cornered by a psycho-stalker-fan in a club. Looking back now, it *was* kinda comical.

"Well, this is a little different," Paxton added.

"Sky thinks I'm cheating on her," Travis confessed, sighing heavily.

"What? Already! Jeez, what'd you do?"

Travis simply handed his phone to Madi who responded with, "Oh, dear."

"Great, way too keep me hopeful, Mad."

"Sorry, but this is like a level four intervention."

"Level four? What's level four?" That sounded bad.

"Girl talk, you wouldn't understand." She took out her own phone and began to punch in numbers then handed Travis his phone back.

"What are you doin'?"

"Saving your ass, Ares." She grinned sassily as she cooed into the phone. "Sky! Hey, It's Madi. How are you, sexy lady? Good. I'm well. Just sitting here listening to your man gush about how much he misses you. Yes. God, yes, all pouty and whiny." She winked back at Travis when his brows went up. "I'm about to send him home so he can get back to doin' what he really wants to be doing, if you catch my drift." Madi elbowed him and laughed. "I know! *Total* horndog." When Travis gaped at her, Madi winked again. "Well, I called you because Hunt has been hounding me about hanging out with you guys, and you know tomorrow's their day off, so I thought we could all go out for dinner and drinks tonight." She held up her finger when Travis looked at her with a, "What the hell are you doing?" look on his face. "Nope, no excuses, lady. You know the old sayin' about all work and no play. Don't leave a girl hanging, Skyla. I need to be around some estrogen every now and again. You see what I'm up against..." Madi paused and her brows went up in victory as she said, "Alright. Wonderful. See you at six."

She hung up the phone and looked at him, blue-green eyes dancing. "You're welcome."

"Th—thank you. That was…" He had no words.

"I know. And this had better be some random nobody that DM'd you because so help me if you hurt that girl, I will break your man parts off and shove them where the sun doesn't shine!" Madi growled down at Travis who balked at the normally sweet Madi's furious tone.

"I swear I don't know who the crazy bitch is."

"Good." Madi looked down at her phone again and began punching numbers.

"What are you doing now?"

"Scoring you some major points, bad boy… I'm sending a huge bouquet of flowers to her… ooh and chocolate-covered strawberries, telling her how amazing she was in bed last night and how much you miss her." Madison giggled as she turned to leave.

"Thank you!" Travis shouted back, feeling somewhat reassured.

"Sounds like we're having double-date night," Hunter said over to Travis and nudged his elbow. "You buying, *bad boy*?"

SKYLA SQUIRMED as she opened the door, nervous but also glad to be getting to see Madison Thomas again. She'd held Travis off as long as she possibly could, fearing being alone with him, knowing she would probably break down into a puddle of tears.

She'd managed to keep him at bay most of the day, keeping busy with all her case prep work, but assured him she would be able to make dinner tonight on time. She didn't want to disappoint Madi; she'd been so kind this past weekend and Sky genuinely liked her. Sky knew she needed to get her head out of her ass and face her "boyfriend" with the question that had been racing through her mind all day. She was ashamed at how a simple—and probably innocent—direct message affected her, but she was also just getting over a two-year relationship so he had to understand. At least, she hoped he did.

Travis came to her home to pick her up, promptly at 5:15 PM, surprisingly in a white limo decked to the nines.

His smile could light up a city it was so bright and the reassurance she needed was almost fully appeased. She grinned back at him as his eyes fell down her frame.

"Wow, where were you hiding that dress? You look gorgeous."

"Thank you, I—" she didn't get to finish because his arms wrapped around her waist and his lips crashed against hers possessively, kissing her passionately and leaving her sex yearning before he pulled back slowly.

"Mmm, I've missed you."

"I see that." She blushed as he cupped her cheek and looked hard into her eyes.

He opened the car door and helped her into the seat, where yet another bouquet of roses sat, this one white instead of red. The card read, "My darling, one for every hour I've died without you." Damn, she hadn't realized how sappy he could be. The earlier bundle had said, "My Aphrodite, your silken love quenches the thirst I never knew my masculine soul needed to be whole. Counting the breaths until I hold you in my arms again, your warring god." He had to be like a closet poet, for sure.

"Travis, these words…"

"Too mushy, I know." He rolled his eyes with a scowl.

"No, surprising and incredibly romantic."

"But completely true," he added and pulled her against his chest.

Having him so close again made her insecurities seem so silly and excessive. She felt she should apologize but didn't know how to begin.

"How was your day, lover?" His lips stilled at her earlobe, and Sky shivered as his breath hit her bare neck. She'd pulled her hair back into a twist, assuming he might take her out somewhere really fancy; she'd wanted to be prepared.

"Incomplete without you," she answered in response to his prior romantic words.

He chuckled and cupped her throat. "If I hadn't promised Madi we'd be there, I'd have Lyle turn this car around right now and take you in this very seat."

Sky attempted not to whimper aloud. "There's always after-dinner drinks."

"Ah, yes, absolutely."

He stroked her throat with his fingertips, leaving her flesh pebbled in goosebumps as she leaned into him and absorbed his solid frame against her own. He felt good, he felt right.

"Sky," he murmured in her ear. "Are we gonna talk about the elephant in the room?" Skyla frowned and looked back up at him, his blue eyes piercing her soul. She felt her body flush and started to speak only to have him touch her cheek with his knuckle, leaving her unable to. "I know that you saw the notification about the DM on my Instagram."

Sky panicked. Dammit. Was that his admission of guilt? She cleared her throat and tried to catch her breath. "I—I mean…"

"I don't know who she is, just so you know."

Sky gulped. *He's lying*, her heart stated. Her instincts told her not to trust him. "So, this is the reason for the flowers and the dinner?"

"No, I—"

"I *saw* you, Travis. I saw you talking to some blonde cheerleader at the game on Sunday."

He got quiet, frowning. He looked thoughtful, like he was choosing his next words too carefully and her inner fat girl began to panic. "Sky, I don't know what you're talking about. Cheerleaders aren't allowed to even acknowledge us. They can get fired for speaking to us."

"Well, she did and you said something back to her. There was an exchange of sorts."

"Ok, so now I can't *talk* to other girls?" His brow went up in question, and Skyla realized what an asshole she was starting to look like. Heat engulfed her as shame riddled her. *Jesus, I sound like a lunatic.* Just as she was about to tell Travis to have the driver pull over, she was gonna be sick, he spoke softly again. "Baby, whatever the case, I honestly don't remember speaking to a cheerleader, and even if I did, I can swear to you that nothing happened. I didn't DM her back. I blocked her, in fact. Here's my phone, I'll show you."

Sky shook her head, closing her eyes as humiliation tore through her soul. It was high school all over again, she was still that apprehensive, self-doubting girl chasing after the football hunk that every girl wanted. "I'm sorry," she whispered and begged herself to simply die so she wouldn't have to see the conviction in Travis's eyes when she was finally able to open her eyes again.

"Hey, there's nothing for you to be sorry for. I know how it looks, but I swear to you, I haven't so much as looked at another girl since you and I have been together. Ask the guys if you don't believe me. Ask Hunter tonight. Ask Madi, too. She—"

"I know. I want to believe that…"

"Hey. Sky. My sweet Aphrodite, look at me."

She couldn't. She didn't want to. She simply wanted the earth to swallow her so she didn't have to feel like an idiot.

Finally, Travis coaxed her back to him and she opened her eyes only to see understanding reflecting back at her. He smiled that smile that took her breath away and all was right in the world.

"There's my sexy girl. Believe it or not, I understand. Trust me, I feel the same way."

"You do?"

"Yeah. I haven't ever felt this way before, either. When I'm not with you, you're all I can think about. And when I'm with you, I feel like I've never been more alive. It kinda makes you a little crazy. I wanted to kill your ex-fiancé. Just the thought of him talking to you made me wanna tear him limb from limb."

"Really?" was all she managed to get out.

"Really! You aren't the only one feeling all this for the first time, so don't feel bad, ok?"

Sky nodded then lowered her head, trying to rein in her feelings.

"But listen to me, very carefully, alright? I'm not your ex, Skyla.

I'm not going to hurt you like he did. I would never do anything to hurt you. There are going to be many women approaching me, talking to me, messaging my social media accounts, throwing themselves at me. I'm used to it, and I know you aren't, but that doesn't mean that I'm interested in them or that I would do *anything* to jeopardize what I have with you. I have to be cordial, I have to be professional, but I will never, *never* cheat on you. I swear that I won't be that guy. I will always talk to you, I will always be here for you, and I will always love you."

Sky swooned as his words hit her where she needed them most. "Oh Travis."

She leaned into him and unleashed twenty-eight years of reservation, self-hate, and doubts and let him heal every scar she'd ever been given, verbally and physically. She thrust her tongue in, warring with his in a passionate dance that left them breathless and aching and before she could get her urges fully out, the door was opening and they were gaping up at a shocked Madi and Hunter.

"Well, well, looks like we interrupted just before they attempted to make a baby."

Madi gasped and swatted at a laughing Hunter. "Sorry, guys. We always did have poor timing."

Skyla's face reddened, and Travis thankfully was the first to recover as he pulled them out of the car and adjusted himself.

"I see you made up fairly quickly."

"All is right as rain," Travis noted and cleared his throat.

"Sky, you look amazing. I love that lace." Madi oohed and aahed over Sky's elegant black lace cocktail dress and pulled her in for a hug.

"You look stunning as always, Madi."

Madi waved her hand, bashfully, but she did look stunning as always, in a form-fitting rust-colored silk halter gown with a train.

"Two fine-looking ladies, dude." Hunter nudged Trav's arm.

"We're damn lucky."

"Luck had nothing to do with it, I'm hung like a—"

"Hunter Lawrence Thomas," Madi scolded and took his arm.

Sky laughed even as Madi and Hunter moved ahead of them and she took Travis's arm, getting a bright grin and a peck on her cheek.

They moved into the beautiful Italian restaurant that Madi had chosen. They were sat right away at a table in the back of the restaurant, far from the crowd in a spacious alcove. Having money came with perks, Sky saw right away as a waiter came right over with waters and menus.

"It is my pleasure to serve you, Mr. and Mrs. Thomas, Ms. Larson, and Mr. Redmond. I'm Vincenzo and if you have need of anything, please do ask."

They started with wine and appetizers, fried calamari, and eggplant rollatini. Then came fresh salads with plump heirloom tomatoes and burrata, sizzling rotisserie meats, chicken, sausage and meatballs, fresh handmade tortellini and pappardelle pasta, and finally, gelato.

Sky had never tasted finer foods and imagined that was about as close to true Italian as she was ever going to get. She was stuffed and enjoying dining with Travis, Madi and Hunter.

Hunter, much to her surprise, had a generous side once he put his over-inflated ego away. He and Madi were sweet together, and she could easily understand why they were attracted to one another; they complimented each other well and laughed a lot. Madi was a gracious hostess, making sure everyone got their fill and didn't want for anything. Skyla was glad Madi had suggested this. It made her realize that despite their money, their big houses, and their hectic and over-hyped jobs, deep down they were just people too, who had the same wants and needs as others did.

Madi and Hunter discussed the fact that they were trying to get pregnant, and Sky wished them luck, touched that they'd included her in on their "little secret." Madi spoke of how proud she was of the team, her father, her husband, and her family as a whole. They'd really given back to the community, donating both their money and their time to veterans, underprivileged children, and victims of domestic abuse to name a few. Sky was blown away by her generosity and how humble she seemed. Madi also mentioned how glad she was that Travis had joined their ranks and spoke of his accomplishments in the few months since he'd come to them. She could see that Travis was truly happy here in Atlanta and was so grateful things were finally looking up for him, despite all that had gone on with Geraci and his men. It was hard to believe that mere weeks ago, they'd been sneaking around and hiding out in a shack in the Rocky Mountains. *My how things have changed.*

Travis's thoughts must have been in line with hers and he laughed. "This was delicious but not quite as good as my little Aphrodite's feasts in the cabin."

"Uh oh, I sense a story coming on here." Hunter's brow raised in question.

"I beg to differ. I never made a feast quite like this."

"I dunno, those chicken and dumplins were mighty hard to compete with." Travis's grin said he was referring to something other than the dumplings.

Sky laughed. "You're just buttering me up, Travis Redmond."

"That's exactly how I like you, baby." He pulled her in for a smooch even as Hunter smarted off with, "Maybe these two could teach us a thing or two about this whole baby-making process."

Travis snorted in a laugh and got them all cracking up. "Now don't get any ideas, Hermes. I'm not into exhibitionism."

"Well damn, it was worth a shot. Sorry, honey." Hunter looked apologetically over at Madi, who rolled her eyes and smacked her head with her hand dramatically.

Once they were done and heading out, Madi pulled Sky in for a big hug. "This was so much fun. We must do it again, I insist."

"I couldn't agree more. I had a wonderful time."

"Enjoy your day off tomorrow, man. I'll be preheating the oven, if you know what I mean." Hunt winked to Travis, who gave him a knowing smirk.

"The key is not to babysit the timer."

Hunter brought his hand up to his chin thoughtfully, jokester that he was.

"Lord, I don't know whether I'm making a child or a turkey," Madi stated.

Sky tried hard to hold back a laugh but didn't succeed.

Finally, she and Travis said their goodbyes and slid back into the limo where Travis pulled Skyla to his chest, resting her head against his pec.

"That was fun," he said.

"It was. Thanks," Sky replied.

"For what?" he asked, looking into her eyes as he stroked her hair.

"For inviting me."

"Madi invited you, so I guess it should be *me* thanking you." He winked and leaned in for a kiss. It was a soft, sensual, slow kiss, unhurried as they savored it. Finally, Travis pulled back. "I'm glad you approve of them."

"Me approve of them? You got it backward, Trav." Sky shook her head.

"Negative, Aphrodite. You need the approval of *no one*. That's what you keep forgetting." And the look in his admiring eyes almost had her believing it to be true.

SKYLA blinked and December was almost over; Christmas was upon them.

She'd gotten to attend her first Atlanta home game—as a player's girlfriend—on the first Sunday of the month. She'd been excited to meet Travis's mother, Fiona, and brother, Tucker, who favored Travis very little, surprisingly. Travis definitely got his looks from his mom—and her eyes. She was thrilled to meet a woman she called "stable" in Travis's life, and they'd all eaten dinner together following the end of the one o'clock game. Tucker still had some bruising and lacerations to his face, but had healed up well considering. He was excited about starting college next semester—Forensics, how intriguing.

Sky had also gotten to meet Madison's mother, Amelia, and fun-loving and blunt-speaking sister, Brooke, at the home game, where the luxury box seats were even nicer than the ones in Cleveland.

The Gladiators had won that game and the next, following a bye week. This past game had also been a win, and they were heading to the play-offs next week in the Wild Card Round. It was as if the shift that had turned her and Travis's life around was affecting every-thing; she was grateful to be witnessing the spectacular show. Travis's skills never ceased to amaze her. He was tough, fought hard for every yard, and crushed every goal he set. He'd beaten a team record as well as a cumulative rushing record. He and the rest of the team had come back from a six-game loss to be undefeated, and now they had a prospective Super Bowl in their future.

They'd had dinner with the team last night, a holiday celebration at Madi and Hunter's where he'd introduced her as his girlfriend which made her heart happy. Their home was extremely luxurious and big, and Sky had enjoyed meeting all the other players, their ladies, and kids. Linc and Valeria's baby boys were little angels, and Sky simply adored how attached Travis was to them. Seeing him holding them and how they'd responded to him made her ovaries ache. He noticed how her eyes glazed over as she'd watched him interacting with the little toddlers. They'd gone home after a scrumptious dinner and drinks to literally tear the sheets *up*.

Geraci had been denied bail and was looking to serve thirty years to life, possibly even the death penalty so long as their witnesses came through. The trial was set to begin in February, despite that his lawyer was attempting to work out a deal with the state. DA Jeffers was leery of any type of bargain and was seeking the max penalty for each charge.

Now, Skyla was sitting in Travis's living room, finally alone with him as they sat on the couch sipping their coffee on Christmas morning. Travis seemed lighter than he had and each day with him made her appreciate him even more, fall in love with him even deeper, and thank God that he'd been planted in her path.

She'd not been sure what to get the man who pretty much had it all. He'd insisted that she not get him any gifts, stating that he'd been given the world when they'd been thrust together in San Antonio almost two months ago. Still, she'd gotten him a few presents, including a customized Yeti with the depiction of a running back and the word "The Mighty Ares" beneath it because she needed something; she couldn't *not* give him gifts on Christmas. He'd loved them all.

She told him the same and balked as he brought out a present from beneath the giant tree, twinkling with multi-colored lights and a star atop it.

"Travis!" she scolded. "We said no gifts."

"Yeah well, you didn't follow the rules, Aphrodite. What makes you think I was going to?" The sly grin he gave her made her want to take him back to the bedroom and violate *all* the rules, despite that they'd already made love like there was no tomorrow. "Besides, this isn't a gift so much as it's Ares staking his claim."

She gaped as Travis took the present, lifted the lid off it, and knelt in front of her. She held her breath as he pulled a velvet box from the package and cupped it, grinning at her as if he were the happiest man alive.

"My sexy Aphrodite," he began and took her hand. "It's been two amazing months since you took me by storm. The guys told me it was too early to propose, even though I really wanted to. They said it was—and I quote—creepy, inappropriate, and in the words of Hunter Thomas, 'highly irrational.' Sooo, I resorted to my own good judgement and decided to show you how much I love you, with something *almost* as good as an engagement ring."

Skyla looked down at the little blue box from Tiffany and Company and gasped as it opened to reveal a gorgeous rose gold olive leaf band inset with diamonds.

"Oh, Trav." She felt tears come to her eyes as she looked back up into the love that shone so brightly in his.

"Skyla Larson, this ring isn't just a promise that you'll be mine. This represents so much more. It's my promise to you. My promise to never disappoint you. My promise to be faithful. My promise to be yours. Baby, I want everything: the wedding, the house, the kids, the white picket fence. I want it all. And I want it all with *you*. But I also know how important your career is, and that you're striving to become DA one day soon. I don't want your plans to change because of me. Our careers are in their prime after all, but I do want you to know what you mean to me. I'm your god and you're my goddess, and it would make me the happiest man on earth if you'd wear my ring and show that to the world."

Sky's heart threatened to explode as he lifted the ring in his thumb and index finger. She nodded vigorously, and he moved it onto the ring finger of her left hand where she admired the sparkle of it in the sunlight.

She looked into the eyes of the man who held her heart as he leaned in to kiss her. She savored his plump lips and how her heart swelled in that moment, knowing that she'd never been happier.

When she pulled back, tears ran down her face as she observed the gorgeous promise her god had made to her, sparkling vibrantly on her finger.

Travis "Ares" Redmond, the god of war, had finally found something worth fighting for; it was the heart of his Aphrodite, Skyla Larson.

EPILOGUE

Skyla laughed over at Travis, rolling her eyes as he sweet-talked their chef into another few shrimp tacos.

"Thank you, Marcel. It's absolutely delicious."

"Of course. I'll be back in un minuto, señor Redmond." Marcel rushed back to the grill, beaming brightly.

"You pig," Sky scolded. "You've had three already, and rice *and* beans."

"You've made me work up an appetite, my goddess." He kissed the back of her hand.

They'd *both* worked up an appetite following a day on the beach and sex in the stone shower, bed, and downstairs on the couch before Marcel came to make their dinner.

They'd come for a week in Cancun to Lincoln's beach house. Travis had a commercial that was filming there, and Geraci's trial started next week so they'd wanted a fun and quick Valentine's Day trip. Linc had volunteered the house and Travis had jumped on it, thanking him profusely for letting them stay.

"Any time, brother. Glad to have someone stayin' in it," Linc had told him.

"Well, it's much appreciated. It's a great place."

Travis had stayed at the beach house before a few other times and always enjoyed the comfort of the home and stunning view. The white sands and blue-green waters eased his mind and the warm sun and crystal-clear pool was refreshing. Having Sky here made it all the more enjoyable.

Vacationing with her for the first time was intensely satisfying. Their relationship had only gotten stronger since he'd given her a promise ring at Christmas. Their team had gone into the playoffs in January, after a stellar end to their season, but lost in week one to the Pats. Even still, Travis couldn't remember ever being happier.

After the awesome time they'd had this week, he couldn't wait to have many more vacations with the woman he loved. They discussed going to Europe in the summer and spending next Christmas at the cabin where their love had originated. He was still trying to plan when and how he would propose, he wanted it to be symbolic and—although she wouldn't approve—extravagant. He was Travis Redmond, after all.

He pulled Skyla to him for a kiss, then grunted as his phone buzzed in his pocket. He started to ignore it—assuming it was just another like or comment from the pics he'd posted earlier on Instagram of him and Sky when they snorkeled with sting-rays—seeing as her lips were bringing his desire back to life, but then Skyla pulled back.

"Baby, your phone's ringing."

Travis groaned and grabbed it. He smiled when he saw Lincoln's name, hit the green answer button, and put it on speaker. "Hey buddy! I'm just sittin' here listening to the ocean and about to eat another shrimp taco made by your amazing chef. Whatever you're paying him, double it, he's totally worth it!"

"Trav...I...Jeez, are you sitting down?" Linc sounded frenzied.

"Yeah, man. You ok?" Trav asked, feeling his gut tighten. He looked to Sky who pulled her lips in with concern.

"Oh Jesus, Trav. It's horrible. It's…" Linc gasped. Was he fuckin' crying?

"Linc! What is it? Is Val ok? The boys?" Bile rose in his throat as he imagined something happening to those sweet little twins, and he thought he might be sick.

"It's not them. Val and the twins are fine. It's…God, it's Hunter. Trav, he's…he's gone."

"Gone?"

"He's dead, bro."

"*What*? No!" Trav felt his panic rise. No. It couldn't be true. It just couldn't be.

"He and Brett were in his new car. They were T-boned."

"Brett?"

"He's fine, not a scratch on him…but Hunter… It hit the side Hunter was on. Travis, he's gone. There— There was no saving him. It's like something out of a nightmare… How soon can y'all get back?"

"We'll leave first thing in the morning."

"Alright. I have more calls to make so I've gotta go. But please, be safe. I'll see y'all tomorrow."

Sky looked back into Travis's stunned face as tears flowed down her cheeks. She covered her face with her hands and sobbed as Travis pulled her to him. "Oh Travis. I'm so sorry. Oh God, I can't believe this."

Travis tried to calm his pounding heart as his mind struggled to absorb what Lincoln had just told them. Their best wide-receiver, their friend, their goofball of a teammate was gone before his twenty-ninth birthday. Travis was sick, physically sick.

Suddenly, Skyla pulled back and gasped. "Oh, Trav. Madi! Oh, God. I can't even imagine what she's going through right now."

And Travis's heart ached as he thought of sweet Madison Thomas, Hunter's wife, now widowed at twenty-eight. She must be devastated, truly.

And Brett…Brett had been in the car with Hunter. And he didn't have a scratch, Linc had said. Brett and Hunter were best friends. Jeez; how guilty Brett must feel.

God, this was bad. So so bad. Just when life had been so good, the unthinkable had happened.

Hunter "Hermes" Thomas was dead.

THE END

SNEAK PEEK AT FALSE START
PROLOGUE

I t was the coldest, most dreary day in February that Brett "Brickhouse" McFadden could ever remember. The wind was unrelenting and the rain was merciless, coming down with such force that it stung his back through his thick, black leather jacket. He stood frigid, like stone, at the graveside service of his best friend and favorite wide receiver, Hunter Thomas. The sound of the torrential rain along with the overhead tarp that whipped continuously drowned out the preacher's eulogy, adding to the already solemn mood of the day.

Brett looked over to Hunter's widow, Madison Hope Thomas, the woman that had been his best friend since they'd first met as children at the ripe age of seven. She was seated in front and to the right of him but not far from his reach or his gaze. His heart went out to her. She looked broken and numb, and he knew that was how she felt because he also felt the same. He'd been in the car with Hunter the day he'd died. He'd been driving Hunter's car when they were hit. He'd been at the hospital when Hunter was pronounced dead. It all seemed like a horrible nightmare that he would wake from at any moment, but he continued to be encapsulated unwillingly in it. He watched the tears stream down Madi's face, a continuous flow of them, or maybe it was the rain, he honestly couldn't tell. She'd given up the handkerchief long ago as it was as soaked as everything else was.

The preacher seemed to be done with his sermon and stepped toward Madi, she stood and wrapped her arms around his neck, sobbing into his shoulder. She'd known the old man most her life, Reverend James Young, he'd been her mentor, her preacher and her baptizer. Brett's heart ached for her. She and Hunter had been married for a little over 5 years and they'd loved each other immensely. Hunter had been an easy going, fun-loving, class-clown type guy. He was the one that made everyone laugh, while Brett was the more serious one of the three of them.

Madi was the girl next door; A smart, beautiful, classy southern woman who was—and always had been—the epitome of perfect in Brett's eyes. He and Madi had been very close since childhood when Brett's father, Drew McFadden, was hired on as GM of the Atlanta Gladiators football team, by Madi's father, Jerry Taylor, owner and president of the Gladiators, the team that Brett currently and Hunter, formerly, played for. Brett and Madi had been raised together, gone to every single school together and then met Hunter in college, quickly forming an ever-lasting bond with him. Hunter had quickly taken to Madi and they'd dated and were married not long after graduation. That day had been the worst day of Brett's life…well, at least, up until today.

Reverend Young had taken turns hugging everyone around the small group of gatherers at the graveside and suddenly and awkwardly hugged Brett. The old man's attempt was short-lived as his small frame couldn't embrace Brett's larger build. Instead, he pulled back and looped one arm around Brett's side and patted his back.

"I'm so sorry for your loss, Brett."

"Thank you, sir," he responded despondently.

"I know how much y'all are hurting right now, but you must take great care of Madi."

Brett couldn't recall how *many* times he'd heard that in the last few days, as if he didn't intend to do exactly that. He'd known what he had to do the minute he saw her in the ER waiting room, the minute she'd seen the look of despair on his face, the minute he'd caught her in his arms.

The look Madi gave Brett when she entered the automatic doors of the ER tore his heart right open. She ran at him and looked into his face. He knew he was as white as a ghost—his friend had just died minutes before as he'd held his hand. Hunter had been in such pain, professing his past trans-gressions, and making Brett promise all sorts of things as he lay dying in a pool of his own blood.

Brett grabbed Madi as she fell to her knees. She breathed in and out rapidly as she bowed her head. "Oh, God! He's gone, isn't he?" She felt like putty in his arms, her voice ragged, on the verge of breaking.

"I'm so sorry, Madi. I—I don't even know what to say."

Hunter had wanted Brett to drive the brand new McLaren that he'd bought. A ridiculous car, but Hunter was proud of it and wanted to show it off. Brett had obliged.

The next thing he remembered was a deafening roar and screeching as time seemed to stand still. He remembered not being able to hear right away then assessing the situation, seeing Hunter crushed into the dashboard thinking he was dead right then and there, seeing red—so much red blood—and realizing Hunter wasn't moving. The next thing he recalled was calling out for help, walking out of the car, the fear, trying to figure out what to do, praying, plead-ing, watching as the firefighters used the jaws of life to get Hunter out, the ambulance ride, the guilt, trying to save face as the EMTs worked on his friend...

Then sitting next to him, telling him that everything was going to be ok, the guilt, the conversation in the trauma bay after the doctor told him that nothing could be done to save him, that it was too late, regretting that it was too late, watching the light fade from Hunter's eyes...

The guilt, the ultimate guilt.

"...so just turn to God in this time of need as He can hear your prayers and knows what you need before you even ask Him for it," Reverend Young stated and gave a weak smile as he patted Brett on the arm.

Brett came harshly back to reality and just nodded his head. The flashbacks were taking a toll on him. He inhaled deeply and moved behind Madi who spoke to Travis Redmond, Lincoln Porter, TJ Rawlins, and Paxton Guthrie. Brett nodded solemnly to his teammates and gently took her elbow with one hand, covering her with the large umbrella he'd been holding the entire time with the other. He pulled her into his side, tightly holding her to him as they walked in the direction of the road.

No words were spoken as he, Madi's mother and father and sister headed toward the car. Brett held the umbrella over her as she stepped robotically into her father's Buick and then slid in beside her, closed the umbrella and placed it on the floorboard next to his leg. She fell into his chest as he wrapped his arms around her and laid her head over on his shoulder sobbing, as she'd done for the last three days. His heart broke once again. *Oh, how many times can a heart break?* he wondered again for the umpteenth time. It was as if the breaks just simply got deeper and more painful as each piece re-broke over and over again.

He looked over to Brooke, Madi's sister, who was seated beside them and frowned. Brooke just shook her head and looked away, propping her chin on her arm, and focused her gaze out the window as a tear fell down her cheek. Madi's dad, Jerry, who sat in the driver's seat, caught his eye in the rear-view mirror, exhaled, and started the car, focusing his gaze ahead. Brett noticed the tears in the man's eyes as he turned his head. Amelia, Madi's mother, shifted her position in the passenger seat and reached her hand out to take Madi's. She gently squeezed and Madi returned it. Amelia frowned as she tearfully looked up to Brett. He just gave her a weak smile. These people were his family, every single one of them. His parents were best friends with Madi's parents. They'd all been as close as two families could be. He'd always treated Madi's mom and dad as his second mom and dad. And now they'd lost one of their own.

The silence was deafening as they rode back to Madi's house. Only the pounding rain and wind seemed not to take the hint. Brett passed Madi a tissue and looked ahead as she sighed, blew her nose, and tried to calm herself. He simply sat and stroked her hair and arm in comfort.

It wasn't long before he closed his eyes and all at once, they were pulling into Madi's garage. They all got out silently, Brett taking Madi gently from the car and cradling her against his side as they walked into the house. Stepping through the mud room, Madi placed her handbag on the side counter and kicked off her shoes, sniffling as she went. She broke away from Brett's side as they entered the kitchen then stopped at the counter and seemed to be at a loss for what to do and where to go from there, staring off into space. Brett slipped his jacket off and placed it on the back of one of the kitchen stools, watching her the whole time. The rest of the family ambled in and removed their wet jackets, covertly watching and waiting.

Suddenly, Madi swung around and looked over to Brett with the most horrific look on her face. As if she'd just realized something terrible, she brought her shoulders up into a shrug and her face crumpled. He moved to her swiftly and embraced her, holding her to his chest as she bawled like a baby. Amelia came up behind her and embraced her, stroking her hair. She shushed her daughter and tried to calm her, but to no avail. Madi was simply overcome with emotion and no attempt at comfort would help at that moment. It was simply going to take time. Amelia pulled Madi, and pulled, and finally succeeded in separating Madi from Brett's embrace at Madi's reluctance. She protested. "No, Brett. I—"

"Shh, hush now, let's go get you out of these wet clothes and into a warm bath, hmm?" Her mother stroked at her cheek and kissed the tear running down it. "C'mon," Amelia soothed her, taking her hand and leading her away and up the stairs.

Madi continued to protest, "But, Brett...I—" She turned and reached for him, but her mother reassured her once more. "It's alright."

"It's ok, Sunflower, I'll be up shortly, ok?" He nodded and smiled in encouragement. She contemplated that for a moment then finally turned and went up the stairs with her mother.

Jerry was the first one to break the silence. "Jesus, I don't know about you, but I could sure use a drink." With that, he walked away and toward the parlor. Brett turned to Brooke, who shook her head again. She grabbed a bottle of pills out of the pantry and laughed humorlessly. "I assume Madi's gonna need these." She headed up the stairs after Madi and her mother.

Brett followed Jerry into the first room adjacent to the front door, the formal parlor. It was where the Thomases hosted a small group and formerly where Brett and Hunter would have some drinks at the end of the night on occasion.

Jerry was pouring scotch into a highball glass and motioned with his eyes to Brett who nodded that, yes, he *did* indeed want one. Brett lit the fireplace and threw some logs in while Jerry grabbed another glass, pouring a fair amount of scotch into it as well. He then grabbed both, handed Brett his glass, and they took a seat opposite one another as Jerry toasted Brett.

"What a week, huh?" He meant it as a rhetorical question and continued. "Damn...I don't even know...just DAMN." He cursed and slammed his fist down on the arm of the large overstuffed Queen Anne chair he sat in. "Sorry," he apologized, "but I hate to see my daughter like this. And I know you do too." Brett just nodded and swallowed hard. "I'm gonna miss that son of a bitch, ya know?" He laughed tearfully. "I know you will too though." He sighed heavily and sat silent for several long moments.

Brett just listened to the rain and the crackle of the fire, trying hard to relax his heavy heart and mind. "I know the next few weeks are gonna be real hard on my Madi. I just appreciate you being here for her, Brett." Jerry reached forward and patted Brett on the knee. "You're a good man, I've always known that, but the way you've been with Madi is truly commendable. She needs you. I guess you see that." Jerry raised his eyebrows and scoffed. Then he fell into silence and sipped his scotch slowly.

Suddenly, the front door burst open and in stumbled Frank Thomas, Hunter's father. He struggled to get his umbrella closed and mumbled curses all the while.

"Well, c'mon in, Frank," Jerry stated. "Would you care for a libation?"

"Damn this weather today," Frank said, slamming his umbrella into the umbrella stand. "Nah, thanks though, Jer. I'm just gonna grab that other casserole for Rita and we'll head on home. She's not doing so well right now." Brett stood to go fetch the dish and motioned for Frank to take his seat. Frank shook his offered hand. "Too bad you couldn't hear the damn preacher over this stupid rain. The flowers were awful beautiful though, huh? How's our girl holding up?"

Brett just shook his head sadly. "Not well, sir, not so well. How about you?"

Frank sadly shook his head in return. "I guess I'm trying to be as strong as I can for my wife, but I never expected to have to bury my only child today." He ambled over to the sofa that Brett had been sitting on as Brett exited the room.

"I'll go grab that casserole for you." Brett excused himself and went to the kitchen, opened the well-stocked fridge, took the medium-sized chicken casserole from the second shelf, and brought it out to Frank who took it.

"Thanks, Brett. I doubt we eat it today but...well, maybe tomorrow."

"No worries, there's so much food in there I don't know if it will ever get eaten. Want to take some more stuff home too?" Frank shook his head. "I can't hardly get Madi to eat anything. Come to think of it, I guess none of us has had much of an appetite..." Brett trailed off, propped his hip against the door jamb and wrung his hands.

Frank sighed. "I guess your folks stayed home today?"

"Yes sir, Momma's sick with a sinus infection, but Dad said to give him a call if any of us needed anything. So please don't be afraid to ask."

"That's mighty kind of Drew. I tell ya, everyone has been so gracious with all of this." Frank teared up a little. Jerry reached over and patted his shoulder then went over to the bar to make another drink, this one for Frank who took it obligingly. The men sat in companionable silence once again. Finally, right before Frank was about to get up, Brooke came to the landing of the stairs.

"Brett, I'm sorry to interrupt, but... Madi, she's refusing to take the Valium. Again." she yelled down at him.

Jerry sighed, and Frank looked over to Brett who nodded, "Ok, I'll be right up," he hollered back up at her.

Brett grabbed his drink, slung it back and downed it, said his goodbyes to Frank, and headed up the stairs.

He wasn't entirely out of earshot when he heard Frank say, "So... how long's Brett been in love with my daughter-in-law?"

He heard Jerry laugh humorlessly and reply with, "Hell, I reckon for as long as he's known her."

FALSE START premieres September 25th.
Pre-order it HERE

AFTERWORD

Thank you *so* much for reading *UNSPORTSMANLIKE CONDUCT*. I hope you enjoyed Travis and Skyla's story.

If so, please leave a review. I appreciate ALL my readers. I couldn't do this without **YOU**!

(If you enjoyed Sky and Travis's story, don't worry, you'll see them again in the rest of the series ;-) This series also ties in with the Sin and Secrets collection—starts in November.)

The next book in the series, *FALSE START*, follows Brett McFadden and Madison Thomas's story and is set for a September 25th release date.

BLURB:

Almighty *Zeus*, thrower of thunderbolts… *Ha!*

Brett "Brickhouse" McFadden may be called Zeus on the Gladiators football field, but when the man who's been his best friend and favorite receiver for over a decade gets killed instead of him, he's completely helpless and left to pick up the pieces **Hunter "Hermes" Thomas** left behind.

The one and *only* constant in Brett's life has always been his hidden love for his first best friend, **Madison Thomas**, the perfect girl he fell in love with at seven—yes, seven—years of age, who also happens to be Hunter's widow. Love is complicated after all!

Now that Hunt's gone, Madi needs him more than she ever has, and Brett feels utterly blessed to be given this second chance, but will the shameful guilt be enough to kill him too?

Madison Thomas, CEO and VP of the Atlanta Gladiators, thought her life was well-established, until the unimaginable happened; the abrupt death of her husband, Hunter. Her overdependence on her best friend, Brett, begins to intensify as the darkest days of her life follow and she finds herself bombarded with the regrets of her past...*and* the unavoidable attraction she's always felt for the perfectly-sculpted "king of the gods".

As new revelations come to light, Madi starts to see that Hunter wasn't the husband—or man—she thought he was. Now, she must storm past the *FALSE START* she was given and embrace the possibility of a do-over with the one she's always wanted—Brett McFadden.

Will the "god of thunder" prove to be the better contender for Hera's heart or will this long-suffering Olympian forever remain fourth and inches from his ultimate goal line?

This book is a second chance/friends to lovers workplace romance that deals with tragic death and has some light BDSM.

ACKNOWLEDMENTS

Thank you, thank you, thank you!

To all who helped kick off this new series! To all my betas, ARC readers, fellow indies, friends and fans—Jamie, Nic, Jen, Emina, Crystal—you guys are A-MAY-ZING! Couldn't have done this without you!

I'm so glad you enjoyed Travis and Skyla and want MORE.

Lots of steam, drama, and fun headed your way. I love you all. Thanks for appreciating my work and characters, it means the world to me :-*

ALSO BY SHANNA SWENSON

~THE SIN AND SECRETS COLLECTION~

RISE: A Sin and Secrets Novella

(Coming November 2020)

~Aurora Rose Reynold's HEA WORLD~

Until Kingston

(Coming 2021)

LEARN MORE AT WWW.SHANNASWENSON.COM

ABOUT SHANNA SWENSON

Shanna Swenson is a cardiac sonographer by day and a weaver of various fictional tales by night.

She's been an avid reader all her life and began writing at the age of fourteen. She finally published her first novel, *Abundance*, after it sat patiently on her laptop for well over fifteen years and she hasn't stopped writing since.

Shanna fits her zodiac sign of Cancer with a capital C and enjoys life's simplest things—sunsets, rain, and coffee—to name a few.

When Shanna's not supporting her fellow indies with her face buried in a book or writing her next novel/novella, she enjoys action and horror movies, pro football, hiking, working out, and traveling with her own "knight in shining armor".

You can find her on the following social media platforms.

Her website is www.shannaswenson.com

facebook.com/shannaswen

twitter.com/shanna_swenson

instagram.com/shannaswen_author

goodreads.com/Shannaswen

amazon.com/author/shannaswenson

pinterest.com/shannaswen

bookbub.com/profile/shanna-swenson